MERLINE LOVELACE

THE FIRST MISTAKE

D1334938

MIRA

First published in Great Britain 2008.
MIRA Books, Eton House, 18-24 Paradise Road,
Richmond, Surrey, TW9 1SR

© Merline Lovelace 2005

ISBN: 978 0 7783 0284 1

63-1208

MIRA's policy is to use papers that are natural, renewable and
recyclable products and made from wood grown in sustainable
forests. The logging and manufacturing processes conform to the
legal environmental regulations of the country of origin.

Printed and bound in Spain
by Litografía Rosés S.A., Barcelona

To Al,
for all the wonderful years of romance
and adventure!
Thank you, my darling.

ACKNOWLEDGEMENTS

With special thanks to:

Lieutenant Colonel Eddie Howard, USAF/OSI, who bravely agreed to interviews, provided invaluable detail on current OSI organisation and missions, and made sure Cleo went into the field properly armed.

Lieutenant Alana Casanova, OSI/PA, and Technical Sergeant Kathleen Matthews, SAF/PA, for expediting my requests for information and access to OSI personnel.

Jon Bowman, Executive Director, Santa Fe Film Festival, who shared his vast knowledge of cinema arts in general and New Mexico's rich film history in particular.

Peter Chapman, Director of Marketing, Lensic Performing Arts Center, for escorting me through his fabulous theatre and helping plot the perfect escape.

1

Cleo North was just escorting a twenty-year-old megamillionaire software wizard into the Las Vegas Convention Center when someone pumped out three quick rounds from a semiautomatic.

The first bullet scattered the crowd streaming into the center. The second dug into the wall a few inches from her client's head. Cleo didn't wait to see where the third hit. Whipping her 10 mm Glock from the holster at the small of her back, she launched herself through the dry November heat.

"Get down!"

Her client hit the sidewalk. Cleo's well-toned one hundred and twenty-six pounds smacked down on top of him. The software guru's glasses flew off. Air exploded from his flattened lungs. Bug-eyed, he squirmed frantically.

"I…can't…breathe!"

She ignored his wheeze but couldn't ignore the fact that he was now in as much danger from the panicked mob as from the shooter. When a knee landed square in her back and a sneakered foot whacked her in the ribs, Cleo decided it was time to get the hell out of Dodge.

Making like Moses, she used arms and elbows to part the sea of terrified humanity, and fought her way into a crouch. The blue steel Glock helped considerably. When the crowd caught sight of the semiautomatic, more shrieks split the air and the stampeding horde swerved enough for Cleo to get a grip on her client's collar. Pumping pure adrenaline, she dragged him nose-to-the-ground around the corner of the building and into a narrow alley.

The alley led to the convention center's loading docks. The rolling bay doors at the end were down and locked, but Cleo's preliminary security sweep had ascertained that at least three other doors opened onto the passageway. Two had panic bars on the inside and couldn't be opened from without. Service personnel and caterers gained access to the convention center through the third, which fire codes required remain unlocked during business hours.

Yanking her client to his feet, Cleo aimed him at the dock steps and spun around to cover his retreat. He made a dash for the service door and twisted the knob with both hands. By the time Cleo reached him, he was pounding on the panel with his fists.

"It's locked!"

Well, hell! So much for fire codes!

She threw a glance back down the alley and nixed the idea of taking her client out that way. The shooter was still out there, and the first rule of personal security was to hustle the protectee *away* from danger, not propel him back into it.

"Get behind that Dumpster," she ordered, shoving him toward the container perched at the edge of the loading dock.

His Adam's apple bobbed like a turbo-charged yo-yo. "Why? What are you going to do?"

"Shoot the lock off the door."

That was the plan, anyway. Cleo had picked, kicked or drilled into a considerable number of locks. She'd never fired at one embedded in a fireproof steel door a good six inches thick, though. Angling to the side to avoid a possible ricochet, she took aim. Before she could squeeze off a shot, footsteps pounded into the alley and stopped.

The good news was the newcomer couldn't see Cleo or her client with the Dumpster shielding them. The bad news was she couldn't see *him*, either.

With a smothered curse, she put a finger to her lips. Her client got the message. His Adam's apple bobbled again as he clamped his mouth shut. Scrunching down, he tried to make himself disappear while Cleo hooked the toe of her boot on the Dumpster's lift arm. Her cushioned soles didn't so much as squeak—thank God and the devious minds at Oakley!

Designed to provide maximum stealth, Oakley assault boots were the footwear of choice among U.S. Special Forces. Cleo and the military had parted ways years ago. Still, she recognized a good thing when the tattooed ex-Special Ops type who served as her personal trainer thumped her with it.

Being blind, however, was definitely *not* a good thing. Confirming that her client was concealed, she hoisted herself atop the Dumpster. Heat shimmered in iridescent waves above the closed half of the lid. The open half emitted a stink. When Cleo shimmied forward on her belly, it also emitted a swarm of pesky little gnats, one of which went straight up her nose. Resisting the violent urge to sneeze it out, she raised her head an inch.

There he was. A dark figure silhouetted against the dazzling sunlight at the far end of the alley. She couldn't make out his face. She didn't need to. The weapon clutched in his right fist was sufficient ID.

He stood unmoving for a long moment, as if sniffing the air for the scent of his prey. When he started down the alley, Cleo's heart thumped against her ribs. The desert heat trapped in the tunnel had sweat stinging her eyes. The gnat trapped in her left nostril had her grinding her teeth against the frantic need to blow the damn thing out.

Trying not to suck it in deeper, she waited until the shadowy figure drew even with the Dumpster. A half second later, she landed on the balls of her squeakless Oakleys, right behind him.

"Hey, pal!"

The gunman swung around, and Cleo launched into her best Jackie Chan spin. On the front side of the whirl, her boot connected with his weapon and sent it flying. On the back side, she connected with a solid wall of muscle.

Damn! The man was a gorilla. And quick, too. Cleo registered that fact at about the same moment his fist wrapped around her ankle. Her boot was still buried in his chest at the time.

Blinking in a desperate attempt to clear the stinging sweat, she didn't try to fight his bruising grip. Instead, she went up on the ball of her other foot. Like a ballerina attempting an awkward arabesque, she used her body weight to thrust forward and send her attacker stumbling backward. *He* used his brutal hold on her ankle to take her along for the ride.

They both went down. His back slammed into the concrete. Cleo's jean-covered butt bounced off his chest. Her right leg remained stretched straight out. She got her left knee under her and jammed the muzzle of the Glock under his chin.

His breath left on a grunt. "Nice takedown, North."

Cleo's eyes narrowed. Shadows still masked the man's face, but there was no mistaking that deep, lazy drawl. Blinking furiously, she huffed out the gnat and dug her gun barrel in another half inch.

"Donovan?"

"Hey, go easy on the windpipe."

"You'll be breathing through a *new* windpipe if you don't talk fast and tell me why you took three potshots at my client."

"Is your client the skinny kid in the Armani suit?"

"He is." Cleo ground the barrel in deeper. "Talk."

He grunted again. "I didn't take three potshots at your client. I took *one* at the pigtailed sleazoid who fired at him. Sleazo is currently lying face-down with several giant-size Expo-ers sitting on him, by the way. No thanks necessary."

Cleo almost believed him. She'd been in the personal security business too long, however, to accept anything at face value—particularly from an undercover agent who still carried the stink of cordite on his button-down oxford shirt.

The fact that she'd indulged in a brief, steamy affair with said agent before he'd dropped out of sight and out of her life didn't exactly add to his credibility. The mere reminder of his abrupt disappearing act made her dig the barrel in another quarter inch.

Jack Donovan gritted his teeth. "Dammit, North! I'm starting to get pissed."

"Ooh, I'm so scared."

She settled her weight more comfortably on his chest. She could make out his features now. The same square jaw. The same nose flattened a little at the bridge, courtesy of some long-ago brawl. The same blue eyes and streaked blond hair.

"Keep talking, big guy. Tell me why you just happened to be strolling into the Las Vegas Convention Center the same time this sleazo you mentioned tried to take out my client."

"I was tailing you. I have been for the past twenty-four hours."

That took some of the wind from her sails. She employed a *very* high-priced technical consultant to equip her with the latest electronic gizmos. The consultant—who also happened to be her stepcousin-in-law, Doreen—had produced the Oreo-size scanner currently clipped to Cleo's belt. It was supposed to snatch pulses from cell phones or any other electronic device within a specified radius, record the patterns and chirp if the same pattern repeated at regular intervals.

There had been no chirping. Definitely no chirping. Cleo would have to have a little chat with Doreen when she got back to Dallas.

"Okay, I'll bite. Why are you tailing me?"

"The Old Man sent me. He wanted to see if you're still as good as you used to be."

"Oh, yeah? What do you think?"

A sun-bleached brow lifted. "What I think is that you've put on a few pounds since the last time you sat on my chest, woman."

"You're a dead man, Donovan."

Laughter rumbled in his chest. "Of course, we were both naked at the time. That does make a difference, Cleopatra Aphrodite North."

Cleo ground her teeth. That's what came of having a dreamy poet for a mother and a father whose job as a hydrologist with the U.S. Agency for International Development had taken him all over the world.

Cleo had heard the story in a dozen different variations. How she'd been conceived while her father worked on a project on the upper Nile. How her mother had been editing a translation of Greek verse at the time. How the moonlight had shimmered on the Nile the magical night the couple had learned she was pregnant.

Her mother had died before Cleo's third birthday, and Cleo had never quite found the heart to tell her pop how unmagical she found her name at times. This was one of them.

"You know," she said, "only two other people know what that middle initial *A* stands for. One of them is dead."

Genuine interest gleamed in Donovan's blue eyes. "Did you shoot him?"

"No, I didn't, but I'm *reeeal* close to pulling the trigger right now."

Jack grinned, and Cleo's breath slid back down her throat. She'd almost forgotten the impact his crooked grin could have on her respiratory system.

Fortunately—or *un*—her client chose that moment to poke his head out from behind the Dumpster. Goggle-eyed, he gaped at the figure between Cleo's thighs.

"Who's he?"

"A hired gun."

"I knew it!" The rest of Harold Dennison's Armani-clad torso popped out to join his head. "I *knew* MetroTech would try to off me! When I turned down their last offer, I figured they'd try something like this. That's why I hired you for additional security."

He danced around Cleo with the same annoying peskiness the gnats had a few moments ago. Sighing, she removed the steel barrel she had embedded in Jack's throat. He in turn released his bruising hold on her ankle.

She pushed herself to her feet and ignored the pat he gave her fanny on the way up. "This particular hired gun isn't employed by MetroTech. He's an air force special agent. I used to work with him in another life."

"An air force agent?" Dumbfounded, the software whiz's jaw dropped. "The *government* wants to off me?"

"No," Jack drawled. "It doesn't."

Rolling to his feet, he brushed off his butt. His tight, trim butt, Cleo couldn't help noticing. *He* hadn't added any pounds since the last time she'd squatted on his chest.

"The man who shot at you is being detained out front until the police arrive," he informed her client. As if on cue, sirens wailed in the distance.

"Here come the cavalry," Cleo muttered, "and the red tape."

Donovan slanted her a sardonic glance. "Still hate filling out forms and completing after-action reports?"

"That's one of the main reasons I left the air force and went into business for myself. I don't report to anyone but the IRS these days."

Unfortunately, Cleo couldn't avoid *all* forms or reports, particularly when firearms had been discharged or public property had been destroyed. Both events occurred with annoying frequency in her line of business.

She showed her P.I. license and permit to carry a concealed weapon to the uniformed cops who responded to the report of shots fired. Jack showed his shield. Naturally, they took his statement first. When he finished, he leaned against the fender of the black-and-white and listened with unabashed interest while Cleo gave hers.

Yes, she'd been hired by Mr. Harold Dennison here to provide personal protective services. No, he hadn't received any specific threats. No, she didn't recognize the pigtailed shooter who'd tried to take him out.

Harold did, however. When the police took him over for a look at the man whose thigh the EMTs had just finished patching up, he let out a piercing shriek.

"Greg!"

The shooter's head whipped around. He looked to be a few years older than his target, which meant he could probably purchase beer legally.

"Do you know him?" Cleo asked Dennison.

"He's my partner. Or was, until we went our separate ways last year."

"You didn't mention an ex-partner as a possible threat during our intake interview and initial threat analysis."

"I didn't think... I didn't consider..." His Adam's apple did the yo-yo bit again. "I bought Greg's share of the company when he left. I thought we were square."

God give her patience! "How much did you pay to buy him out?"

"Three and a half million."

"And how much are you selling your new software for?"

"Around fifteen million."

Cleo rolled her eyes. The clearly disgruntled ex-partner was more expressive. After several pointed remarks, he flipped Dennison the bird. His finger was still at rigid attention when the EMTs rolled him away.

"We need to talk," Jack said while the police went over Dennison's statement with him. "I'll wait for you at your hotel."

"I'm at—"

"The Mirage." Grinning, he tugged on a hank of her hair. "I'm in the room next to you, so close I can almost hear those cute little snorts you make in your sleep."

She pinned him with an icy stare. "I do not snort."

"If you say so. See you later, Cleopatra."

She spent the next two hours filling out reports and hovering next to Dennison while he demonstrated his new software to a standing-room-only crowd. After twenty minutes of computer-speak, Cleo decided maybe police reports weren't so bad, after all.

She topped off the day by witnessing the deal representatives from the hardware giant Metro-Tech cut with her client. Fully recovered from his near-death experience, the software wizard demonstrated a surprising sense of street smarts by levering their offer up to eighteen million.

Everyone emerged from the meeting happy. The MetroTech reps clutched an assignment of copyright in their collective, sweaty paws. Harold left with ideas for a new product already spinning in his busy, brainy head. Cleo had a fat check tucked in her back pocket.

So fat, in fact, that she hooted when Jack indicated the Old Man wanted to talk to her about doing a little work for the United States Air Force.

"The United States Air Force can't afford me."

"That so?" He scanned the contents of the minibar in her room and decided on a Diet Coke. "What's the going rate for security specialists these days?"

With a smug smile, Cleo produced the check and waved it under his nose. She still owed him for that crack about the few extra pounds.

He let out a long, low whistle. "That much, huh? Maybe I should think about a career change."

"Maybe you should."

They both knew it wasn't going to happen anytime soon. Donovan was career air force. He'd joined right out of high school, spent years as a military cop, earned both a bachelor's and a master's in criminology. Along the way he'd cross-trained into special investigations, gone through Officers Training School and worked his way up to the exalted rank of major. Now a top agent with the AFOSI—Air Force Office of Special Investigations—he was blue to his bones.

Cleo was anything but.

She'd been looking more for adventure and travel than a lifelong commitment, when she joined the air force right out of collge. She'd scored high enough on the Air Force Officer Qualifying Test to make her eligible for the special investigations field, and had jumped at it. Mostly because she thought Special Agent North sounded cool and James Bondish.

Only after she'd been sworn in and completed Officers Training School did she discover that AFOSI agents worked much more than spy stuff. Long, grueling months at the OSI Academy gave her a thorough grounding in basic law enforcement, investigative techniques, forensic sciences, intelligence operations and protective services.

She'd graduated as a rookie investigative agent, then spent another long apprentice year that included rotations through the unglamorous world of fraud and computer crime, as well as the spook world of counterintelligence and force protection. Another three years as an investigative agent followed, working cases that ran the gamut from counterfeit military IDs to high treason and desertion in the face of enemy fire.

If Cleo hadn't balked at the restrictive military

regulations governing everything from completing case reports to the size of the little stud earrings women were allowed to wear, she might have hung in there after completing her initial four years of service. By then, though, she'd become fed up with the bureaucracy. She'd also butted heads with just about every officer in her chain of command, up to and including the general who headed the Air Force Office of Special Investigations.

Now General Barnes apparently wanted her back. The same General Barnes who'd suggested she consider turning in her OSI shield. Rather pointedly, as she recalled. Cleo hid her thrill of satisfaction behind a casual inquiry.

"What kind of job does the Old Man have in mind?"

"He didn't say."

Jack glugged his Coke. Cleo refused to dwell on the smooth action of his throat muscles. Instead, she concentrated on the nice, round red mark her Glock had made just under his jaw.

The drink downed, he crinkled the can and pitched it into the wastebasket. "All the Old Man told me was that it was a seven burner."

He launched the bomb casually, but it hit with laser-guided precision. Cleo went stiff.

A seven burner was General Barnes's private label for a hot case. So hot an agent dropped everything else to run it to ground as quickly as possible. It also generally meant the case had the highest implications for national security.

Donovan had hooked her. He knew he'd hooked her. She saw his utter confidence when he sauntered across the room and curled a knuckle under her chin.

"I've reserved two seats on the red-eye back to Washington. It doesn't leave until ten forty-five tonight. Any suggestions on how we might kill the next three or four hours?"

She had a good number of suggestions. All of them involved getting naked and sweaty. Unfortunately, naked and sweaty led to unexpected complications. Where Jack Donovan was concerned, anyway.

Ignoring her body's instant scream of protest, she backed away from his touch. "I'm not government anymore. I don't do red-eyes."

Besides which, she didn't want to appear too eager.

"I need to head back to Dallas tonight and take care of some loose ends. I'll catch the shuttle to Washington early tomorrow morning."

Jack didn't try to dissuade her. In fact, she was sure she caught a flicker of relief in his baby blues. The one time they'd actually followed through with the naked and sweaty thing had left him as wary as it had Cleo. It had also left him with a bullet hole in his right shoulder, but that hadn't been her fault. Not completely.

"Your call," he said with a shrug. "I'll see you at headquarters. Two o'clock sharp. Don't be late. You know the Old Man."

"Yes, I do."

Cleo kicked herself all the way to the airport.

She wasn't some giddy adolescent, for God's sake! She could differentiate between a nice, healthy roll in the sheets and eternal love. She was also currently uninvolved and—all right, she could admit it—more than a little horny since ending things with the lawyer she'd been dating off and on for the past six months. Unless she wanted to enter into a long-term relationship with a vibrator, she needed someone other than squeaky voiced millionaire clients in her life.

Once she was aboard the Dallas-bound jet, though, her thoughts turned from Jack Donovan to the man who'd sent him. General Barnes didn't know it, but Cleo had gone to considerable trouble to engineer this face-to-face meeting.

What *she* didn't know was how the heck her fierce determination to reopen a case almost a decade old had escalated to a seven burner.

Resting her head against the seat back, she closed her eyes. The case had been consigned to the dead file for years, but the grisly scene at the Willow Bend Apartments still played out inside her head in vivid Technicolor.

Blood and gore had covered the walls.

Drenched the Berber carpet. Splattered the TV screen. The knife had been embedded in the victim's bowels when the local police had called the OSI to the scene. Cleo had identified the dead woman instantly. She'd interviewed Air Force Sergeant Debra Smith only three days earlier.

Debra's killer had sat slumped in an armchair only a few feet from his victim. She'd recognized him, as well. Staff Sergeant Thomas Mitchell. Debra's boyfriend. He'd used a 9 mm German-made Kurtz to blow his brains out.

The stench of death had clogged Cleo's nose and throat. The still-slimy deposits on the walls and carpets had brought her gorge up. She'd barely made it out of the apartment before puking.

At least she hadn't contaminated the crime scene. Small consolation compared to the knowledge that she'd botched her investigation and directly contributed to Sergeant Smith's savage murder.

2

The flight from Vegas to Dallas took two hours. The drive from the airport to Cleo's two-bedroom condo in the northwest corner of the city required another forty minutes and considerable cunning on her part.

Contrary to the repeated assertions of her friends and associates, she didn't harbor any particular death wish. But she *had* learned to drive in Bangkok when her father worked a dam construction project in conjunction with the Thai government.

Thai drivers subscribed to a simple philosophy. He who leaned on the horn the hardest and stood on the accelerator the longest owned the road. Dallas suburbs didn't present the same challenges as the countryside around Bangkok. There were no plodding water buffalo to careen around or benjo ditches to suck in the careless. There were, however, plenty of Texas road hogs to contend with.

Cleo would prefer a water buffalo anyday.

After doing battle with I-635, she took the North Dallas Tollroad and exited just south of Plano. Urban sprawl had converted most of the surrounding hayfields to strip malls and pricey housing developments. Cleo's condo unit sat at the edge of a creek lined with cottonwood trees, which was great viewwise and not so great when the trees shed and thick, cottony puffs clogged air conditioners.

Peeling into her coffin-size garage, she squeezed out of the black MG and took the stairs to her living quarters. The warning light on the elaborate security system her stepcousin/technical consultant had installed glowed a nice, steady red.

"Mary had a little lamb."

Okay, the nursery rhyme was hokey, but Cleo had this small problem with numbers. They tended to reverse themselves in her head for no discernible reason. Voice recognition took care of that minor inconvenience.

Once inside, she vectored straight to the kitchen and dumped her leather carryall on the counter. The flashing red light on her answering machine indicated a new message since her last check. It was the same one her dad left on her machine every time he called. Cleo's mouth curved as she listened to the time-honored litany.

"Hiya, kiddo. Call me. *Tachi-dao.*"

A man of few words, her father.

Still smiling, she picked up the phone, hit speed dial and ambled over to the fridge. A quick glance showed that her choices ranged from leftover Chinese to leftover pizza. She was reaching for the carton of fried rice when the phone clicked and a breathless voice came over the line.

"Hello?"

Cleo smile morphed into a grimace, but she kept her reply friendly. "Hi, Wanda. How's it going?"

"Oh, Cleo, the most awful thing has happened!"

Her heart stuttered and stopped. A dozen disasters flashed into her head, not the least of which was that her dad had suffered another bout of the angina that had scared her shitless the first time he'd gone white and clutched his chest.

"What's wrong?"

"You won't believe it!"

"Wanda! What's happened?"

"They delivered the new drapes I had made for your father's den this afternoon. They're chartreuse. Chartreuse! I know the sample I picked out had more green to it."

Cleo prayed for patience. She still couldn't believe big, buff Patrick North had fallen for this dithering twit, much less married her after a whirlwind courtship that had lasted all of three weeks.

But he had, and Cleo loved her father too much to let him see that Waffling Wanda drove her straight up the wall.

"If the drapes aren't the color you want, send them back."

"I can't." The older woman paused. "Can I? I mean, they're custom-made."

"Send them back."

"I don't know...."

Here it came. The hesitation, the uncertainty, the agonizing indecision.

"They *do* hang well. And your father swears he likes the color. I just don't know...."

Eyes rolling, Cleo thumped the fried-rice carton down on the counter. "Why don't you leave them up for a few days and see if they grow on you?"

"That was your father's suggestion, too."

So go with it!

"I guess I could do that," her stepmother conceded after more dithering.

"Great. Is Dad there?"

"Hold on, I'll get him."

Cleo swallowed her irritation as she waited for Patrick to come on the line. For so long it had just been the two of them. He'd taught her to enjoy sushi and squid and Szechwan peppers so hot they peeled away the lining of her mouth. She'd watched him build dams, put in irrigation systems to reclaim drought-stricken fields, teach villagers how to purify their drinking water. He was her hero as well as her pal and confidant.

He was also the reason she'd chosen Dallas as the base for the security consulting business she'd started up after parting company with the air force. Her dad had retired here, and Cleo had wanted to keep an eye on him.

Now, Patrick insisted, he had Wanda to handle that task. Cleo didn't need to fuss or worry about that one small episode of angina anymore.

Whenever he made that ridiculous assertion, she'd bite her lip so hard she'd taste blood, but always managed a cheerful nod. If marriage to Wimpy Wanda gave him pleasure—as it so inexplicably did—Cleo would fight to the death to protect that happiness. Unfortunately, that meant she had to refrain from strangling the woman.

"Hiya, kiddo. What's happening?"

"Hiya, Pop. Not much."

"You're home earlier than you expected. Did you finish that Vegas job?"

"Yeah, I did."

Between forkfuls of cold fried rice, she filled him in on the details. She also let drop that she was leaving for Washington, D.C., early in the morning.

"D.C.? Why?"

"My old boss at the OSI wants to talk to me about a possible job."

Patrick's rich chuckle came over the line. "I thought you swore up and down you'd never get sucked into the military establishment again."

Cleo didn't tell him she wanted to be sucked. Or that she had, in fact, arranged the sucking.

"I'm just flying up to hear what the general has to say."

"Okay. Make sure you stop by here when you get back. You have to see these great new curtains Wanda had made for my den."

"Will do."

"*Tachi-dao.*"

A smile curled around her heart as she repeated the phrase they'd adopted as their own years ago. It was from an ancient Ryukyu Island proverb that warned travelers to maintain a sharp sword. For father and daughter, it was shorthand for *Be careful, Stay safe, I love you.*

"*Tachi-dao,* Pop."

Carrying the rice carton with her, she headed for her office. Her stepcousin-in-law Doreen kept it up-to-date with the latest in electronic data gadgetry, but Cleo didn't bother to boot up the flat-screened behemoth perched on her desk. Tonight she wanted to review a paper file.

It was right where she'd tucked it, inside her upper left-hand desk drawer. Setting aside the rice, she swiped her hand on her jeans and spread the contents of the file out on her desk.

There wasn't much to spread. The official investigation was buried deep in OSI archives. All Cleo had were notes she'd made from memory, a memo detailing a chance meeting, and the info she'd pulled up on one Alexander Sloan, Colonel, USAF, Retired.

She skimmed the notes she'd reconstructed of the original investigation done at Luke Air Force Base, Arizona. Sergeant Debra Smith gets into an argument with her boyfriend, Staff Sergeant Thomas Mitchell, at the on-base, all-ranks club. The argument escalates to shouts and a perceived threat of physical violence. The on-base police are called. An incident report is filed.

Because a threat had been communicated, the OSI assigns Special Agent Cleo North to investigate. Her investigation reveals Smith and Mitchell had been dating for almost a year. Both possess spotless records. Both are also nervous about the impact of the argument on their careers.

Very nervous, or so it seemed to Cleo at the time. But because the incident didn't meet the threshold for a substantive investigation, her supervisor had overruled her gut feeling that she'd missed something.

Determination: lover's spat.

Investigation zeroed.

After entering a brief, one-page synopsis of the incident into the data system, Cleo was off the case.

Cursing, she squeezed her eyes shut. She could almost see herself signing off on the report. Christ! How could she have been so damn green?

Granted, it had been one of her first investigations. But she'd gone through all those long months of training. She'd aced the OSI Academy, soaked up practical experience with each of her rotations. She couldn't count the hours she'd logged in criminal ops, fraud, counterintelligence. The OSI wanted their operatives to learn the trade from the ground up.

Cleo had learned, all right. The hard way. Blowing out a ragged breath, she skimmed the last few lines of her notes.

September that same year. Sergeant Smith found at Willow Bend Apartments, multiple stab wounds, pronounced DOA at E.R. Staff Sergeant Mitchell, also DOA, cause of death self-inflicted gunshot wound. Determination, murder/suicide. Investigation closed.

Guilt over her failure to substantiate the danger to Debra Smith had almost eaten Cleo alive. She swore she'd never ignore her instincts again. The hard-nosed approach to investigations she'd developed after the Smith case had made her the stuff of legend within the OSI. That same bulldog attitude had also ruffled feathers. More than one official in the OSI chain of command had breathed a sigh of relief when Captain North decided to leave the air force and go into business for herself.

North Security and Investigations had started small. Just Cleo and an answering machine. But she'd hit the market at a time when executive kidnappings and terrorist threats were sending the demand for private security consultants through the roof. Particularly security consultants with her training and connections.

Three days after her Web site had gone up, a Dallas firm had hired her to work the advance security for one of their executives scheduled to attend a conference in Venezuela. Two weeks after that lucrative job, she'd been on a plane to Atlanta to conduct an undercover investigation of an employee theft ring at a major food distributor's plant.

The years since had been good. Her company was still small—just Cleo, her part-time office administrator and Doreen, her stepcousin-in-law with the uncanny affinity for all things electronic. But Cleo had developed hundreds of contacts in the security business, including the hired guns she brought in when she needed backup on a case. She'd kept so busy and been so successful financially that she'd managed to bury her lingering guilt over the Smith case—until her chance meeting with Debra's sister.

It was one of those crazy coincidences. A casual conversation struck up while waiting in the McDonald's line at the Atlanta airport. Friendly enough until the woman Cleo had been chatting with spotted two young airmen right out of basic training. Her murmured comment that her sister used to be in the military had produced a smile and a nod from Cleo. The sister's name had frozen the smile on her face.

But it was the comment some fifteen minutes later, while the two women nursed cups of coffee and relived the stark horror of Debra Smith's death, that stopped the breath in Cleo's throat.

Debra had called her sister a few days before she died. She'd sounded worried, almost scared. Debra hadn't come right out and said so, but the sister had formed the impression she'd gotten involved with someone else on base. She said Debra mentioned a pilot with a funny nickname. The Roman or the Greek or something along those lines.

Cleo had jetted straight back to Dallas and worked her extensive networks until she came up with a name. Colonel Alexander Sloan, USAF. A onetime jet jockey whose handle was the Greek. From Alexander the Great, she was informed.

Now retired, Sloan lived in New Mexico. He also happened to be serving as honorary chairman of the Santa Fe Film Festival. Propping her elbows on the desk, Cleo stared at the photo she'd pulled from a glossy, online brochure advertising the festival.

"Handsome bastard, aren't you?"

Steel-gray eyes stared back at her. They were set above chiseled cheekbones and a granite jaw with a dimple in the center. Cleo had dug up reams of information about Alexander Sloan, civilian. What she wanted now was access to his military dossier. For that, she needed the OSI.

Shuffling the papers into the file, she stuffed it back in the desk drawer.

She was jerked awake before dawn the next morning by a shrill yip and the scrabble of clipped claws on the hardwood floors.

"Oh, crap!"

Before she could yank the sheet over her head, four paws landed on her chest. A blast of puppy breath hit her in the face, followed almost immediately by a wet tongue slurping across her lips.

"Arrgh!" Dragging up the sheet, Cleo put it between her mouth and the wiggling fur ball. "Go away!"

Fur ball took that as an invitation to play. His lips rolled back. Needlesharp teeth locked on the three-hundred-thread-count Egyptian cotton. Emitting fierce growls and more blasts of doggie breath, the miniature schnauzer engaged in a ferocious tug-of-war. The excitement affected the animal's kidneys, as Cleo had known it would. Spurts of puppy pee spattered the sheet.

"Baby! Stop that!"

Flipping on the bedroom lights, the willowy, silver-haired widow who served as Cleo's part-time office manager crossed the room and scooped up the joyously wiggling schnauzer. "You know Cleo isn't at her best before her first cup of coffee."

She didn't even come *close* to her best until her second or third cup. Holding the sprinkled sheet between thumb and forefinger, she pushed herself up on one elbow and squinted at the clock.

Good Lord! It was 5:50 a.m.

"What are you doing here so early, Mae?"

"Baby has an appointment to get clipped this morning. I decided to pop into the office beforehand and go through the mail." Tucking her pet under one arm, the older woman pursed her lips. "If you'd let me know you were flying home last night, I could have had it all sorted and prioritized for you."

That was why Cleo had hired her, she reminded herself. She *needed* someone to organize her office and handle the paperwork she herself loathed. What she didn't need was someone organizing her life. Unfortunately, both came packaged in the same slender martinet.

Mae was a retired accountant. She'd buried one husband, divorced another and could almost shoot her age in golf. She was currently dating a cardiologist, but had developed a severe case of the hots for Cleo's forty-something trainer. Which was why the tattooed biker and former Special Forces type insisted he and Cleo work out at a gym these days. Mae struck terror into Goose's heart.

"I'll put the coffee on," Mae announced as Cleo crawled out of bed.

"Thanks. I'll grab a quick shower and take a cup on the run."

"Run to where?"

"The airport. I'm catching the early shuttle to Washington."

"Washington? What happened to Las Vegas?"

"That job's done. *Fini. Completo.* The check for final payment is on my desk."

Remembering Jack Donovan's soundless whistle when he'd eyed the check put a smile on Cleo's face. She hadn't felt the least compulsion to inform him that most of her clients didn't pay anywhere near as well as well-heeled software geniuses. Some couldn't pay more than a token fee, like the desperate single mom who'd begged for help finding her runaway daughter. Cleo wasn't in this business for the money. Still, it didn't hurt to let Jack—and the Old Man—know her services wouldn't come cheap.

Intent on making the early shuttle, she almost

collided with Mae, who blocked the path to the bathroom.

"How long will you be gone?"

"I'm not sure. Why?"

"Your dad's birthday is this weekend. Wanda was hoping you'd go over the menu with her."

"We've gone over it twice already."

Mae's eyes were sympathetic as she tugged on one of Baby's ears. The super-efficient office manager could only take Wanda in small doses, too.

"She's got a good heart, Cleo."

"I know."

"And she loves Patrick."

"I know."

"Can't you try a little harder to overlook her, uh…"

"Wimpiness? I try. Believe me, I try. Gotta hustle, Mae."

November in Washington, D.C., was a different proposition from November in Vegas or Dallas. A damp chill hung in the air. Passengers hurrying in and out of Reagan National Airport hunched deep in their jackets.

Thankful she'd opted for a warm black knit turtleneck with her jeans and caramel-colored wool blazer, Cleo dropped her carryall in the back seat of a rental car. Exiting the airport, she zipped south on Route 1 and crossed the Potomac into Maryland via the Woodrow Wilson Bridge.

The traffic gods were kind. Less than a half hour after departing the airport, she wove a zig-zag path through the concrete barriers protecting the entrance to Andrews Air Force Base. The sprawling installation served as home to a military airlift wing, which operated *Air Force One* and a host of other VIP support aircraft. It also provided a spillover location for functions moved out of the Pentagon over the years in the continuing series of bureaucratic shell games intended to eliminate layers in the Department of Defense. Among the agencies that now made their home at Andrews was the Air Force Office of Special Investigations.

The gate guard checked Cleo's driver's license against an access roster and issued a temporary base pass. Once cleared through the checkpoint, she drove down the Avenue of Flags.

The physical location of the headquarters hadn't changed much since her last visit more than four years ago, but the OSI's mission had definitely taken some new twists. In addition to its traditional counterintelligence, criminal investigation and technology protection roles, AFOSI was now the DOD executive agent for the Defense Cyber-Crime Center, a forensic lab that provided computerized evidence processing, analysis and diagnosis. Additionally, specialized antiterrorism teams were dispersed at locations around the world to counter threats against air force personnel. Several of the teams, Cleo knew, had gone into Iraq ahead of the main body of troops.

She pulled into a visitor's slot outside the two-story building housing the headquarters, and checked in with the security specialist manning the front desk. One visitor's badge and two escorts later, she was escorted into the inner sanctum of Brigadier General Samuel Barnes.

Every one of Sam Barnes's twenty-eight years of service showed on his craggy face. He'd long ago caved to DOD regulations and stopped firing up his beloved pipes, but kept one clamped between his teeth most of the time. As the general's executive officer ushered Cleo into his office, Barnes removed an elaborately carved pipe, centered the bowl in an ashtray and rose to his feet.

Jack Donovan untangled his rangy length and rose as well. Like Barnes, he was in dark blue uniform pants paired with a light blue, long-sleeved shirt.

Resisting the instinct to salute her old boss, Cleo offered her hand instead. "Sir."

The *sir* just slipped out.

"Good to see you, North." Barnes folded her

hand in his bear-size paw. "How are you enjoying civilian life?"

"Pretty well, actually." She couldn't resist. "No standardized interview forms or after-action reports. No cares about hair length. No uniforms."

Okay, Barnes didn't need to know she'd pretty much traded one uniform for another. Turtlenecks and thigh-hugging jeans constituted her standard duty uniform these days. In his honor, though, she'd added the Pendleton wool blazer and exchanged her squeakless Oakleys for Bruno Maglis with three-inch stacked heels. Her version of kick-ass chic. She also liked the fact that the boots put her eye to eye with the general.

"Want some coffee?" he asked cordially.

"Yes, sir. Black."

He signaled to Jack, who filled a china mug emblazoned with the OSI shield. Having Donovan wait on her pretty much made the trip for Cleo. Giving him a bland smile, she took the chair the general indicated. Barnes sat opposite her. Jack ranged off to the side.

The OSI commander didn't waste any time getting down to business. "I understand you were approached by Marisa Conners's personal assistant to provide additional security at the premiere of her new movie next month."

"Yes, I was."

"I also understand you turned Miss Conners down."

"That's correct."

"Why?"

Cleo could have responded that her business decisions were private and confidential. She knew that wouldn't cut it with the Old Man. Besides, she wanted this job for reasons of her own. Reasons she wasn't ready to reveal to Barnes or anyone else at this point.

"I provided event security for Miss Conners at Cannes a couple of years ago. The woman has an ego the size of Brazil and the personality of a pit bull with his nuts caught in a mousetrap. I decided then that hell would freeze over before I would work with her again."

"Consider it frozen."

"Come again?"

"Let me put it this way. We'd like you to reconsider your decision."

"Why? Ms. Conners is a civilian, unaffiliated with the Department of Defense. What does the OSI care about her security arrangements?"

The general fingered the pipe resting in the ashtray. He was choosing his words carefully, Cleo knew, telling her only what he'd decided she needed to know.

"The premiere of Miss Conners's movie coincides with the Santa Fe Film Festival, where she's being honored as one of the guest artists.

The festival's honorary chairman is former air force."

Cleo's pulse skipped. The face in the glossy brochure leaped into her head.

"Right. Alex Sloan."

"You know him?"

"Not personally. I did some homework before turning down the Conners job," she said with perfect truth.

"Then you know the festival draws movie stars and film crews from all over the world."

"So I understand."

"The United States government has a particular interest in a sound engineer on one of those crews," Barnes said slowly. "He's made significant improvements in swept-frequency acoustic interferometry."

"Excuse me?"

"It's a new sound technology that measures and differentiates between sound-wave transmissions. If perfected, it could allow us to bounce noninvasive waves at a closed container, for example, and determine its contents via the return-wave signatures. I don't need to tell you the implications of such a technology for Homeland Security and the war against terrorism."

No, he didn't. Cleo's agile mind was already making the leap. Airport security screeners could aim harmless sound waves at closed suitcases and receive instant, computerized readings on contents. Bomb squads could use differing sound waves to detect and, if necessary, detonate explosive devices at safe distances.

No wonder the Old Man had designated this a seven burner!

"So what's the problem? Why aren't we going after this sound engineer?"

She didn't realize her slip until the general cracked a smile.

"I mean you," she corrected. "Why aren't _you_ going after him?"

"We intend to. There's one minor problem, though. He's North Korean."

"Uh-oh."

"Right. Uh-oh."

The pipe made the trip from ashtray to lips. Barnes sucked on the stem for a moment before anchoring it in the corner of his mouth.

"Given the current tension between Pyong-yang and Washington, the United States can't approach this man directly. Instead, we approached the chairman of the festival. Colonel Sloan has agreed to facilitate 'opportunities' for the engineer to interface with CIA operatives and scientists from Los Alamos Labs there in New Mexico. We don't want anything to disrupt or draw undue attention to the festival."

Cleo's blood began to tingle. She was close. So close. She reached for the mug and hid her excitement behind another swig of coffee.

"By disruption, I assume you mean Marisa Conners."

"Correct. Your task is to keep her pampered, preoccupied and safe while our guys milk information from this engineer."

"Assuming I agree to take the gig, which I haven't."

"If an appeal to your patriotic sense of duty doesn't work, the government's prepared to match whatever fees Miss Conners pays you."

"And if that doesn't work?"

Barnes didn't blink. "You might experience difficulty in the coming months renewing everything from your driver's license to your permit to carry a concealed weapon."

Cleo tried her best to look pissed off at the out-and-out blackmail. Forehead creased, she thumped her fingers on the ceramic mug.

"Okay, here's the deal. If I take the job, I want full cooperation from local, state and federal agencies and access to whatever data I deem necessary for my client's protection."

"Of course."

She set the mug aside, all-business now. "I don't know if you've heard the hype about Miss Conners's new flick. It's *way* out there."

"A modern take on the New Testament," Jack interjected, entering the conversation for the first time. His mouth kicked up at the corners. "I understand it makes Mel Gibson's *Passion of the*

Christ look like a Disney flick. Word is Ms. Conners plays an earthy, erotic Virgin Mary."

Cleo gave a small snort. The earthy, erotic bit was right on target. The virgin part missed the mark by at least two decades.

"According to the media buzz," she informed them, "several religious organizations have expressed outrage over Miss Conners's portrayal of Mary. That could be a clever PR ploy on the studio's part, of course. Given the rise of ultra-right-wing hate groups in this country, though, the threat can't be discounted."

She was preaching to the choir, she knew. The OSI and other intelligence agencies were up to their collective asses in hate groups and terrorists, both homegrown and foreign.

"If I take this job, I want a complete list of all organizations or individuals that might pose a direct threat to Miss Conners."

By federal statute, the OSI was prohibited from collecting data on such groups unless they posed a direct, viable threat to the air force. But the OSI could get the information from the FBI or the Department of Homeland Security a good deal easier than your average, garden variety P.I. could.

"I also want background dossiers on everyone connected with the festival. That includes the chairman."

Particularly the chairman.

Barnes shrugged. "No problem. I suspect we have something on Sloan somewhere."

Ha! The OSI had something on just about everyone who ever wore a blue suit.

Which was why Cleo had turned down Marisa Conners's initial offer of employment. She knew Conners's temper and histrionics had made her a pariah among the select community of top security consultants. She also knew the self-centered star would insist on getting her way. Cleo had figured the actress would whine about her safety at the festival, which she had. She'd also guessed the festival chairman would ask his air force connections to pressure Cleo, which *he* had.

The good ole boy network was alive and well.

Still, she gave in with a show of something less than graciousness. "Okay, I'll take the job. If I end up putting a bullet through Marisa Conners, though, I'm going to name you both as accessories after the fact."

"Fair enough. Donovan will act as your control here at headquarters."

"Control?"

"Sorry. Liaison."

The general buzzed for his executive officer and stood. Cleo got the message. The papal audience was over.

The exec escorted her to the door. She maintained a straight face, but a fierce, satisfied smile kept trying to sneak past her guard.

She was in.

Phase One complete.

The two men stood silently as Cleo departed. The general scowled at her back. Jack admired her ass.

When the door thudded shut behind her, Barnes clamped his lips around his pipe stem and sent his subordinate a considering look. "That was too easy."

"Think so?"

"I know so. I headed Criminal Investigations when Cleo North packed a shield. I still have the battle scars."

Jack sported a few scars, too, one of them courtesy of a Speer 200-grain Gold Dot hollow point. Cleo tended to have that effect on people.

"Feed her whatever data she asks for," the general instructed, "but run it through the analysis folks first."

"And tell them to look for...?"

"Damned if I know!"

Hiding a grin at the irritated growl, Jack left his boss's office. He couldn't admit it to Barnes, but the thought of working with Cleo North again had his blood pumping almost as fast as it had when she'd pounced on him behind the convention center.

With every stride he took down the tiled corridor, the years rolled back. Jack could still remember Cleo in her rookie days: smart, determined, as quick with a comeback as she was on the draw. From all reports, she'd aced her way through the academy. And she'd pretty much set the OSI community on its heels when she'd reported for duty on her first assignment.

By then the infamous picture of the OSI's newest recruit had flashed across every screen in every detachment. Some intrepid soul had spotted the provocative ad in a mail-order lingerie catalog, scanned it into his computer and zipped it around the globe at the speed of light.

Contrary to everyone's expectations, the rookie agent had laughed when told of the ad. She'd worked her way through college, it turned out. Modeling lingerie was only one of the many part-time jobs that had helped pay her tuition costs. If anyone posted a shot of her in her red-and-yellow-striped Wiener Hut uniform, though, she swore she'd hunt them down and hurt them.

Jack still had a printout of the ad tucked away somewhere. Much creased and fraying at the folds. He didn't need to dig it out to call up a mental picture of Cleo North in skimpy lavender lace. The image jumped into his mind whenever someone mentioned her name.

So did the searing image of Cleo with her head thrown back, her back arched and her sweat-slick thighs straddling his.

Even after all these years, the memory

slammed into Jack like a fist to the midsection. Christ! He couldn't believe he'd jumped the woman's bones in the middle of the one and only op they'd worked together.

And what a fuckup that mission had turned out to be. In every sense of the word.

He could still feel the giant ferns slapping at his face as he followed their contact through the Honduran jungle. Still hear the stutter of gunfire that erupted when they ran smack into a nest of heroin processors. Cleo had managed to dodge bullets and machetes, but Jack had taken a slug to the shoulder before they'd battled their way out of that one.

They'd had to hole up in a cave for two days and nights before the area cleared enough to call for an extraction. For the idiocy that followed, Jack could only blame pumping adrenaline and the high from the painkillers he'd gulped down after Cleo plugged the hole in his shoulder.

The fact that she had been assigned to his team was bad enough. The air force tended to frown on such matters as fraternization within the ranks. What made it worse, though, was that they were on a mission. One that could have gotten them both killed. They were damn lucky they'd made it home from that botched operation.

Jack had always wondered what might have happened if Special Agent North hadn't turned in her shield shortly after that mission and his ex-wife hadn't gotten drunk and driven her car into a tree a few months later.

The guilt that stayed buried in his gut despite his every attempt to root it out had pulled him right back into the same vicious cycle of trying—and failing—to help Kate climb out of her alcoholic pit. By the time he'd put his own life back on track, Cleo had set up shop in Dallas and hit the ground running in the security consulting business. She had also reportedly gotten it on big time with an outfielder for the Texas Rangers.

The outfielder had lasted a year or two. The lawyer she'd been dating until recently less than that. From all reports, she was between studs.

Which was why Jack's pulse had kicked up several notches when the Old Man said he was sending him to Las Vegas to see if Cleo North was as good as she used to be.

She was. She most definitely was.

In every way, shape and form.

She was also up to something. Now all he had to do was figure out what.

3

Cleo took the call from Donovan early the next morning. She was on her cell phone advising Mae that she would fly directly from D.C. to L.A. when he beeped in.

"Just wanted to let you know I got that list of religious hate groups and individuals on the watch list you wanted. I kept it unclassified so I can zap it to your computer."

"That was quick."

"We aim to please."

She heard the smile in his voice. Dammit! All these years, and he could still get her wet. Over a cell phone, no less.

"I also had our threat analysis group do a computer search, looking for hits on Marisa Conners and the title of her new movie. There's a lot of chatter out there, but nothing to raise the worry factor above pucker level."

"Thanks." She kept her tone casual. "How about the background dossiers on the folks working the festival?"

"Alex Sloan was easy, being former military. I gathered what I could on the rest of the committee members, the full-time director and the key volunteers."

"You do good work, Donovan."

"Yeah, I know."

There was a pause. Cleo's thoughts bounced between a ten-year-old murder case, the job she'd just agreed to do, and the agent who'd once pushed all the right buttons.

"You know how to reach me," he said after a few moments.

"Right."

She turned in the rental car, hopped the shuttle to the terminal and made a beeline for the closest data port to download the file Donovan had forwarded. The damn thing was huge, eight megabytes. She was still downloading when her flight was called.

She made it to the gate just as they were closing the passenger list. Once aboard, she drummed her fingers on her laptop and waited until the flight attendant gave the go-ahead to use electronic devices.

She was anxious to get Phase Two underway. She'd be more anxious if it didn't involve Marisa Conners. Cleo supposed she should feel guilty for using the star this way, but couldn't work up so much as a twinge.

It hadn't taken much to bait the hook. A few calls to friends who worked in the film industry. Casual reference to the outrage expressed by ultraconservative religious groups over Conners's newest flick. Subtle hints that the star should take a hard look at her security.

The movie's advance buzz had added credence to those hints. The tabloids were already screaming gleefully about sacrilege and heresy. *Time* and *Newsweek* had both run pieces touting protests by the Catholic Council of Bishops over Marisa's depiction of a twenty-first century Mary in the throes of sexual ecstasy during a not-so-immaculate conception.

The statements issued by the studio's PR machine were designed to keep the controversy boiling. Unfortunately, the hype could well stir up more than controversy. Cleo's preliminary research had turned up FBI statistics linking more than sixteen hundred hate crimes to religious bias.

Rolling those statistics over in her mind, she waited impatiently while the airliner climbed to cruising altitude. Finally, the flight attendant gave the green light and computers pinged to life all through the cabin. Cleo clicked on Donovan's file and went to the list he'd compiled of right-wing religious hate groups. Using her thumb, she scrolled through page after page.

The list read like an alphabet soup of bigotry, intolerance and violence. The BOA—Brothers of the Apocalypse—believed responsible for dozens of black church bombings. The CLR—Christian League of the Resurrection—which preached retribution against Jews for killing Christ. The WCW—the World Conference of Witches—a satanic cult that advocated human sacrifice. The NLR. The JJR. The DRO. And, of course, Al Qaeda.

Donovan's list was longer and definitely scarier than the one Cleo had compiled from her own resources. She cross-referenced his data with hers and set up a filter for the handful of groups with a specific focus on the cult of the Virgin Mary.

After the groups came an even longer list of lone crusaders. There were so many out there. Quiet. Seething. Absolutely convinced their beliefs were right and everyone else's were wrong.

Their ranks included a Florida minister on trial for shooting a doctor outside an abortion clinic. A Detroit teen charged with inciting his buddies to rape and sodomize a nine-year-old Muslim girl. The as-yet unidentified stalker who'd declared open season on Catholic priests as punishment for their "fall from grace." Cleo scrolled through the list, highlighting those she'd ask Donovan to track for last known address.

Her computer battery ran out somewhere over Arizona. Frustrated, she moved the pointer over the file labeled "Alex Sloan" before shutting down. The urge to see what Donovan had sent ate at her, but she'd have to wait to review that file after her meeting with Marisa Conners. At least then her head wouldn't be buzzing with hate groups and vicious crimes committed in the name of God.

The film star lived in a sprawling, Spanish-style mansion in the foothills above L.A. Cleo followed the directions Miss Conners's assistant had supplied when she'd called to say she'd reconsidered the Santa Fe job, winding upward until she gained a spectacular view of the smog layer blanketing the city.

The house was easy enough to find. Gaining access to it was even easier. Cleo punched the call button, supplied her name and drove through gates a VW Bug could have crashed. Security at the front door wasn't much better. A maid ushered her in without bothering to ask for any ID to confirm she was who she said she was. Cleo followed the maid inside, where Marisa's current personal assistant greeted her.

"Ms. North. It's a pleasure to meet you."

A tall, Nordic type with muscles to spare, Peter

Jacobsen took her hand in a surprisingly gentle grip.

According to the info sweep Cleo had run to update her file on Marisa Conners, Jacobsen was relatively new to the star's entourage. Not surprising, since Conners appeared to go through employees like toilet paper. The update also indicated this particular assistant's duties included boinking his boss on a regular basis.

Cleo let her glance slide over the sculpted contours of Jacobsen's knit shirt. She wouldn't mind being boinked by an assistant like this one. Where the heck did she go to trade in Mae?

"Marisa was thrilled when I told her you'd changed your mind and agreed to provide additional security during her trip to Santa Fe."

Cleo forged a polite smile but couldn't quite bring herself to return the sentiment.

"We don't have much time," she said instead. "The film festival kicks off next Wednesday. I need you to brief me on any personal communications Miss Conners has received concerning her new movie, written or otherwise."

"She's received several," the blond hunk admitted. "Most of them of the shame-on-you variety. I've got copies of the letters and transcripts of calls to the studio PR department ready for you."

"I'll also need a list of public appearances Miss Conners intends to make while in Santa Fe, and a detailed agenda for the festival."

"I've got those waiting, too."

Cleo eyed Jacobsen with new respect. Brawn, beauty *and* brains. A definite step up from the doped-out rock star Marisa had crawled under the sheets with in Cannes.

"I'll take a look at what you've pulled together before I do my intake interview with Miss Conners."

He shot a glance at the sleek gold-and-silver number banding his wrist. A Baum and Mercier, Cleo noted. The Neiman Marcus of handcrafted Swiss watches. For services rendered, she guessed.

"Miss Conners has an appointment with her hairdresser at two and a talk show taping at three. I've scheduled you to meet with her at one, before she leaves for the studio."

"That'll work."

Cleo used the short interval before her session with Conners to review the documentation Jacobsen had compiled, and interview members of her client's support staff. Besides Jacobsen, the team included the live-in maid, a health and fitness advisor who appeared to spend most of his time in the kitchen feeding carrots into a blender, and Miss Conners's media consultant.

The last was blade-thin, with spiked black hair and a barracuda smile. Like Jacobsen, J. L. Evans was also new to Marisa's entourage, having replaced the harried PR rep who'd accompanied the star to Cannes a few years ago. She brought Cleo up-to-date on the plans to premiere *The Redemption*, and expressed considerable delight at the adverse publicity generated so far.

"We got great mileage out of the letter from the Council of Bishops. Anything that hints of censorship starts the Fourth Estate salivating."

Plucking the bishops' letter from the stack Cleo had fanned out on Peter Jacobsen's desk, J.L. gave it several loud, smacking kisses. The sheet of paper settled back onto the pile, bearing the brand of her bloodred lipstick.

"What we need now is something to feed the masses," she said. "You know. Movie stirs howls of outrage. Star threatened by right-wing fanatics. Death stalks premiere of new flick."

"The outrage is certainly there," Cleo agreed, swinging a booted foot. "As is a generous helping of disgust and numerous promises to boycott the film. At first glance, though, none of these communications conveys a direct threat to Miss Conners."

"They do if we put the right spin on them."

"Putting a spin on things is your job. Mine is gauging the risk to my client. My initial assessment is that the situation warrants increased security awareness but—"

"No buts." J.L. spiked a hand tipped with vampire nails through her coal-black shag. "We want to play this one like it's for real."

Cleo's foot stilled. Her eyes narrowed to slits. "I don't *play* it any other way. Do we understand each other on that point, Ms. Evans?"

"Er, yes."

She treated the woman to another few seconds of ice and picked up where she'd left off.

"As I was saying, the situation warrants increased awareness. But until I run the names of all these people through my databases and check out the security at the festival, I'm not prepared to state what, if any, increased protection Miss Conners will require in Santa Fe."

J.L. tried to recover. "I'm sure your analysis will be thorough."

Damn straight it would. Cleo may have finessed her way into this job, but she'd give it her professional best—a point she forced herself to keep in mind when the phone on Jacobsen's desk buzzed. He took the call and flashed an apologetic glance her way.

"Marisa's running late. Would you mind conducting your interview while she finishes up in the spa?"

Cleo minded, but experience had taught her this was par for the course with Conners. Shrugging, she gathered up the letters and transcripts. Both Jacobsen and Evans accompanied her to the mini-spa at the rear of the house.

Marisa was working out on a Stairmaster. Sweat ringed the armpits of her hot-pink bodysuit. Her trademark auburn mane was scraped back in a ponytail that bounced with every step.

Cleo gave her credit for the fact that she hadn't succumbed to the Hollywood mania for industrial-size boobs. She'd invested heavily in her lips, though. Inflated with collagen, they pooched and puffed as she threw a glance over her shoulder. Jade-green eyes performed a swift inventory and glommed onto Cleo's boots.

"Gucci?"

"Bruno Magli."

"Hmm."

That was it. No hello, nice to see you, it's been awhile since Cannes.

"So what's the drill?" she huffed, pumping away. "Same as last time?"

"Same as last time."

Cleo slid a hip onto the edge of a massage table. She'd briefed Marisa extensively prior to the trip to Cannes. Few of the details had registered. She didn't expect them to this time, either, but she went through the standard spiel about the parameters of event security, her need for free access to Marisa's suite once the star arrived in Santa Fe, even the bit about protection being a team effort.

"In that regard, Mr. Jacobsen's been very helpful."

Marisa slanted her assistant a catlike look. "Peter's pretty handy to have around."

Yeah, Cleo just bet he was. "He gave me copies of the letters and transcripts of the calls the studio's received regarding your role in *The Redemption*. I'll see the studio security folks after I leave here, then bump the info they give me up against the data I've called. In the meantime, I need *your* take on the situation."

It helped if the client was scared or if someone else had just made the news. An executive kidnapping tended to get the attention of other corporate bigwigs. Ditto a celebrity stalking or murder. Client cooperation generally increased in direct proportion to the possibility of ending up dead or stuffed into the trunk of a car.

Marisa didn't appear unduly worried about either. Her main concern seemed to be the fact that she'd be stuck in what she considered the boonies for four days.

"I only agreed to appear at the festival because the studio said the timing fit with the movie's release. You know. December. Christmas. Mary and all that."

"I get the connection."

Ponytail swishing, she humped away. "Poor choice for a premiere, if you ask me. Up in the mountains. All that snow. Not even a major airport for reporters and reviewers to fly into."

Cleo bit back the suggestion that the studio might have chosen Santa Fe to launch *The*

Redemption for exactly that reason. The advance buzz had not been kind.

"I'm flying to Santa Fe on Sunday to do the on-site assessment and prepare for your arrival," she advised her client. "If I see anything that worries me, I'll let you know immediately."

"If you don't, J.L. may have to stir things up a little more."

"Exaggerating the threat won't make either one of us very popular with the folks in Santa Fe."

Annoyance flickered across the star's face. "So talk to them. Make sure they understand I'm going to squeeze all the coverage out of this visit I can."

Cleo intended to. She'd have to walk a fine line, though, and downplay inflated press releases without discounting the very real potential for disruptive activity or violence.

All the while, she'd have her eye on the event chairman who, coincidentally, was working with government spooks to gain access to a revolutionary new sound technology. The same man who might or might not have been involved with the murdered Debra Smith.

The next few weeks looked to be real interesting.

While her client went off to get beautiful and do her talk show, Cleo drove to Whitehorn Studios for a meeting with the head of security.

After that useless session, she wrangled a one-on-one with the chief of the Los Angeles FBI Field Office. Responsible for some eighteen million people residing within a forty-thousand-square-mile area, the L.A. office was one of the busiest in the Bureau. Its agents also constituted a living, breathing databank on celebrity stalkers. Cleo picked up a number of good tips, but no information or threat specific to her client.

She booked a seat on a 7:50 p.m. flight to Dallas. While waiting for the flight, she found a plug and recharged the laptop's battery. Once airborne, Cleo entered her notes from the day's activities. Only then did she open the file Donovan had zapped her regarding Alex Sloan.

His official air force photo jumped out at her. Standard head and shoulders, blue service dress uniform with wings and ribbons, a flag in the background. The same steel-gray eyes that had stared out at her from the film festival brochure, but in a younger, leaner face.

Scrolling through the files, Cleo skimmed the biographical data Donovan had extracted and undoubtedly sanitized. Most of it she already knew.

Born Alexander Sloan forty-six years ago next month.

Twin brother, Marcus, aka Marc Sloan.

Boys adopted at birth by Major General Harrison Sloan, United States Army, and wife, Rebecca.

Cleo didn't have to go far to make the connection. Alexander, aka the Greek, had been named for Alexander the Great. She'd bet Marcus got his tag from the Roman emperor Marcus Aurelius. Since Major General Sloan was the author of a dozen or so ponderous works on ancient military history, it was a pretty sure wager.

Interesting that both sons had followed in their father's martial footsteps. Marcus had gone the Naval Academy route, but opted out of the military after one tour. He now headed an engineering firm that retrofitted civilian cargo vessels for military use.

Alex had attended the Air Force Academy, trained as a fighter pilot and earned a Distinguished Flying Cross in the first Gulf War. Early promotion to major. A high-viz job with the secretary of defense. A superstar in the making until his first wife was diagnosed with breast cancer.

Reading between the lines, Cleo guessed Sloan had put his career on hold to be with his wife during the last stages of her illness. She might have given him max brownie points for that if he hadn't married again less than a year after his wife's death. A younger woman this time, twelve years his junior. Almost the same age difference as between Cleo's dad and *his* second wife.

Grimacing, she skimmed the one-page, computer-generated report showing Alex Sloan's various assignments. The Luke Air Force Base entry brought her straight up in her seat.

"Whoa!"

Her pulse jumping, Cleo zeroed in on a small, innocuous entry listed under secondary duties. Although officially assigned to the Fighter Operations Center, Lieutenant Colonel Sloan carried the duty title of Chief, Harvest Eagle Program.

Instantly, her mind clicked back to the decade-old murder investigation. Staff Sergeant Mitchell had worked on the same program. She was sure of it.

She remembered asking about Harvest Eagle. Remembered being told it was the unclassified designation for a highly classified project taking place somewhere out in the Arizona desert. She never did learn the details. She didn't have a need to know.

Her blood began to pound. The roar of the jet's engines faded. The unanswered questions that had haunted her for years now took a different shape and form.

Had Mitchell worked for Sloan? Did Debra Smith meet the colonel through her boyfriend? Did Mitchell discover his girlfriend was fooling around with his boss, stab her to death in a fit of rage, then shoot himself rather than face prosecution for murder?

Cleo snapped down the laptop lid. She intended to get some answers. Next week. In Santa Fe. The right ones this time.

She owed Debra Smith.

4

Saturday afternoon passed in a flurry of activity in preparation for Santa Fe. Saturday night was reserved for Patrick North's birthday party.

The party was in full swing when Cleo arrived at the two-bedroom patio home her dad had purchased on his retirement from the Agency for International Development. Souvenirs of his overseas assignments were scattered throughout the house. Intricately carved African masks vied for wall space with Aztec temple rubbings and Thai batiks. A six-foot-tall Egyptian obelisk doubled as a coat rack. Woven Peruvian carpets softened the glazed white tile.

Cleo's favorite item was missing, though. The stuffed crocodile with the beady eyes and

chipped front tooth no longer graced the entry-
way. In its place was a statue of a fat little cherub
wearing a nauseating smirk.

"Hiya, kiddo."

Patrick North strode down the hall to greet
her. Big, buff, his rust-colored hair streaked with
silver, he'd been Cleo's one, unshakable constant
through a childhood spent junketing around the
globe.

"Hiya, Pop." Going up on tiptoe, she brushed
his cheek with a kiss. "What happened to Elmer
the Croc?"

"Elmer's been retired to the attic. Now that
Wanda's finished redecorating the den, she's
starting on the foyer and living room."

"Oh. Great."

The obelisk would go next. Cleo would bet
money on it. With a silent farewell to the much
chipped marble, she passed her dad the gift she'd
bought him.

"Here, this is for you. Happy birthday."

Like an eager kid, he went right for the ribbons. Both father and daughter had always at-
tacked their Christmas and birthday presents.
This time, though, Patrick gave a rueful grimace
and stopped himself just in time.

"Wanda wants me to open the presents after
dinner." Hooking his arm over Cleo's shoulders,
he steered her toward the patio. "Come on, kid,
let's go grab some ribs."

In keeping with the instructions on the invitations, everyone was decked out in western wear. Almost everyone, that is. Goose, Cleo's tattooed trainer, was in his usual black leather. His biker vest and leather pants sported enough chain to anchor the *Queen Mary*. Grinning, he tipped his beer in greeting.

Cleo didn't know much about Goose, aka Dave Petrowski, other than the fact that he'd served with the USAF Special Forces for an unspecified period of time at locations he declined to disclose. In his current incarnation, he was a part-time physical trainer, a full-time Harley devotee and president of the North Dallas Chess Club.

That was where Cleo had met him. She'd accompanied her father to the club's championship match, intending to hoot and cheer for him. She'd ended up hooting for the bald giant who'd defeated Patrick in the first round.

Three weeks later she was sweating and grunting with him in training sessions that left her aching in every muscle. One of these days, she vowed as she returned his grin, she'd take the man down.

She and Patrick were headed Goose's way when the biker's grin went south. The hand gripping his beer turned white at the knuckles. Cleo glanced to the right to see what had put that look of desperation on his face and spotted a trim figure with a miniature schnauzer tucked under one arm bearing down on the biker. Goose threw a frantic look over his shoulder, searching for an escape route, but it was too late. Mae had him cornered.

Cleo couldn't watch this. She swung around.

And immediately wished she hadn't.

The sight of her fifty-three-year-old step-mother in a frilly, red-and-white checkered skirt that skimmed her dimpled thighs was bad enough. Wanda had to go and add tasseled cowboy boots and a Kilgore Rangerette–style cowboy hat perched at a jaunty angle on her permed curls.

"Look at my bride," Patrick murmured, his seamed face wreathed in wonder. "Isn't she something?"

Cleo's heart melted. She could live with the dithering. She could put up with the indecision. She might grind her teeth to stumps if forced to go shopping for more than an hour or two with the woman, but what were a few stumps compared to the goofy smile on her father's face?

"Yes, Pop, she is."

The birthday party wound down around eleven. Cleo hit the rack early, made it to the air-port by 10:00 a.m. on Sunday and landed in Albu-querque just after two.

The hour-long drive to Santa Fe gave her a

taste of a New Mexico winter. She could sum it up in three words—high, dry and *cooooold*. As she neared Santa Fe, the city's seven-thousand-foot elevation took those factors and multiplied them by what felt like a factor of ten.

The breath-stealing altitude made for a searing blue sky. Not a cloud puffed on the empty stretch. Sunlight glittered like glass on the snow-covered mountains ringing the capital. Cleo followed I-25 into the city and fell instantly in love.

Snow dusted the pueblo-style buildings, giving the adobe structures the look of frosted gingerbread houses. Long strings of dried red chilies dangled from exposed roof beams. Wreaths made from the same ubiquitous peppers decorated walls and doors. Sacks that looked like brown paper bags but were probably some weather-resistant polymer lined walkways and rooftops. The luminaria would throw off a magical glow at night, as would the lights strung through the trees in the plaza at the center of town.

The five-star El Cortez Inn sat right off the main square. Cleo could only guess at the strings the festival committee had yanked to squeeze her into the exclusive hotel on such short notice. She'd requested a room adjoining those her client would occupy. The mini-suite she was shown to overlooked the plaza and contained a canopy bed, a kiva fireplace and a safe large enough to store her Glock in its hard-sided case along with several spare boxes of ammunition.

Nine-eleven had made it tough to carry her own weapon when she traveled, but Cleo didn't mind the hassle. She'd filled out all the forms, declared the weapon and ammunition to the airlines and shipped them via her checked baggage, as required by Transportation Security Agency regulations. She'd also shipped a full complement of active and passive security systems. Before she installed any of her own devices, though, she needed to check out the hotel system. After stashing the Glock in the safe, she went in search of the director of security.

She found him in an operations center lined with enough monitors and circuitry to launch the space shuttle. A retired cop, he was more than happy to strut his stuff.

"Our guests tend to be high end and receive protection to match. Our surveillance system is state of the art. Hidden Elektron cameras provide fifteen-second sweeps of all public areas, elevators and hallways. We also have eyes into all service areas."

His pride and joy was a recently installed microwave alarm system. Like a man caressing a nubile young mistress, he smoothed his thorny palm over the desk-size console.

"Each guest room is equipped with silent motion detectors. The electronic door key we give the guest at check-in contains a special code. The key deactivates the alarm when the guest unlocks the door, resets it again on exit. Anyone else enters the room, a red light pops up on this console."

"What about the cleaning staff?"

"We change the housekeeping access code every twenty-four hours, and the maids get keys only to the rooms they're scheduled to service that day. Even with that, they have to signal us before they enter a room."

He ran through the fire protection systems, the medical equipment available in house, emergency team response times and a summary of security incidents for the past year. Cleo made the appropriate noises, but her mind was already on the additional defenses she would install when she gained access to Marisa's suite.

That would have to wait until the next day, as the suite was occupied. With the afternoon fast giving way to dusk and temperatures dropping, Cleo settled for a brisk walk around the downtown area to imprint its layout on her mind, and dinner at a restaurant the concierge recommended.

The Sena House had once been home to a Mexican patriarch and his family, which reportedly included twenty-eight children. Shops and boutiques now crowded the enclosed hacienda just a block off the plaza. The restaurant tucked into a corner of the hacienda was strung with Christmas lights and fragrant with the scent of the mesquite logs snapping and crackling in the fireplace. Cleo downed a platter of blue corn enchiladas topped with a green chili sauce and served with confettilike chorizo that left her gasping for breath.

She lingered over a crusty, honey-soaked sopapilla and coffee. She wanted to relax, but the tension that always infected her right before a mission or a challenging case had her by the throat. Idly stirring the thick black brew, she ticked off the tasks remaining before Marisa's arrival.

Cleo had to meet with the festival folks to verify the schedule and security arrangements. Do a face-to-face with her contact at the Santa Fe PD. Conduct a sweep of Marisa's suite. Check out the offensive and defensive driving skills of the chauffeur assigned to the actress.

Scope out Alexander Sloan's lair.

The spoon halted in midstir. Her fingers went tight on the pewter stem.

Marisa Conners came first. Cleo intended to do whatever it took to ensure the star's safety while in Santa Fe. In the process, though, she might finally pay her debt to a long-dead sergeant.

Too wound up to sit any longer, she signaled

for the bill and walked back to the hotel through the cold, star-studded night.

Cleo had arranged to meet with the festival's executive director early Monday morning. With the kickoff event scheduled for Wednesday afternoon, the festival office was a scene of controlled chaos. Volunteers manned phones and computers. Escorts were being given last-minute updates on arrival times. The part-time publicist fielded questions and issued press credentials to a crew that had evidently showed up without advance notice.

"Sorry to catch you at such a busy time."

Joe Garza waved aside her apology. He was a genial New Mexico native with a background in communications, eyes the same shade as his faded denim shirt and a silver belt buckle the size of a Frisbee. As Cleo soon discovered, the silver-haired movie buff also possessed a bone-deep love of the cinemagraphic arts.

"Most of the hard work is done," he assured her. "Now comes the fun part."

Ha! Wait till he had his first face-to-face with Marisa.

"I've read the background material you sent Miss Conners about the festival," Cleo told him. "I understand you've accepted more than two hundred films for judging this year."

"We have. Our festival is getting bigger every year, partly because of the terrific support from

sponsors and local residents like Shirley Mac-
Laine, Judge Reinhold and Val Kilmer, partly because of New Mexico's rich cinema history. The
tradition goes all the way back to Thomas Edison," he told her, obviously warming to a favorite subject. "Edison's film company shot a fifty-
second short at the Isleta Pueblo in 1898. Since
then, our state's glorious natural light and
dramatic scenery have lured a steady stream of
filmmakers."

"I saw the numbers in the brochure. More than
a hundred major feature films shot wholly or
partly in New Mexico in the past decade."

"Those numbers go off the chart when you include indies, shorts and documentaries. We
started the festival to return the favor by show-
casing many of those films. The two hundred
submissions we accepted this year compete for
honors in eight different categories."

Holding up his hand, he ticked them off. "Best
feature, best short, best documentary, best American independent, best Latino, best Native, best
Southwest." Frowning, he waggled his fingers.
"I'm forgetting one. Oh, right. Best art matters
entry."

Whatever that was. Cleo's knowledge of the
film industry was pretty much limited to the security end of the business, although she'd gotten
a taste of the glamour side of it at Cannes. A sour
taste, unfortunately.

"We've sold over twenty thousand tickets to the showings," Joe confided. "Since most folks attend more than one showing, that equates to about eight thousand attendees."

And any one of those eight thousand could represent a threat to Marisa Conners. Not a number Cleo could dismiss lightly.

"Our biggest problem is finding venues to show all those films." With a nod at the map tacked to the wall, he indicated half a dozen locations highlighted in vivid yellow. "Luckily, we have several colleges and universities with good-size auditoriums. We also utilize the Mission San Miguel. It's one of the oldest in the United States, no longer used for religious services but perfect for small showings. As far as I know, we're the only film festival that shows movies in a church."

Cleo refrained from comment. She'd studied the schedule, knew *The Redemption* would premiere at the downtown center for the performing arts. Smart decision by the festival committee. No sense pouring oil on the fire.

When she inquired about the center's status, Joe waxed poetic. "It's actually the old Lensic Theater, located just off the plaza. The theater is a thirties-era gem, completely restored to its former elegance."

"I'll need access to the theater to check out the security before Miss Conners's appearance."

"No problem. Just tell me when you want to do a walk-through and I'll arrange it for you."

"This afternoon around two would work for me."

"I'll set it up."

The executive director hooked his thumbs in his belt. Fingers tapping against the turquoise-studded buckle, he rocked back on his heels and seemed to be choosing his words carefully.

"We scored big this year with *The Redemption*. First time we've premiered a major film during the festival. Given its pre-release hype, it's sure to draw a huge crowd."

"Let's hope it doesn't draw the wrong kind of crowd."

"Yes, well, there is the worry of demonstrators to contend with, especially since Santa Fe's population base is heavily Catholic. That's why we're glad you're handling Miss Conners's security." His blue eyes twinkled. "I did some checking, too. You've got quite a reputation in the business."

She chose to take that as a compliment. "Thanks."

Their private session over, he introduced Cleo to the full-time managing director, several of the volunteer artistic directors and a somewhat frantic press coordinator. But not to the man she particularly wanted to meet.

"Alex Sloan rarely makes an appearance at the office," he explained in response to her casual query. "He and the other board members serve primarily in an advisory capacity. You'll meet them all at the private party the Sloans are giving to kick off the festivities."

Swallowing her disappointment, Cleo spent another hour going through the festival's security plan with the managing director, reviewing the specifics of the events Marisa was scheduled to participate in, and fixing the location of the various venues in her head.

She kicked off the afternoon with a visit to the police department to establish a contact. That done, she conducted her initial walk-through of the Lensic Performing Arts Center.

The restored movie palace was located on San Francisco Street, a stone's throw from the main plaza. The exterior facade was adobe, but the fanciful turrets and arches looked more Spanish than pueblo to Cleo.

The lobby proved even more lavish than the exterior. Neck craning, she drank in silvery columns and brilliant red, green and gold ceiling squares. She was memorizing the lobby layout when the theater's young marketing and PR director came out to greet her.

"Ms. North. Welcome to the Lensic."

Paul Blackman's smile and firm grip won Cleo's instant approval. So did his enthusiasm for the facility he escorted her through.

"The theater was built by Nathan Salmon, a Syrian immigrant who peddled goods out the back of a wagon in the 1890s. He was stranded in Santa Fe during a snowstorm, fell in love with the city and opened a dry-goods store here some years later. Salmon amassed a fortune and, to show his appreciation to the people of Santa Fe, decided to build the most magnificent movie palace in the West."

"Looks like he achieved his goal."

Blackman grinned at the comment. "We restored the theater to its original grandeur, but left off one or two of the more exotic touches."

"You could have fooled me," Cleo murmured as they passed through a vestibule dominated by two massive crystal chandeliers.

"Back when the Lensic was built, a huge striped awning hung from the auditorium ceiling, giving it the appearance of an Arabian tent."

The eight-hundred-seat auditorium still had a fanciful air, Cleo thought. Moorish arches, colorful tiles and plaster rosettes decorated the walls and adorned the proscenium arch above the stage.

"Rita Hayworth, Roy Rogers and Judy Garland all performed on stage here. In 1940, the Lensic hosted the premiere of *Santa Fe Trail*. Ronald Reagan, Errol Flynn and Olivia de Havilland arrived via a train chartered especially for the big event."

"So history repeats itself with the premiere of *The Redemption*."

"On a somewhat smaller scale," Blackman admitted with a sigh of regret for the glamour days. "Still, we're pretty jazzed about hosting the film's first public showing."

Cleo would have been jazzed, too, if the movie hadn't gotten her client crosswise of a half-dozen hate groups. Thinking of the long list Donovan had sent her, she skimmed another glance around the auditorium. She'd loaded the theater's floor plan into her laptop and had memorized the location of every exit. Still, it was one thing to plot escape routes from an empty building, but another altogether when that building was crammed to capacity.

"The 1991 renovation extended the stage by forty feet to accommodate live symphony, ballet and operatic performances," Blackman explained. "We also added space under the stage to allow for a larger orchestra pit, trapdoors, dressing areas and offices."

"I need to crawl around down there."

"Sure. I'll take you down."

"Where does this door lead?" Cleo asked as they emerged in the theater's bowels.

"It's an emergency exit that opens onto Burro Alley."

Blackman punched in a code and leaned on the escape bar. The door opened onto a narrow lane that ran the length of the theater.

"There used to be a row of hitching posts along

this alley. Farmers would bring produce or wood into the city to sell door-to-door. When they finished, they'd tie their burros here, put a blanket over the animals' heads and go off to do their own shopping or hit the cantinas."

Cleo wasn't as interested in the history of the narrow lane as in the fact that it provided the most direct route back to El Cortez Inn.

She spent another half hour prowling the theater, and made arrangements for a second walk-through the day of the premiere, before leaving to check out the rest of the venues.

At each site, she evaluated escape routes and identified choke points. Santa Fe's narrow streets and high pedestrian traffic worried her. The stretch limo Marisa had insisted on would make fast, tight cornering really tricky.

As a result of Monday's reconnoitering, Cleo reserved all of Tuesday afternoon to work with the limo driver. She'd requested someone trained in defensive, evasive and, if possible, offensive vehicular tactics. Randy Scalese filled all three categories.

The former University of New Mexico tackle looked like a walking mountain in his bulky sheepskin jacket. Thumping the limo's hood with the same pride a racehorse owner might show in his prize stallion, he enumerated the vehicle's hidden assets.

"She's got a smooth belly, as you requested. Reinforced with a second plate."

Cleo hunkered down to check the panel riveted across the vehicle's undercarriage. Sealing the vehicle's cavity made it easier to spot signs of tampering, and tougher to plant explosive devices. The additional plate also increased protection from mines and other nasty little surprises.

"Both front and back bumpers are also reinforced," Scalese confirmed. "They're not up to armored vehicle standards, but they'll plow through most barriers."

"What about the tires?"

"Run-flats, per your instructions."

The engine was powerful enough to best a bulldozer in a tug-of-war, and the array of installed electronics would have made Doreen, Cleo's stepcousin-in-law turned gadget freak, drool.

"I assume you park the limo in a locked garage at night."

"I do. And I remain with it at all times when I have to park on the street or in an open lot."

"Good. As an extra measure, I want you to deploy these little babies whenever you're in wait mode."

"These" were handy-dandy electronic trip flares, custom built to Cleo's specifications. The military used similar devices for perimeter defense of forward locations or to mark the positions of mines.

If triggered by motion, heat, sound, light or any other of a dozen programmable alerts, the tiny, two-inch sensors beeped a warning on a handheld unit. If radio silence was required, the sensors could be set to emit a special ultrasonic alert. The military dropped them by air, fired them from a grenade or shoulder launcher, or scattered the sensors manually in groups of up to two hundred and fifty. Cleo had found that six or seven formed a darn near impenetrable shield around a parked vehicle.

When she was satisfied that Scalese knew how to deploy, program and activate the sensors, it was time to put both driver and vehicle through their paces.

"Okay, let's see what this baby can do."

She and Scalese headed out of the city. They found a deserted dirt road, where she tested the driver's responses to emergency situations.

By the time they'd finished, slush coated the windshield and Scalese's once gleaming Lincoln looked like some primordial beast that had just crawled out of a swamp. He didn't seem to mind the dirt, however. Resting his hamlike fists on the wheel, he grinned.

"That was fun."

"A real blast."

She sincerely hoped they wouldn't have to ex-ecute a J-turn or breach a barricade. If they did, at least she knew the burly tackle could execute the maneuvers.

"What now?"

She made a show of consulting the list of venues. "We need to check the rest of the sites. And the residence of the festival chairman," she added casually. "He's hosting the kickoff party tomorrow night. I want to know how to get there and back in the dark."

She also wanted a visual on the residence, along with a fix on any and all close neighbors. Cleo didn't anticipate paying Alex Sloan a late night visit of the unannounced variety, but a girl never knew....

The retired colonel lived on Barranca Road, in an aerie set high in the Sangre de Cristo Mountains. The road up to his residence turned and twisted like a snake with a severe case of indigestion. Gulping, Cleo eyed the sheer drop-offs and tried not to think of conducting evasive maneuvers on these hairpin turns.

The house itself was constructed from a terra-cotta adobe that melted into the snow-draped sandstone cliffs behind it. Massive bronze gates ornamented with ancient Anasazi designs guarded the driveway, which wound through a small forest of pine and piñon.

"Drive on past," Cleo instructed. "Slowly."

Squinting to see through the shadows on the

snow, she spotted at least two surveillance cameras mounted in the trees beyond the gates. And there, almost buried in the drifts, the faint red eye of an infrared beam.

Her boy Alex evidently took no chances.

Smart man.

She had Randy take the limo up until the road switched back enough to give her an eagle's-eye view of the property below.

"Pull over a minute."

Randy edged toward the snow-covered shoulder. Cleo dug a pair of binoculars out of her tote, shouldered open the door and stepped out onto what felt like the top of the world.

Her breath plumed in the icy air and her lungs had to fight to pull in the thin oxygen. Planting her rear firmly against the muddy hood, she brought up the high-powered glasses. A roll of her thumb adjusted the focus and brought Sloan's multilevel adobe dwelling into view. Slowly, she scanned the house and grounds.

She had only a vague idea what real estate ran to in Santa Fe, but she'd bet this particular chunk had set Sloan back six or seven hundred thousand. *Not* the kind of house most retired air force colonels could afford.

Alex Sloan had invested wisely over the years, though. Cleo had pored over the financial disclosure statement Donovan had sent with the colonel's background file. The statement was required of all senior officers in sensitive positions and showed Sloan had built up a nice portfolio of mutual funds and low-risk bonds. He'd also purchased some six thousand shares in his brother's company, buying in initially at a little over three dollars a share. Sloan Engineering now traded at more than five hundred dollars a share on the NASDAQ.

Wondering why the heck her own investments tended to go in exactly the opposite direction, Cleo took a fix on the windows, balconies and exits visible from her position. She had almost finished the sweep when the glint of sunlight on glass drew her gaze. A small structure was tucked away at the back of the property, almost hidden among the pines. A casita, it was called in these parts, constructed of the same terra-cotta adobe as the main house.

A guest cottage? Servants' quarters? Whatever its function, the cabin was occupied. Footprints stamped down the snowy path leading from the house. Another trail of footprints led into the pines...and disappeared.

Interesting.

Cleo kept the binoculars trained on the shadowy depressions until the heat from the limo's engine cooled and the metal under her rear went from cozy to distinctly uncomfortable. Butt cheeks numb, she pushed away from the fender.

"Okay," she said, sinking back into the heaven of heated leather, "let's head back down."

Reversing, Randy found a spot wide enough to wedge the limo around. When they approached Sloan's gates again, he slowed and shot Cleo a questioning look. "Want me to turn in?"

She was tempted. Very tempted. She could say she was doing advance recon prior to Miss Conners's arrival. She'd catch Sloan off guard that way and be able to assess the man without a party crowd to distract her. On the other hand, she'd counted on that party crowd to distract *him*. Regretfully, Cleo shook her head.

"No. We'd better check out the last venue and head back to town."

"What is the last venue?"

"Bishop's Lodge. Best I can tell from this map, it's not far from here."

"Not far at all," Randy drawled, "if you're a crow."

Non-crows, Cleo discovered, had to drive back *down* the narrow, winding road, travel a few miles by highway, and crawl *up* another track just as twisty.

They got down okay, but Randy started darting glances at the rearview mirror after they'd left the short stretch of highway and started back up again. Cleo threw a look over her shoulder at the nondescript gray sedan some fifty or so yards behind them.

"When did we pick them up?"

"Halfway down Barranca. I figured we'd lose them when we turned off on the road to Bishop's Lodge, but they're still with us. Could be they're just going to the resort, like us."

"Could be."

She scanned the road ahead. The two-lane blacktop cut through the hills like a scar. Stands of blue spruce and aspen thrust up between snow-dusted red boulders, and banded the pavement on both sides.

"There's a turnoff just ahead." She squinted at the signpost half buried in the snow. "State Road 12. Where does it go?"

"It loops back to the highway, but most of the road is unpaved."

"Take it and we'll see if our friends follow."

They did. They also closed the distance between the two vehicles to less than ten yards.

Eyes narrowed, Cleo swiveled around. Both the driver and the individual riding shotgun wore wraparound mirror sunglasses and bone-white arctic parkas. The kind designed for maximum concealment in snowy conditions.

Randy picked up on the significance of the parkas a few seconds after Cleo did. Frowning, he cut his glance back and forth between the road ahead and the rearview mirror.

"They aren't skiers. Not in that gear."

"That's what I'm thinking."

The First Mistake 91

She was also thinking about the Glock still in the safe in her hotel room. She didn't usually carry unless she was covering a client.

"Want me to lose them?" Randy asked.

"I'd rather find out who they are."

"Fine by me. Just tell me what you want me to do."

She eyed the twisting road ahead. As Randy had warned, pavement had already given way to gravel.

"Hit the gas and take the next two turns the same way you did during our practice runs."

"Yes, *ma'am!*"

His size-thirteen tromped down on the accelerator. Tires spun. Dirt and gravel spewed out behind the rear wheels. The limo shot forward with all the speed and grace of an Abrams tank.

Grabbing the grip above the passenger door, Cleo hung on through the first turn. The second slammed her against the door. She waited only until Randy had three of the four wheels in contact with the road again before punching the button on her seat belt.

"Slow down enough for me to bail out."

He tore his glance from the road. "Huh?"

"Now!"

His boot hit the brake. Cleo wrenched the door handle. Icy air whooshed through the crack.

"Take the limo around the next turn," she

shouted over the rush of the wind. "Leave it crossways across the road and run for the trees."

She hit the snow at the side of the road, rolled to her feet and sprinted into a stand of aspen.

5

Cleo was behind a silver-barked aspen, sucking in her gut to make herself invisible, when the gray sedan careened around the curve. The vehicle whizzed right past her and shot into the next turn.

Abandoning her cover, she plunged through the trees. Brakes squealed. Tires screeched. She rounded the curve just in time to spot the gray sedan fishtail wildly and rock to a stop mere inches from the limo. Before the tires finished spinning, the two men jumped out. The sight of their weapons had Cleo sucking in another breath.

Holy shit! Those goons carried some serious firepower.

The driver sported a semiautomatic with a lethal-looking silencer screwed into the barrel. His passenger held an assault rifle in close to his body in a way that told Cleo he knew how to use it.

Who the hell were these guys? And why were they on her tail?

Cleo intended to find out. First, though, she had to lead them away from Randy Scalese.

"Hey!"

Her shout cracked like a whip in the frigid air. Both men whirled. Cleo didn't stick around long enough for them to get her in their sights. Zigzagging through the aspen, she plowed through the fresh snow.

The altitude got to her sooner than she'd anticipated. Within moments, the thin, icy air stabbed into her lungs. Moments more and she was wheezing like an old bicycle pump.

Damn! She'd better schedule a high-altitude training session with Goose after this gig. She needed a better gauge of how fast and how far she could go in conditions like these.

Not as far or as fast as she wanted to, obviously. Dragging in a gasp that went down like broken glass, Cleo scrapped Plan A and improvised Plan B. She'd hoped to lead these clowns well away from the limo, circle around and head back to their vehicle to do a little search. The way her heart was chugging, she wouldn't make another fifty yards.

Okay, fine. She couldn't charge forward much farther. She'd have to go up. Up had worked in Las Vegas.

She plowed on until she spotted a branch thick enough to suit her. Huffing, she ran past the branch, stopped dead and jumped into the air. A full-body twist brought her back down with her boots planted squarely in the snowy holes she'd just made.

Retracing the deep tracks, she dashed back to the branch. Her gloved palms slapped against the tree limb. The neat somersault she executed would have won a grunt of approval from Goose, who tended to communicate primarily in monosyllables.

Going into a tuck, Cleo caught her knees on the branch. Mere seconds later, she'd righted herself and was wedged tight against the trunk. It didn't hide all of her, but she counted on her highly visible footprints to distract the men, who came charging through the trees. She also counted on the thin, brittle branch she'd ripped off to provide her with a counterforce to their arsenal.

She let the first of her pursuers chug by below, thrilled to see his breath was coming as hard and fast as hers. She dropped like a cat behind the second.

Her arm whipped around his throat. Jerking him back, she dug the sharp, jagged end of the stick into the vulnerable spot right below his jaw.

"What the—!"

His startled exclamation spun his partner around. The silenced semiautomatic took an instant bead. From behind her living shield, Cleo stared into the unwinking red eye of a laser-guided sight.

"Drop your weapons," she barked, angling away from the lethal beam. "Both of you."

For added emphasis, she tightened her choke-hold and dug the stake in a little deeper.

"Jesus!"

The man she held pinioned dropped his assault rifle. The laser beam aimed by his companion didn't waver, however. For a throat-closing moment, Cleo thought he intended to shoot right through his partner. Her heart did a jerky little dance just under her ribs until the semiautomatic hit the snow.

"Okay, boys. Let's have it. Who are you?"

She loosened the pressure on her captive's windpipe enough for him to respond, but the stake remained buried in the soft tissue just under his jaw.

"CIA," he gasped.

Cleo didn't ask for identification. She wasn't about to allow either of them to reach inside their parkas.

"Care to tell me why we're playing tag?"

Laser Man responded this time. Assault Rifle Guy was too busy gulping in air.

"We'll answer that when you confirm your identity."

Confirm, huh? That meant they'd already run the Lincoln's tags, contacted the limo agency and obtained a tentative ID on both driver and passenger. That also meant they had access to state or police data systems and were probably the government men they claimed to be. She wasn't quite ready to let them off the hook, though.

"Why don't you tell me who you think I am?"

"You're Cleo North," he snapped. "Private security consultant. Current residence, Dallas. Eyes, brown. Height, five-eight. Weight, one twenty-three."

He was a few pounds shy, but why sweat the small stuff?

"You're also former air force OSI," the operative growled. "Special Agent Donovan informed us you'd be operating in the vicinity."

Jack's name took all of the fun out of things. "If you'd IDed me, why the heck did you jump on my tail?"

"You were observed conducting surveillance of a particular residence on Barranca Drive. We wanted to talk to you about it."

"So you chased me through the woods with weapons drawn?"

A flush mounted Laser Man's cheeks. His mirrored sunglasses shielded his eyes, but Cleo had a hunch they weren't real friendly.

"You conducted evasive maneuvers, abandoned your vehicle and took off. We were merely following."

"Suuuure you were." Edging away from Rifle Guy, she tossed her stick aside. "Let's see some ID."

They both stared at the jagged branch, one in disbelief, the other in disgust.

"IDs?" Cleo drawled.

She took her time studying their credentials, mostly to annoy them. Rifle Guy's identified him as Andrew Modesto. Laser Man was Charles Porter. Then again, you never knew with CIA. The IDs were probably as phony as the polite smiles she got when she returned their credentials.

"We'd better continue this conversation back at our vehicles," she advised. "My driver might be getting a little anxious."

Scalese was more than anxious. They spotted him following their tracks through the woods, a jack handle clutched tight in one fist and a tire chain dangling from the other. The tension in his shoulders eased when Cleo trudged into view, apparently unharmed and on sociable terms with her pursuers.

His glance shifted back and forth between the two parka-clad men. "Who are your friends?"

"They're good guys," Cleo assured him with only a slight mental cramp.

She left it to the two agents to identify themselves, which they declined to do. Apparently Scalese didn't have a need to know.

"What's going on?"

Cleo fed the driver a variation of the same line the two men had fed her. "They spotted us checking out the high-dollar properties on Barranca."

"And thought we were casing them?" Scalese didn't try to hide his skepticism as he eyed the assault rifle slung over Rifle Guy's shoulder. "That's some neighborhood watch the folks up there have going for them."

"Yes," Porter—Laser Man—replied, "it is. Would you return to your vehicle, sir? We still have some questions for Ms. North."

Randy looked to Cleo for guidance. At her nod, he turned and plowed back the way he'd come. The other three followed as far as the road. When the limo door thudded shut behind the driver, Porter picked up where they'd left off.

"Why were you conducting a surveillance of Alex Sloan's residence?"

Cleo debated her answer and decided the truth would work. "Colonel Sloan and his wife are hosting a private cocktail party for the film festival VIPs tomorrow evening. My client plans to attend."

"And?"

"And I don't take clients *in* anywhere until I'm satisfied I can get them *out*." She tucked her hands into the crooks of her arms. "Your turn, Porter. Why is the CIA running cover on Sloan's residence?"

She already knew part of the answer. It had to do with the new sound technology. What she didn't know was why the Company had set up operations so far from town. Were they planning to lure the North Koreans out here? She would have thought they'd approach the sound man at his hotel in town, using the bustle of the festival to mask the contact.

Porter dodged her question by keying the transmit button on the small radio clipped to his shoulder. He moved far enough away to shield his brief communication, but his jaw had torqued tight when he returned to Cleo.

"That's all for now, Ms. North. You're free to go."

"Funny," she mused. "I kinda thought it was the other way around."

Porter dragged off his sunglasses. His eyes held all the warmth of a granite tombstone. Obviously, the man lacked anything resembling a sense of humor.

Cleo left him and his cohort with a careless wave and a promise to go a little gentler on them next time.

The first call caught Donovan in the shower. He had his back to the tiles and the water going full blast. The scalding stream had almost needled away his bitch of a day.

Head cocked, he counted the rings. His terse

invitation to leave a message came on, followed by a request from the OSI Ops Center that Major Donovan contact General Barnes. Immediately.

"Shit."

Closing his eyes, Jack let the water work its magic for another five minutes before stepping out, toweling off and padding naked into the bedroom. The Ops Center patched him through to the general's quarters.

"I just got a call from Henry Philbrook," Barnes announced grimly.

Jack's mind formed an instant profile. Henry Philbrook. Deputy director, CIA. Career bureaucrat. Genuine prick.

"Seems *Ms.* North took on two of his operatives."

The unnecessary emphasis had Jack swallowing a grin. He knew how much it pained the Old Man that Cleo was a civilian. All these years, and he still couldn't get past the fact he hadn't been able to keep one of his most promising—and bullheaded—young agents in uniform.

"Who won?" he asked.

"Who do you think?"

"My money's on Cleo."

"You pegged it. She got the drop on them with a stick."

"Come again?"

"You heard me." There was a huff, followed by

the clack of teeth chomping down on a pipe stem. "She took down two CIA operatives with a sharpened stick."

Jack couldn't help himself. He burst out laughing.

The general waited in pained silence until he got himself under control again. "Philbrook said his guys spotted Cleo checking out Alex Sloan's residence with high-powered binoculars."

"Best I recall, Sloan is hosting some kind of function at his house in connection with the film festival. Cleo would want to recon the site before taking her client in."

"That's what she told Philbrook's boys."

"They're not buying it?"

"*I'm* not buying it."

Neither did Jack.

"I want to see what you gave her on Sloan," Barnes growled. "And what you didn't give her."

"Yes, sir."

"Have the file on my desk first thing in the morning."

"Will do."

When Jack hung up, the warmth of his shower had dissipated, but he barely noticed the goose bumps on his still-damp back and shoulders.

What the hell was Cleo up to?

He knew her. Better than she thought. They'd only worked one op together, but those weeks in

Honduras had given him an insight into the woman that would remain forever branded on his psyche. And on his shoulder.

The woman was smart, independent and sexy as all hell. She was also sly, stubborn and a major pain in the ass when she wanted to be. Jack had a feeling this would turn out to be one of those times.

Cursing, he yanked open a dresser drawer. He'd pulled on clean shorts and was tugging a T-shirt over his head when the phone shrilled again. His answering machine clicked on after two short rings, reminding him he hadn't erased the earlier message.

"Jack? Jack, are you there?"

He froze, the cotton twisted around his upper torso. Every muscle in his body corded.

"Jack, iz me."

Oh, Christ. She was drunk again. He could hear the booze, the whining self-pity. He tugged down the twisted T-shirt and braced himself for the crying jag that would come next.

"Pick up, Jack. *Please* pick up."

There they were, right on cue. The hiccuping sobs. The noisy sniffles.

Jaw locked tight, he slammed the dresser drawer shut. After all the years and all the hurt, she could still tie him in knots. He was halfway across the room when the sobs gave way to bitter, corrosive anger.

"No, 'course you're not there. You never were. Not when I needed you, you bastard."

Blowing out a jagged breath, he lifted the receiver. "What do you want, Kate?"

6

Cleo picked up the key cards for Marisa's suite at eight-forty Wednesday morning. Before letting herself into the rooms, she made a swing by housekeeping to borrow a stepladder.

"Is there something we can assist you with?" the head housekeeper inquired.

"No, thanks. I'll get this back to you in a couple of hours."

The VIP suite was exquisite. Four rooms—sitting area, separate dining room, bedroom, bath—all done in pale wood, wrought iron, and earth tones that evoked a haunting sense of the ancients who'd once inhabited this region. Depositing her handy-dandy bag of tricks on the massive slab of red stone that served as a coffee table, Cleo took a good twenty minutes to commit the layout of the rooms and furniture to memory.

Satisfied she could find her way around the suite in total darkness, she opened her bag and extracted her search tools. The flashlight, screwdrivers and selection of mirrors were hardly high tech. Just part of the grunt work of securing a site. She didn't really expect to find any hidden microphones or explosive devices, but she worked her way methodically through the four rooms anyway.

Unscrewing the ceiling vents, she searched the air ducts. Wall vents and electrical sockets were next. Floors came last. As she replaced each bolt and screw, she coated it with a drop of specially treated silicone. The sealant dried as thin and transparent as Saran Wrap, but the fluorescent dots would light up like orange fireflies under a black light. Cleo could instantly spot any broken or missing seals.

The physical search completed, she conducted an electronic sweep. As she tested the telephone and electrical lines, she suspected Laser Man, Assault Rifle Guy and friends were doing the same thing at the hotel across the plaza. According to the roster Cleo had obtained from Joe Garza, executive director of the film festival, the North Korean crew was scheduled to check into La Fonda this afternoon.

Which again begged a question. Since the North Koreans were booked into a hotel in town, why had the CIA gone all hyper when they'd spotted Cleo scrutinizing the outside of Alex Sloan's residence? Maybe she'd find the answer to that question tonight, when she poked around *inside* the place. Along with some answers to the questions about Debra Smith's brutal murder.

Her jaw set in a mix of determination and anticipation, Cleo finished checking the electrical and phone lines and went to work on the appliances.

By 10:50 a.m., she and Randy Scalese were on their way to Albuquerque to pick up Marisa, the star's media consultant and her personal assistant.

Cleo used the hour-long drive to give herself a stern pep talk. Just because Conners had disregarded her advice and waded into the crowd at Cannes didn't mean she'd do it again. They'd both learned from that experience. Marisa had discovered how quickly an adoring crowd could become a mob, and Cleo had learned to gauge the dangerous degrees of adulation. Hopefully, she wouldn't have to put that hard-won experience to work in Santa Fe.

Leaving Randy with the limo, Cleo checked the arrival gates and made for the security checkpoint. The flame-haired star strolled down the concourse a short time later. With a wave to the ogling security personnel, Conners stepped into a barrage of lights and cameras.

Cleo hid a cynical smile as the star postured and posed for the local paparazzi. Marisa Conners had honed her sex kitten pouts and sloe-eyed glances to a fine art. Stunning in white leather pants and an ankle-length duster of the same creamy leather lavishly trimmed with fox, she fielded questions while her handsome, muscle-bound personal assistant went to claim their luggage.

"Miss Conners! Over here!"

Curling her chin into the fox, she gave the photographer from the *Albuquerque Journal* a ten megawatt smile. "Yes?"

"What's your response to the recommendation by the archbishop of the Albuquerque diocese that his parishioners boycott *The Redemption*?"

He got what Cleo suspected was the studio-supplied, bad-publicity-is-better-than-no-publicity response.

"I respect the archbishop's sense of responsibility toward his parishioners, but I'd invite him to view the film before he forms an opinion of it."

"Miss Conners," one of the TV reporters called out. "Is it true you and James Cox, your co-star, got it on during the making of this film?"

"James and I are friends. Just friends."

"His wife seemed to think otherwise when

she sued him for divorce and you for alienation of affections."

"James and Caitlin have since reconciled. It was all a big misunderstanding."

And great PR for *The Redemption*, Cleo thought as she turned in a slow circle to scan the crowd attracted by the cameras and lights. Grudgingly, she gave her client points for keeping her cool through the flurry of questions that followed. Until the last one, that is.

"Miss Conners! Is that real fur you're wearing?"

"Yes."

"So you don't concur with many of your fellow actors who've spoken out against animal cruelty in the entertainment industry and the slaughter of helpless creatures for mere adornment?"

Marisa pretended deafness, but sent her media consultant a get-me-the-hell-out-of-here look. J. L. Evans stepped in.

"Sorry, folks. Miss Conners has appointments in Santa Fe. Here's my card. Call me if you want to arrange additional interviews."

Hitching up her fox-trimmed collar, the actress stewed all the way to the limo. "God, I hate these friggin' animal rights nuts. One of these days I'm going to fire back and ask when was the last time they ate a hamburger. Or if their shoes are *real* leather."

Cleo ignored the outburst and introduced the

new arrivals to Randy Scalese. Marisa acknowledged the driver with a sulky nod. Obviously
impatient to get under way, she searched behind
her. "Where's Peter?"

"He's claiming your luggage," Cleo replied.

"There's a lot of it. You'd better go help him."

"I don't think so."

The woman knew darn well Cleo's responsi-
bilities did not include hauling suitcases. She
needed to remain with her client and keep her
hands free of encumbrances.

"Send the driver, then."

"Randy stays with the vehicle at all times."

"J.L.!"

"I'm on it."

The blade-thin brunette darted back into the
baggage claim area. She returned a few minutes
later with Jacobsen, two porters and a near mountain of luggage. Somehow, Randy levered all the
cases into the trunk.

The scene at the hotel was a repeat of the one
at the airport. Media crowded the hotel entrance.
Fans and gawkers stood elbow to elbow with the
reporters and photographers. Flashes started flaring the minute the limo pulled up.

Cleo exited the vehicle first and scanned the
crowd. As instructed, Peter left the limo next. He
moved forward, acting as vanguard so Cleo
could take up a position to Marisa's rear. Your

everyday, average, dime-store security specialist could conduct a forward surveillance. It took considerable training and concentration to guard against an attack from the sides or the rear while keeping your client in view at all times.

Marisa, of course, hammed it up for the cameras. Waving and blowing kisses, she floated into the hotel. El Cortez's manager waited just inside. So did Joe Garza and the festival's publicity director. The two festival officials escorted their guest artist to her suite, went over the agenda and generally gave her the royal treatment.

Pumped by all the attention, Marisa was in a friendlier frame of mind by the time they left. Kicking off her boots, she dropped onto the plush suede sofa. "How long do I have before the first scheduled interview?"

J.L. consulted the agenda. "Forty minutes."

Marisa's gaze shifted to her personal assistant. The tip of her tongue passed over glossed lips. "That's long enough."

Peter Jacobsen returned his employer's glance. The air between them suddenly went supercharged.

"I need to show you both how the security system works," Cleo stated.

"Do it quick."

Still on a high from her reception downstairs, Marisa didn't bother to pretend an interest in the security system. Peter could listen for both of them. That's what she paid him for—to take care of all the annoying details North kept trying to force on her.

She supposed she should pay attention. North knew her stuff, as Marisa had discovered the hard way in Cannes. Ignoring her security consultant's urgent advice, she'd given in to impulse and answered the strident calls of a fan for an autograph. Turned out the idiot wanted more than a signature. He'd gone for Marisa's hair, intending to yank out a handful as a souvenir. He'd had her by the roots when Cleo doubled the jerk over with a swift knee to the groin.

The incident had made headlines all over the world. Marisa couldn't complain about the publicity, although she didn't like coming across as a helpless twit. Maybe that was why she had such mixed emotions regarding Cleo North. There was grudging admiration, laced with a healthy dose of resentment and pique at how the woman had stolen the spotlight in Cannes.

That wouldn't happen again. Marisa would make sure of it. Right now, though, she had more important matters on her mind than security systems and silent alarms.

Leaning against Peter's shoulder, she wedged her hand between his belt and the small of his back. His buttocks were rock hard. She loved the feel of them, so tight and smooth and hot. She dug her fingers in, squeezing. He managed to keep a straight face until North and J.L. were on their way to the door. Before it clicked behind them, she'd yanked down his zipper.

"Jesus, Marisa! Let me set the dead bolt."

"Screw the dead bolt." She kept him in place by the simple expedient of wrapping her palm around his cock. "Better yet, screw me."

She dropped to her knees and used her strategic handhold to tug him down with her. Peter issued a growled warning when his knees hit the Berber.

"One of us is about to get a serious case of carpet burn."

She was wet by the time he got her out of her leather pants. Damn near gushing when he rammed into her. She liked it like this. No fuss. No frills. Plenty of sweat. She didn't need foreplay. Had never been the kind for kissing and cuddling.

Gritting her teeth, she squeezed her vaginal muscles. Peter grunted and wrapped his big hands around her knees. He knew she liked it fast and hard, knew exactly how to take her to a screaming climax. Yanking up her legs, he hooked her calves over his shoulders and surged forward again and again. Between thrusts, he used his thumb. The pressure on her clit came as close to pain as it did to pleasure.

Groaning, Marisa rode the tight, spiraling sensations as long as she could.

* * *

An hour later, anticipation of her first meeting with Alex Sloan filled Cleo's head as she dressed for the welcome cocktail party. Dark brown hair swept up in a sleek French twist. Billowing black chiffon palazzo pants. A tuxedo-style jacket shimmering with paillettes at the cuffs and lapels. Her compact little ten-shot Glock 29 tucked in its holster and Velcroed to her right ankle.

Not bad, she thought, pirouetting in front of the mirror. Not bad at all. She'd splurged a bit on the outfit. Okay, more than a bit. What was the point of pulling down outrageous fees if a girl didn't treat herself once in a while?

At five-thirty, Randy buzzed to let her know he'd brought the limo around. Cleo tossed a black wool coat over her arm, set her security alarm and rapped on the door to Marisa's suite.

J.L opened it. The media consultant also wore black, unrelieved except for the red slash of her nails and lipstick. With her inky hair and pasty face, she reminded Cleo of an anorexic Elvira. Hunky Peter Jacobsen, on the other hand, looked tanned, healthy and good enough to eat. Which, Cleo thought wryly, Marisa had no doubt already done.

The star herself dazzled the eye in a short-waisted satin jacket and a matching lace skirt, both in bright peacock. The skirt swirled around her thighs. The jacket buttoned well below the swell of her breasts.

She'd clipped her dark-red curls back at the nape, leaving the long column of her neck exposed. No jewelry, Cleo noted, other than the square-cut aquamarine weighting down her right hand. The stone was a good twenty carats.

Marisa's narrow-eyed glance took in every shimmering paillette on Cleo's cuffs and collar. "Valentino?"

"Ungaro."

"Hmm."

"Ready to go?"

With Peter in the lead and Cleo to the right and slightly behind her client, the small cavalcade swept through the lobby. Heads turned. Elbows nudged. Whispers rippled and flowed. Like a queen, Marisa accepted the homage while ignoring the peasants who gave it.

Her volunteer escort for the evening waited in the foyer, shifting nervously from foot to foot. A student majoring in moving image arts at the College of Santa Fe, he'd won this coveted duty by slaving every weekend for the past four months at the festival offices.

Marisa must have still been feeling mellow. She actually got the kid talking about himself and his studies during the drive to Alex Sloan's place. Cleo sat up front with Randy and soon tuned out the patter about optics and the aesthetics of lighting. She kept her eyes on the road ahead, but her mind pinged back and forth between her current client's security and the sergeant she'd failed almost a decade ago.

Heart thumping, she prepared to launch Phase Two of her plan.

Up close, the Sloan residence was even more impressive than it had been when Cleo viewed it through binoculars. The pueblo-style architecture flowed and curved at several different levels. Intricately carved wood trimmed the windows and framed the porches and decks. Luminaria were lined up along every horizontal plane, outlining the entire structure in flickering gold candlelight.

Massive wreaths of bright red chilies decorated the tall double doors. Randy edged past rows of parked vehicles to deposit his passengers right at the chilies.

"Nice little shack," Marisa commented as Peter helped her from the limo.

Their host greeted them in the foyer. His shoulders squared in a way that hinted at his military background, Alex Sloan strode forward.

"Welcome to Santa Fe, Miss Conners."

Cleo's first view of the retired air force colonel generated two immediate impressions. One, the various photos she'd assembled of the man did *not* do justice to his particular combination of gray eyes and jet-black hair just touched with silver at the temples. He was gorgeous, in the best

Pierce Brosnan sense of the word. What's more, he radiated the kind of controlled masculine power that was far more compelling than mere looks.

Two, he was smooth. He didn't bat an eye when Marisa detached herself from Peter without so much as a backward glance and draped herself all over his arm.

"Your home is fabulous," the redhead gushed. "So…so Santa Fe."

"Thank you."

Only the faintest hint of dryness colored Sloan's rich baritone. Tucking his guest's arm against his side, he acknowledged Marisa's careless introduction of the members of her party. His assessing glance took in J.L.'s near-death thinness and Peter's impassive expression before settling on Cleo.

"So you're North Security and Investigations." His mouth curved in a small smile. "I've heard of you. We have a mutual friend in General Sam Barnes."

"I don't know if I'd classify the general as a friend," Cleo replied. "*Fiend*, maybe."

Sloan's smile stretched to a real grin, but before he could comment, an impatient Marisa reclaimed his attention. "I hope you're going to give me a guided tour of your home. I want to see all of it."

"Certainly. Or better yet, I'll get my wife to

show you around. Patrice is the one who designed and decorated the house."

Marisa wasn't about to let him palm her off on his wife. Pouting, she pressed her breasts against his arm and clung to him as the others pinned on the name tags waiting for them on the hall table.

When they were all tagged, Sloan escorted them into an open living room framed on three sides by soaring glass. The windows gave breath-stealing views of snow-capped mountains awash in the light of the rising moon. The glass walls did not, however, provide so much as a glimpse of the little casita tucked among the trees at the rear of Sloan's property.

Cleo turned away from the view and focused her attention on her client. Accepting a flute of champagne from a passing waiter, she pretended to sip it while she drifted through the crowd. Her mind clicked away as she attached faces to the names on the list of attendees she'd been given.

New Mexico's lieutenant governor was there, representing her boss who, she explained to Marisa with an apologetic smile, was out of town. Santa Fe's mayor and his wife had also turned out, as had the festival's main organizers and financial backers.

Several of the other guest artists had made an appearance as well. Cleo spotted the film director who would be honored for his four decades of searing black-and-white documentaries depicting human frailty in its many guises. She also picked out the short, chunky character actor who had appeared in dozens of B-grade westerns.

No North Koreans, though. Evidently they numbered among the many whose work was being shown and judged at the festival but hadn't made the cut for hobnobbing with the VIPs.

Cleo completed almost a full circuit of the living room before she encountered her hostess. The colonel's second wife fit the image Cleo had formed from the snippets of information she'd gathered. Mid-thirties. Silver-blond hair. A skilled potter and generous supporter of the local arts. Not beautiful in the classic sense, but striking. Her ankle-length suede skirt, off-one-shoulder silk peasant blouse and magnificent squash blossom necklace indicated a woman with an unshakable sense of her own style.

Smiling, she offered her hand. "I'm Patrice Sloan. I don't think we've met yet."

"No, we haven't. I'm Cleo North."

"I saw you come in with Miss Conners's party. Do you work with her?"

"Only when absolutely necessary."

"I beg your pardon?"

"I'm a private security consultant," Cleo explained. "Miss Conners hired me to provide additional security during her visit to Santa Fe."

"Did she?" Patrice Sloan's glance flicked to the

woman still snuggled up against her husband. "She isn't expecting trouble, is she?"

"No, just taking normal precautions."

"I suppose that's wise considering the controversy her performance has stirred up." A faint crease formed between the woman's eyebrows. "Alex and Joe Garza and the others have worked so hard to get ready for this festival. It would be a shame if something happened."

"I'm sure nothing will."

Eager to explore, Cleo engaged the woman in polite chitchat for a few more moments before asking for directions to a powder room.

"There's one off the kitchen and another in the hall. If both of those are occupied, you're welcome to use the guest room. It's up the stairs to the left."

"Thanks."

Sauntering through the dining room and kitchen, Cleo moseyed into a study redolent with the scents of leather and of mesquite from the fire crackling in the stone-fronted fireplace. Her attention was riveted instantly by the desk sitting before the windows.

It was a man-sized piece, with memorabilia lined up with military precision on the hand-tooled leather blotter. She smiled at the carved soapstone eagle with wings spread. Appropriate for a full bird colonel. Her glance went to a brass-framed photo of a mustached general in full dress uniform flanked by two straight-backed young sons. Even as boys, Alex and his twin brother had been handsome as sin.

Champagne in hand, Cleo drew a finger along the edge of the leather blotter. Just as casually, she tested the center drawer. She wasn't surprised that the drawer was locked. Sloan didn't strike her as the careless type.

Anxious to get a glimpse of Sloan's private lair, Cleo waited until she'd spotted another guest going into the powder room in the foyer before trying its door handle.

"Oops, sorry," she called in answer to the muffled response. "I'll use the upstairs bathroom."

Over the heads of his guests, Alex watched the trim figure in black mount the spiral staircase. He'd speculated about Cleo North since the day Joe Garza had notified him their guest star might back out of the festival at the last minute due to concerns over her personal safety. Alex suspected those concerns were more PR hype than anything else, but he'd called Marisa Conners himself and ascertained that she'd requested the services of the same security consultant who'd accompanied her to Cannes.

When informed that Ms. North had already turned down the Santa Fe job, Alex had done some digging, then called Sam Barnes. The old boy network still functioned with the same efficiency it had during Alex's days in uniform.

And Ms. North, it appeared, functioned at her own level of efficiency. Which was good, he thought. Very good. He didn't doubt she'd have a very plausible excuse ready when he caught her prowling through his bedroom.

His pulse quickening, he worked his arm free of Marisa's grasp. "Excuse me a moment."

"Sure." She tipped her champagne flute. Her green eyes held his over the rim of the sparkling crystal. "But only for a moment."

With a smile, Alex looked beyond her to her big, beefy assistant. The man didn't return his smile.

With a murmur to his wife that he had some business to attend to and needed her to cover for a while, Alex wound his way through the crowd to the stairs.

7

Cleo reached the top of the stairs and slid a hand into the pocket of her palazzo pants. Aiming the small, palm-size device in her pocket at the surveillance camera mounted midway down the hall, she thumbed the switch.

She hadn't used the scrambler downstairs. There, the crowd had covered her seemingly aimless wandering. Upstairs, she was alone and all too visible.

Keeping an ear tuned to the babble of conversation drifting up the stairs, she fished in her other pocket for a roll of precut transparent strips. The size of a small Band-Aid, each strip contained a hair-thin wire that amplified and transmitted sounds. Cleo peeled off two strips and smoothed them flat on the oak floorboards before screwing a miniature receiver into her right ear.

Early warning system in place, she roamed the second floor at will. The guest suite was almost as large as her Dallas condo. The flat-screen TV in the home entertainment center took up most of one wall. Cocking her head, she skimmed the titles on Sloan's collection of CDs and DVDs. She didn't spot any porn, but then no self-respecting pervert would leave the good stuff out.

The master bedroom boasted a king-size bed with a headboard constructed of slender, white-trunked aspen, and a spa surrounded by glass. Come daylight, the view of the mountains from the universal gym and freestanding shower would be spectacular. Evidently Sloan and his wife didn't worry about the view from the outside looking in. They hadn't bothered with curtains or blinds for the windows.

Cleo did a quick check of the suite's walk-in closet. Sloan's air force uniforms hung toward the rear, neatly zipped into breathable, moth-resistant garment bags. The midnight-blue mess dress still sported his silver aviator's wings and rows of miniature medals. Cleo didn't really expect to find anything in the colonel's underwear or sock drawer linking him to the murdered Debra Smith, but she poked through the built-ins anyway. She'd finished with the top two drawers and was reaching for the third when the distinctive thud of footsteps reverberated through the miniature receiver. Whipping out the earpiece, she tucked it back in her pocket and headed for the bedroom door. Just across the threshold, she came nose to nose with Alex Sloan.

He didn't back off. Neither did she. For a second or two, they played chest tag.

"Lost, Ms. North?"

"Just scoping out the upstairs. I like to map out alternate options for extracting my client should the primary exits become unusable."

"Did you find satisfactory means of extraction?"

"One or two. If necessary, I could toss Marisa through the guest room window into a snowbank. The slope behind the house is considerably higher than in front. Or I could lower her from the balcony of this room. I noticed you keep a fire escape ladder curled up on the deck."

"Like you, I always like to have a backup plan. Must be our military training."

"Speaking of the military..." Cocking her head, Cleo matched him stare for stare. "I looked over your bio and saw we were both stationed at Luke at the same time. Strange we never ran into each other."

"Luke is a big air patch."

"You worked the Harvest Eagle Program, didn't you?"

He didn't so much as flicker an eyelash, but

Cleo sensed the shields going up. Even the unclassified name of the hush-hush activity raised alarms.

"Yes, I did. You're remarkably well informed, Ms. North."

She waved a hand breezily. "All part of the job. I investigated a case involving one of the Harvest Eagle people. Staff Sergeant Mitchell. Maybe you remember him."

"No, I... Oh, wait. Was Mitchell the one who shot himself?"

"He was. After he butchered his girlfriend, Sergeant Debra Smith."

She said the name slowly, deliberately, watching for his reaction. All she got was a headshake.

"That was a bad business."

Cleo's job required an ability to analyze statements and interpret body language. The colonel's didn't hint at deep, tortured guilt in connection with the decade-old murder.

"I should get back to the party," he said. "Would you care to join me? If you're finished up here, that is."

"I'm finished."

For now, she added silently as he tucked her arm in his. Her fingers tested the corded muscle under the worsted wool of his sleeve. Evidently that universal gym wasn't just for show. Sloan worked out.

When they neared the top of the stairs, she

glanced up and caught his gaze aimed at the V of her tuxedo jacket. The gleam in those gray eyes told her something other than that the paillettes decorating her collar and lapels had snared his interest.

"We'll both be busy during the festival," he commented. "Maybe you should stay over afterward. Let me show you around Santa Fe."

Cleo's pulse skittered, but she couldn't decide whether Sloan was playing games or seriously coming on to her. But she began to understand why Debra Smith might have been attracted to this man ten years ago. In a hand-tailored suit, he was sex on the hoof. Put him in a uniform, add the potent aphrodisiac of rank and power, and he'd send any woman's temperature off the chart.

"I'll think about it," she answered archly.

Over the shoulder of one of her guests, Patrice noted her husband's return. She also noted the hand he put to the small of his companion's back to steer her through the crowd. Excusing herself, she moved to intercept them. Her smile included them both.

"Have you been giving Ms. North a tour of the house, Alex?"

"I have. We've also been catching up on old times."

"Oh?"

"Ms. North is former air force. She was stationed at Luke at the same time we were."

"Really?" A flicker of movement by the window drew her gaze. "Oh, no, Alex! Sylvia Delacruz has Miss Conners hemmed in at the bar."

With a nod to the dark-haired woman at his side, Alex went to the rescue. The cornered movie star greeted him with undisguised relief, and Patrice turned her attention back to their guest.

"Were you in the security business at Luke, Ms. North?"

"Call me Cleo. Yes, I was with the Office of Special Investigations."

"Counterintelligence or criminal investigations?"

"Criminal investigations at first, followed by CI and fraud. I was brand-new at the time. Still on my probationary period as an agent."

"I'm an avid fan of Ludlum and le Carré," Patrice admitted with a small laugh. "I'm addicted to all that cloak and dagger, secret agent stuff."

"It could get exciting at times. Other times, it was just grunt work."

"I imagine so. Would you excuse me? It looks like the mayor needs his drink refreshed."

Cleo eyed her hostess as she glided over to her guest. The cool, elegant blonde didn't strike her as the type to gobble up thrillers, or to take such an interest in her husband's career that she'd know about the inner workings of the OSI.

Then again, maybe there was something in said husband's past linking him to an OSI inquiry—like an investigation of the murder of a woman he might have had an affair with.

Cleo knew she was stretching here. Really stretching. But she'd learned the hard way to go with her gut. Whipping out her mental checklist, she added Patrice Sloan to the number of folks she intended to get to know better in the next few days.

The lieutenant governor left the cocktail party a little past nine. The rest of the guests began to filter out soon afterward. Cleo waited patiently until Marisa joined their ranks.

The star was in a mellow mood during the drive back to the city. And why not? She'd wrestled around under the sheets with her assistant this afternoon and by Cleo's count she'd downed at least five glasses of champagne this evening.

Cleo flicked a glance in the rearview mirror. Her client was snuggled up next to Jacobsen. J.L. made a production of looking out the window. The young volunteer escort tried gamely to make conversation while Marisa's tongue played peekaboo with her lover's ear.

Catching Cleo's eye in the mirror, the handsome assistant twisted his lips in a cynical smile.

That wasn't all he twisted. Apparently he could torque his employer's temper as well as her hormones. Cleo discovered that interesting fact when she prowled the hotel corridor for her final check of the night.

J.L. was tucked away in her room on the other side of the suite Marisa shared with Jacobsen. The shouts, not quite muffled by the suite's door, indicated all was not perfect in Conners-land. From the sound of it, the actress had worked up a full head of steam and was releasing it in short, angry bursts.

"I didn't *fawn* all over him!"

Jacobsen's reply was low and muted.

"It's image," Marisa shrilled. "I'm telling you, it's all image!"

Yeah, right, Cleo thought.

Evidently Peter agreed with her assessment, as the sound of glass shattering followed his inaudible reply. Thinking she'd better intervene before hotel security arrived on the scene, Cleo rapped on the door.

Her client yanked it open. Her hair tumbled around her angry face and her green eyes were anything but friendly.

"Everything okay?"

"Yes. Go away."

Marisa woke up the next morning feeling like warmed-over crap. The champagne had left her with a pounding headache. The fight with Peter had left her edgy and disgruntled.

Her rotten mood stayed with her all day and into the evening. It didn't improve when a small band armed with signs denouncing *The Redemption* showed up in front of her hotel just in time to make the six o'clock news. Of course, the media had to turn a few ultraconservatives into a nationwide commentary.

Friday morning brought more protesters, apparently gathering steam for the premiere that night. It also brought another forum featuring all three of the festival's guest artists. Marisa wasn't thrilled at having to share a dais with a director who had yet to shoot a feature-length film and a character actor whose name she had trouble remembering.

She kept a smile on her face and gave every appearance of interest when an intense female with long, stringy gray hair got the nod to speak into the audience mike.

"Mr. Panovitch, would you say your preference for black and white in your films reflects a sense that there's no color in death? Or life, for that matter?"

Who the hell cared? And why wouldn't a woman her age have the sense to hack off that waist-length tangle?

Marisa closed her ears to the convoluted, long-winded response. Christ, she ached for a cigarette! At Peter's insistence, she'd given them up a few months ago. She'd given up Cloud and quaads, too, which were a hell of a lot harder to do without than cigarettes.

She could use a lift right now. God knew she hadn't gotten one from Peter last night. She couldn't believe he still had such a burr up his butt over that cocktail party. So she'd flirted with the film festival's chairman? It wasn't as if she'd fucked the man.

Like she had her co-star, James Cox.

Marisa shifted on her folding chair. Peter had never mentioned the rumors circulating in the tabloids. But she knew he suspected she and James had been going over more than their lines in their trailers during the filming of *The Redemption*.

Peter also suspected James had supplied the Cloud that had sent her spiraling into respiratory distress, too. He was right. That sordid little episode had almost landed her in the hospital. It had certainly ended the affair.

Thank God Peter been there when the shoot ended. He'd helped her through the depression, the delusions, the lingering vertigo resulting from the drugs.

Still, that wasn't any reason for the man to go all Neanderthal and possessive on her. He was her administrative assistant, for God's sake. He knew how important it was for her to maintain her image as a sex goddess. That was the reason—the *only* reason—she'd crawled all over Alex Sloan.

"Ms. Conners?"

"Yes?"

She gave the man who'd claimed the mike an automatic smile. He looked innocuous enough. Rust-red hair trimmed to relative neatness. One of those pointy Van Dyke beards the under-thirty set seemed to be addicted to these days. Wire-rim glasses. A performing arts major, she guessed, although he looked a little past college age.

"How do you sleep at night, knowing you've profaned something so many of us hold dear?"

So much for innocuous. Marisa hung on to her smile. "I assume you're referring to my portrayal of the Virgin Mary in *The Redemption*?"

"I am."

The studio response came smooth and easy. "I assure you, there's nothing profane about my portrayal. I was merely trying to celebrate Mary's essential womanhood."

Why couldn't these dumb fucks accept she'd just been playing a part? Had viewers watched Anthony Hopkins in the *Silence of the Lambs* and come away convinced he devoured human flesh?

Probably.

"Aren't you worried you'll burn in hell for desecrating the Virgin's image?"

"No, I'm not."

The moderator tried to nudge him aside, but he refused to yield the mike. "That's what happens to blasphemers, you know. They burn in hell."

"Blasphemy is in the eye of the beholder," Marisa snapped. "So is art."

"You don't really consider *The Redemption* art?"

"Yes, I do."

Seriously annoyed, Marisa searched the room. Where the hell were the festival organizers? They were supposed to handle hecklers like this.

Relief feathered through her when she spotted her high-priced security consultant making her way down the aisle. Cleo had her sights set on the speaker. She'd hustle him away fast enough.

Marisa wasn't stupid. She'd sensed the disdain under North's mask of professional neutrality after that incident in Cannes. She knew darn well she shouldn't have waded into the crowd against Cleo's advice. Knew, too, she shouldn't have panicked when that souvenir hunter buried his fist in her hair. More shaken by the incident than she'd wanted to admit, Marisa had passed the rest of her time at Cannes in a drug- and alcohol-induced haze.

The situation was different this time around. *The Redemption* was bringing the nuts out of the woodwork. She wasn't up against mere souvenir hunters this time, but fanatics fueled by hate and bigotry. That's why she'd insisted on Cleo North. The woman knew her stuff.

Feeling suddenly, ridiculously naked, Marisa resisted the urge to shrink back in her chair as North approached the man at the microphone.

"Excuse me, sir."

Cleo kept her voice low and her tone polite, but she was fully prepared to take the guy down if he made a suspicious move. Her glance flicked to his name tag.

"You've made your point, Mr. Martin. It's time for someone else to have a turn at the mike."

The heckler shrugged and turned to make his way back to his seat. Deftly, Cleo steered him toward one of the exits.

"I'd like to talk to you a moment. This way, please."

He went with her willingly enough. She got him off to a quiet corner.

"Are you from around here, Mr. Martin?"

"Yes."

"May I see some ID?"

His blue eyes narrowed. They were a bright, almost startling turquoise. Tinted contact lenses, Cleo bet.

"Why do you need to see my ID?"

"I'd just like to verify you're who your name tag says you are and that you're a registered participant at the film festival."

"Why?" he asked again, more belligerently this time.

"Because your comments to Miss Conners could be construed as conveying a threat."

"I was just expressing my opinion."

"Let's see some ID."

Digging into his back pocket, he produced a photo ID identifying him as a student at the University of New Mexico. He also produced a New Mexico driver's license with a picture of the same face with a somewhat bushier beard. The address was local.

Cleo made a show of entering the pertinent information in her notebook before handing back his IDs. "You might want to temper any future remarks to or about Miss Conners, Mr. Martin."

With a careless shrug, he stuffed his cards back in his wallet. "Are we done?"

"For now."

She watched him depart the auditorium before flipping through her notebook for the number of her contact at the Santa Fe PD. After a brief recap of the incident, she provided Detective Salazar with the pertinent details.

"His name is Andrew Martin. He's a local. Resides with his parents at 2250 Old Cerrillos Road. Currently enrolled as a graduate student in cinematic arts at the University of New Mexico, Albuquerque campus."

"Got it. We'll check him out and get back to you."

"Thanks."

Frowning, Cleo hit the end button. The brief exchange inside the forum had shaken her client. She hadn't missed the wariness in Marisa's face when Martin refused to relinquish the mike—or her relief when Cleo moved in and politely hustled him away.

Maybe now the actress would take her personal security more seriously. Granted, it wasn't an easy task for someone who made a living by putting herself out there for the public. Marisa had to walk a fine line between being accessible to her fans and accepting that not everyone admired her or her work. Particularly her work in *The Redemption*.

Chewing on in the inside of her cheek, Cleo slipped her cell phone into her blazer pocket and checked the agenda for the rest of the day. The schedule was packed. After this forum, Marisa would meet with media and then lunch with a selected group of festival attendees.

Following lunch she was giving a workshop and appearing at a tribute tea, where she'd greet the public and sign autographs. Tonight she'd attend another cocktail party prior to the gala premier of *The Redemption*. A champagne and chocolate extravaganza courtesy of Whitehorn Studios would follow the showing.

Cleo had a thousand tasks that needed doing before the premiere. Her mind was clicking through her mental to-do list when Peter Jacobsen made his way toward her.

Worry clouded his Nordic features. "Did the police have anything on that character?"

"They're going to check him out and get back to me."

"Keep me posted on what you find out."

"I will."

As Jacobsen cut a path back to the auditorium, Cleo wondered about his relationship with Marisa. Evidently they'd put their little lovers' spat behind them, yet the suppressed violence she'd heard in their exchange Wednesday night brought to mind another lovers' quarrel. One that had ended in murder and suicide.

The lack of progress on the case that had brought her to Santa Fe gnawed at Cleo. Despite the packed schedule, she'd try to grab a few moments alone with Alex Sloan tonight.

She'd follow up on his veiled offer to show her around Santa Fe, see how far he'd take things. If he was willing to cheat on his wife with Cleo, maybe he'd cheated on her with other women.

Maybe with Sergeant Debra Smith.

8

Marisa's entire support entourage was kept hopping for the rest of the day. Radiating waves of nervous energy, J.L. Evans popped up everywhere. Cleo had to admire the publicist's skill as she funneled media to Marisa for interviews, directed fans to the star's various venues and staged a seemingly endless series of photo ops.

Peter Jacobsen stayed on the go, too. Quietly efficient, he shepherded Marisa from event to event. While she was onstage or giving interviews, he had his cell phone plastered to his ear.

As busy as they were, though, both Evans and Jacobsen provided Cleo with extra sets of eyes. She'd coached them on what to look for as they transitioned about, which were pretty much the same things she looked for herself. A face without a smile. A hand tucked in a pocket. A briefcase or piece of luggage left unattended near Marisa's path.

Randy Scalese proved his worth, as well. Outfitted for duty in a spiffy black chauffeur's uniform, a string tie and a Stetson banded with gleaming silver conchos, the limo driver whisked Marisa's group from event to event. He managed to avoid most of the traffic, zipping around the choke points.

Cleo stuck close to her client throughout Friday morning and afternoon. Her first break came at the conclusion of the tribute tea. The star retreated to her suite to recharge her batteries for the evening's events. Cleo saw her settled in and took off to take care of the to-do's on her list.

Her first order of business was to review the security arrangements and crowd control plan for the premiere with the festival's director. Her second, another walk-through of the theater itself.

This time Joe Garza joined her. With the Lensic's engaging young marketing director again acting as guide, Cleo and Joe inspected exits, checked placement of equipment and reviewed the seating charts.

"Marisa will be seated in the front orchestra, close to the aisle, right?"

"Right." Joe indicated the precise seat. "Alex Sloan and his wife will flank her to the right, her volunteer escort will be on her left."

That ought to put Marisa in a great mood. Nothing like being escorted to the gala premiere of her new film by a volunteer instead of her sexy co-star. The studio had debated flying James Cox in for the evening, but had put him on the talk show circuit instead. Cox would be hawking *The Redemption* on *The Tonight Show* in preparation for its nationwide opening tomorrow.

Cleo had enough on her mind without the additional furor Cox's presence would have stirred. Given the rumors about his supposed affair with Marisa, his arrival on the scene would have sent the media into a feeding frenzy. Thank God they'd dodged that bullet!

Frowning, Cleo surveyed the stage. It was more retracted than she remembered from her first visit and now gave a clear view of the orchestra pit below.

"Will the stage remain back like this during the film showing tonight?"

"This is how we usually configure it for movies," Paul Blackman confirmed. "That way, we can bring the screen right down to the edge of the stage to form a solid visual line."

"So where *is* the screen?"

He hooked a thumb skyward. "We keep it rolled up when not in use."

Craning her neck, Cleo searched among the light racks and fly bars. In the dim recesses she spotted a long, heavy-looking black case suspended from two struts.

"Doesn't rolling damage the screen?"

"Not that one. It's state-of-the-art Velux. Several layers of melted vinyl pellets mixed with binding chemicals and coated with layers of reflective paint."

Cleo professed herself suitably impressed.

After another check of the backstage and understage areas, she followed the two men to the control center at the rear of the theater. Like everything else in the newly refurbished performing arts center, the booth screamed high-tech. She tried to look knowledgeable as Paul and Joe fell into raptures over the five deck DMC platters, Dolby speakers, computer-controlled lighting and a revolutionary new acoustical system.

"The ACS employs electronic signal processors and embedded microphones," Blackman informed her. "They create different acoustic qualities for various performances. A symphony needs a reverberation time of two seconds, vocal performances only one second."

Oooh-kay.

"Then you have the dancers," the young PR director continued. "We need to silence their footfalls so as not to distract from the artistry of their performance. This system allows us to create different acoustic qualities for each medium."

Shoving back the lapels of his jacket, Joe hooked his thumbs in his belt. "The system was state of the art when it was installed a few years ago. The Performing Arts Council may have to take another look at it after that Korean sound crew demonstrates their wave enhancement technology."

That snagged Cleo's interest. "The North Koreans are going to share their technology?"

"Share? Not hardly! But they're giving a demonstration at La Fonda." He checked his watch, an elaborate affair of turquoise and silver that rivaled his belt buckle in artisanship. "Should start in about twenty minutes. Care to attend?"

Hell, yes, she'd care to. "Let me make another quick pass through the lobby area and we'll head over to the hotel."

La Fonda Hotel sat on the northeast corner of the main plaza. According to the informative Joe Garza, an inn, or *fonda*, had occupied that same spot since the city was founded in 1607 and had long marked the terminus of the famous Santa Fe Trail.

The sprawling adobe structure currently in place was once part of the Atchison, Topeka and Santa Fe Railroad's chain of Harvey Houses. It now housed several hundred guest rooms, an array of expensive boutiques and a covered courtyard restaurant humming with the lively strains of mariachi guitars and the scent of sizzling fajitas.

The conference and breakout rooms were on the lower level. Cleo followed Joe down a flight of creaky wooden stairs, dividing her attention between the uneven steps and the array of goods displayed in glass-fronted niches. A multistrand necklace in lapis and gold caught her attention. Instant lust flooded through her.

Normally, Cleo wasn't into jewelry. She didn't have much occasion to wear it in her profession. But the handcrafted gold butterfly clasp was a work of art and the cobalt-blue beads were the exact color of Jack Donovan's eyes.

The thought stopped her in her tracks. Well, hell! Where had that come from?

With everything else on her mind right now, the last thing she needed was to let Special Agent Donovan back into her head. Not to mention her life. Scowling, she followed Joe Garza down to the breakout room set aside for discussion of "Techniques in Sound Editing and Projection."

The first person she spotted in the crowded room was Assault Rifle Guy. Otherwise known as Andrew Modesto, if she remembered correctly. The CIA operative looked a little different from their last meeting. The arctic snow parka and mirrored sunglasses were gone, for one thing. So was the pointed stick Cleo had jammed into the soft tissue just under his jaw.

Today he'd decked himself out in what she guessed was supposed to be sound engineer hip. His jeans rode so low they looked as if they were about to fall off. The V-neck of his cable sweater showed a thatch of curly chest hair. And as if that swatch of hair wasn't bad enough, he actually wore a beret. Not the military, I'll-kick-your-ass kind. This was one of those artsy versions, pancaked flat against the side of his head. The thing even had a little nib sticking out in the center.

Grinning, Cleo followed Joe to some empty chairs a couple of rows behind Modesto's. She plopped down, scanning the room for his buddy. Yep, there was Laser Man. Also sans parka and sunglasses. Sans beret, too, thank God!

Porter flicked a single disinterested look in her direction and glanced away again. His show of nonchalance didn't impress her. She knew darn well he'd be on the horn to his superiors to advise them of her presence ten seconds after the seminar broke up—assuming he wasn't already transmitting some coded signal.

Idly, Cleo wondered how many others in the room were CIA. Or scientists out of Los Alamos Labs, just a hop, skip and a jump from Santa Fe. She'd conducted a little private research of her own since Jack and the Old Man had sprung this business on her. She knew Los Alamos was doing all kinds of stuff with sound, some of it open and aboveboard. Most of it, she'd bet, ultra hush-hush.

All of it, she soon decided, was way above her level of expertise.

The Canadian sound team holding the floor when Cleo and Joe arrived wrapped up their presentation ten minutes later. She'd understood maybe three words in ten. The North Korean presentation was even worse.

They'd brought along a translator, but his halting explanations of such technical terms as wave field synthesis and ADAT cords almost crossed Cleo's eyes. The charts and diagrams the crew projected onto the screen behind them didn't help at all. Not until they played a clip of a documentary for which they'd done the sound editing did she really appreciate their achievement.

The cinematography was jerky and distracting. The dialogue was in Korean. But every syllable resonated with astounding clarity. Cleo found herself holding her breath as the background music swelled to a crescendo. The notes didn't assault her eardrums, as did those that blared from so many of today's surround-sound speakers. Instead, the chords seemed to vibrate against her inner core.

"Christ!" Joe muttered. "Do you hear that?"

Hear it, schmear it. She *felt* it. Every wood-windy trill and smooth, brassy slide. The incredible sensation had to result from the varying sound wave patterns the Old Man had talked about. It blew Cleo away that the same technology used to produce these sounds could be employed in the war against terrorism. If and when Laser Man and Rifle Guy managed to steal it, that is.

Deciding not to mess with them or their attempts to effect a technology transfer, she pushed herself to her feet. "I'd better get back to Marisa."

"Fine." Joe flapped a distracted hand. "I'll see you later."

She left him hunched forward in his seat, elbows on knees, totally absorbed. Laser Man appeared every bit as engrossed. Cleo gave him only a passing glance as she departed the breakout room.

The lapis necklace, however, got another long, lustful perusal. Pausing on the stairs, Cleo stooped and squinted into the glass-fronted niche in a futile attempt to read the price tag.

The thud of footsteps on the creaky steps brought her upright again. Too quickly, as it turned out. Her left boot heel slid off the tread. Cleo threw out a hand to catch the railing, and snagged Alex Sloan instead.

Or rather, he snagged her. His fingers closed around her wrist. Counterbalancing her weight with his, he kept her from tumbling ignominiously down the stairs.

"Thanks."

He descended to her level, a smile in his gray eyes. "You're welcome." Releasing her wrist, he nodded toward the glass-fronted showcase. "I saw you admiring this piece. It's beautiful."

"Yes, it is."

So was he, dammit! Okay, maybe elegant was the more appropriate adjective. Or maybe Cleo just had a thing for lean, sculpted features, wavy black hair, hand-tailored pinstripe suits and Brioni ties.

She knew it was a Brioni because she'd bought one exactly like it for her dad a few weeks ago. Naturally, her inquisitive twit of a stepmother had nagged her to find out the price. Just as naturally, Wanda had choked when an exasperated Cleo had told her that it cost more than a horse, but less than a house.

She'd exaggerated, of course. A little.

"I know the jeweler who designed the necklace," Alex commented. "Her shop is right around the corner."

"Is it?"

He'd just handed her the perfect opening. Deciding this was as good a time as any to find out if he had, in fact, been coming on to her Wednesday night, Cleo tipped her head. "Maybe we should add the shop to the guided tour you promised me after the festival."

She didn't exactly flutter her lashes, but she

came darn close. Marisa didn't have anything on her.

After a startled moment, Alex looked amused. And interested. "Maybe we should."

His glance drifted to her mouth. Cleo was pretty sure now she hadn't read more into Sloan's offer to show her around Santa Fe than he'd intended. Just to clinch the matter, though, she dropped her voice to her version of a husky murmur. "I didn't ask. Will this be a private tour?"

The amusement in his gray eyes deepened. Lifting a hand, he drew his thumb along the line of her chin. The pad was curiously callused for someone as smooth and polished as Alex Sloan.

"Which would you prefer, Brown Eyes?"

She pursed her lips and pretended to give the matter serious consideration. "Private, I think."

His thumb made another pass. "I'm sure that can be arranged."

Well, that blew away the last of her doubts. The colonel gave every indication of being willing to cheat on his wife with Cleo. The question yet to be answered was whether he had cheated on Patrice with Sergeant Smith.

Before she could probe further, the crowd began to pour out of the breakout room. Cleo threw a glance over her shoulder, caught Assault Rifle Guy's startled gaze and quickly put some space between Sloan and herself.

Not quickly enough, evidently. Beneath his

silly beret, Modesto's brows hooked together. Cleo guessed another report would soon zing its way to CIA headquarters. Former Special Agent North was once again observed conducting close surveillance of Alex Sloan. Very close.

Cleo played and replayed the scene on the stairs as she walked the short distance from La Fonda to El Cortez. Dusk was coming on fast, and the December air sliced into her lungs like a razor.

The fire shooting sparks up the chimney of the massive fireplace in El Cortez's lobby took some of the chill from her nose and toes. The gift basket waiting for her at the concierge desk looked as though it might take the cold from every other appendage. Delighted, Cleo surveyed the artistically arranged assortment of tortilla chips, queso and salsa, all nestled in an exquisite pottery bowl shaped like an ancient Anasazi turtle god.

"Where did this come from?"

"It was delivered earlier this afternoon. There's a note tucked inside the cellophane."

"Thanks."

Cleo toted the basket to her room, shed her coat and gloves, and skimmed the note from Patrice Sloan. The message was as coolly polite as the blonde herself.

She'd enjoyed meeting Cleo. Looked forward

to chatting with her again. Hoped she liked the bowl, one of Patrice's own creations.

Dipping a chip in the salsa, Cleo checked her watch. She had a whole forty minutes before Marisa's entourage would have to leave for the cocktail party. Just time for a shower and a quick change. Munching away, she emptied her pockets and unstrapped her ankle holster.

She'd wear the black tuxedo jacket again, this time paired with a slim, floor-length black skirt slit to the thigh on one side. The Glock would go into a holster tucked at the small of her back.

Her hair got a quick shampoo, blow-dry and upsweep. Bowing to the occasion, Cleo pulled on a pair of black panty hose and applied her makeup with a more liberal hand than usual. Her feet went into pointy-toed pumps trimmed with the same shimmering paillettes decorating her jacket. The stiletto heels didn't exactly put them in the kick-ass category, but they did provide Cleo an extra three inches of height to sweep the crowds.

The miniature camera hidden in the brooch she clasped high on her shoulder would help with that, too. She was adjusting the shimmering crystal pin when the phone rang. The news imparted by Paul Salazar, her contact at the Santa Fe PD, wasn't good.

"Your guy Martin gave you a false address," the detective announced. "The couple living at

2250 Old Cerrillos Road never heard of him. Neither has the DMV, for that matter."

She didn't like the sound of that. "Let me guess. He's not registered at the University of New Mexico, either."

"You got it."

"Did you run the name and physical description I gave you through NCIC?"

The FBI's National Crime Information Center databases contained information on everyone from missing children and known members of violent gangs to international terrorists. It also housed lists of individuals known to be associated with right-wing religious hate groups.

"We did," Salazar confirmed. "No hits."

Frowning, Cleo chewed over the information. Martin had gone to the trouble of providing himself with a fake identity. Yet he'd grabbed the mike *and* the spotlight at the forum this morning to publicly heckle Marisa.

He must have known Cleo would check out his license and ID. Obviously, he wasn't concerned she'd come up blank when she ran them.

Which could well mean, she thought with a sudden lurch in the vicinity of her stomach, he didn't intend to use that particular identity again.

Like a bird dog picking up a scent, the trained investigator in her went into full quiver mode. Up to this point, the threat to Marisa had consisted of faceless names and shadowy organizations on a computerized list. Cleo now had a face, but he'd given a fake name.

This Martin character could have a hundred reasons for shielding his real identity. Only one concerned Cleo.

"I passed Martin's description to the officers working the premiere tonight," Salazar informed her. "They'll keep a watch for him."

"Thanks."

She stood for a moment, her mind racing. Ten years ago she'd ignored her instincts and bungled one of her first investigations as an OSI agent. A young sergeant had been brutally murdered as a result.

Cleo had learned from her first, tragic mistake. She listened now when her inner alarms started to ping, and they were pinging like mad at the moment.

Her gut told her the cops would be watching for the wrong man tonight. When and if the individual she'd spoken to this morning popped up again, she suspected his hair wouldn't be a rusty-red, his eyes wouldn't be a bright, startling turquoise and his name tag wouldn't read Andrew Martin.

Sliding her Glock into the holster at the small of her back, she went to break the news to her client.

9

Agitated, Marisa paced the living room of her suite. "What do you mean, the guy's not in any computer?"

"There's no record in local, state or federal databases of an Andrew Martin residing at the address he gave me."

Marisa didn't like hearing the news the second time any better than she had the first. Careless of her elegant side-sweep, she raked a hand through the red curls.

She was dressed for the night's festivities in an eye-popping gold Lurex bodysuit that hugged her slender curves like Saran Wrap. Everyone had gathered in her suite—Peter, J.L., Marisa's volunteer escort for the evening, the additional

PR rep sent by Whitehorn Studios to coordinate the cocktail party and the premiere. The little bomb North had dropped a moment ago had riveted the attention of the entire group.

She wanted them to be aware of the situation, Cleo had announced calmly. All of them, including the bug-eyed volunteer.

"I don't understand." Frowning, Peter followed Marisa's progress as she paced back and forth across the room. "Why would this guy, whatever his name is, register for the conference with a fake ID, then draw attention to himself at the opening forum this morning? Given the situation, he must have known we'd check him out."

"I've been asking myself the same question. The only answer I've come up with so far is that he wanted us to do just that."

"Why?"

"Could be person or persons unknown hired him to play mind games with Marisa. Shake her up as punishment for her role in *The Redemption*."

If so, he was doing a damn good job of it. Marisa was strung wire tight. Her entire body vibrated with nervous energy.

"Or," Cleo postulated, shifting her glance to J.L. and the studio rep, "it could be someone hired him to stir things up and generate more hype for the movie."

J.L. led the chorus of indignant protests, but it

was obvious her wheels were already clicking away. "Whoever he is, he's too good to pass up. Several local stations taped the forum this morning for the six o'clock news. The rest of the paparazzi will be out in force this evening. They'll eat up the fact that there appears to be some mystery surrounding this heckler."

Her thin face alive with the possibilities, J.L. jumped out of her chair. "I've got to zap out a release and get it distributed. What's the name of your contact at the police department?" Flapping a hand, she rushed for the door. "Never mind, I don't need it. I'll just go with 'spokesman.' That keeps the focus on us."

The studio rep was right on her heels. "Good thing you got a transcript of the tape. That 'burn in hell' bit will take on more ominous overtones now."

The "burn in hell" bit sounded considerably more ominous to Marisa now, too. Her movements jerky, she took another turn around the sitting room while North gave a recap of her activities in the past half hour.

"I've asked the Santa Fe PD to put on extra officers for tonight. I've also asked them to send a fingerprint team to dust the mike and the table Martin sat at this morning. I doubt they'll get anything off the microphone. Too many people handled it. But they might be able to lift a set of prints from the table's undersurface."

"What about the tape from the session?" Peter asked. "I read somewhere that voiceprints are now as definitive as fingerprints."

"I've sent a copy of the tape to the FBI. They'll run it through their database. I've also asked my air force contacts to put some pressure on the bureau to expedite the search. Hopefully, they'll have something for us in a few days. With the stepped-up efforts to collect and analyze voice data since 9/11, though, it may take longer. The CIA, the Defense Intelligence Agency and our domestic collection sources have maxed out several supercomputers with the phone conversations snatched from the airwaves."

Marisa wasn't impressed. She was the one putting herself on the firing line. "That's it? That's all you can do?"

"No, that's not all. I've also dug into my personal bag of tricks. See this pin?"

Angling into the light, she displayed the glittering leopard draped over the shoulder seam of her black jacket. The overhead spots raised arcs of brilliant fire from the Swarovski crystals decorating the piece.

"There's a miniature wireless camera hidden in the leopard's eye. The camera displays on this screen."

Digging what looked like an ordinary compact out of her jacket pocket, she flipped up the lid.

"The screen will also display e-mail and voice messages. I'll have immediate access to updates from the police or the FBI."

"If and when they have anything," Marisa pointed out acidly.

"Let's hope we get a hit on the voiceprint." With a confident smile, Cleo clicked the receiver shut. "Ready to go?"

Marisa stabbed a hand through her hair again. Hell, no, she wasn't ready. She felt nervous. Edgy. As brittle as cracked glass. She knew she'd take a beating from the critics and reviewers tonight. The ones who'd seen the advance rushes had already skewered her. Now she had to deal with this crap about a mystery man.

She needed a hit, but she knew Peter would go all stiff on her if she popped anything stronger than an aspirin. She'd have to settle for a drink.

She was on a straight vector for the bar when he scooped up her coat and intercepted her.

"We're running late. Why don't you wait and have a drink at the cocktail party?"

"Why don't *you* get off my ass?"

His expression didn't alter, but Marisa saw his knuckles whiten on the shaved Danish mink.

"We've had this discussion before, as I recall. I'll get off your ass anytime you say the word."

Hissing, she curled her nails into her palms.

She didn't need him hassling her. She didn't need *anyone* hassling her. Not tonight, of all nights.

"I want a drink. I intend to have one." To reinforce her point, she flashed a smile at her appointed escort. "How about you?"

Hooking a finger in his collar, the volunteer tugged at his formal white bow tie and glanced from Marisa to Peter and back again.

"Well, I…"

"Scotch or bourbon?"

"Er, vodka, if you have it."

"We have vodka." She sailed past Peter. "We most definitely have vodka."

Marisa went from edgy and angry to just plain angry as the evening progressed.

Peter sulked all through the pre-theater cocktail party thrown by the studio at a lively Spanish restaurant. Not that anyone but Marisa recognized it as a sulk. His smile was as easy as always, his conversation more intelligent than listeners expected from someone with as much muscle as the reigning Mr. Universe. Nor did he keep his distance. He was right there when Marisa needed him, discreetly in the background when she didn't. Yet she sensed the coolness, the withdrawal.

Dammit, why couldn't he be satisfied with the great sex? Why did he keep pushing her? He was starting to act like a keeper, for God's sake—or worse, a jealous husband.

She'd already chalked up one failed marriage. She'd also helped precipitate the near breakup of at least one other. She still couldn't believe her *Redemption* co-star had admitted their affair to his wife. Or that James had mistaken Marisa's greedy lust for love.

Caitlin Cox had made James crawl before she took him back. He was still crawling, if the rumors held any grain of truth. No way would Marisa give anyone that kind of control over her, Peter included.

Sending him a tight smile, she tossed down the rest of her drink. A moment later, she hooked elbows with Alex Sloan. The foot-stomping flamenco music in the background gave her the perfect excuse to press her breast against his biceps and breathe into his ear.

"You're looking particularly handsome tonight, Mr. Chairman."

Cleo kept a close eye on her client as she worked the crowd.

The mob was considerably larger than the exclusive enclave that had been invited to the Sloans' welcome soiree. Everyone registered for the conference could purchase a ticket for this event. Including Andrew Martin, or whoever the hell he was.

Cleo stayed within striking distance of her client, but kept on the move. Her three-inch heels allowed her to use the camera tucked inside the glittering leopard to survey the crowd's perimeters. Eardrums vibrating to the lively beat of the guitars, she flipped open her compact and blinked. The LCD screen magnified and displayed the scene so vividly she got a great view of one of the waiter's nose hairs.

"Ugh."

Angling her shoulder, she swept the camera to either side. She picked up the image of a very intent Patrice Sloan and zoomed along the blonde's line of sight just in time to spot Marisa nuzzling Alex Sloan's ear.

Uh-oh. Cleo had heard just enough of the angry exchange in her client's suite Wednesday night to know this cuddly, sex kitten act wasn't going to play well with Marisa's sleep-in office assistant. Wondering how it was playing with Alex's wife, Cleo worked her way through the crowd. Thankfully, the flamenco music crashed to a crescendo and died just as she reached the woman.

"Hi, Patrice. I wanted to thank you for the gift basket. The salsa just about took off the roof of my mouth, but the bowl is gorgeous."

"I thought you might like it." Elegant in black lace and suede, she gave Cleo a cool smile. "Did you know the turtle is the Anasazi symbol for earth?"

"No, I didn't."

"According to the ancients, a turtle dived down to the bottom of the ocean and brought mud up on his back to form the continents."

That was pretty interesting, actually, but at the moment Cleo was more curious about the woman's reaction to seeing Marisa come on to her husband. She let her glance slide to the couple across the room.

"The colonel certainly seems to have charmed my client."

"Alex is a charming man. When he wants to be."

The inflection was dry, the delivery droll. Cleo pounced on both.

"I don't think you have anything to worry about. Marisa...well, let's just say she turns it on and off like a light switch."

Patrice slanted her a cool look. "I assure you, I'm not worried about my husband. He's only taken one mistress that I know of."

Somehow, Cleo managed to keep her jaw from dropping while her thoughts scrambled all to hell and back. Did Sloan's wife know about his possible affair with Sergeant Smith? Had Patrice confronted her husband? Forced him to end the liaison? Let something slip that fueled Staff Sergeant Mitchell's murderous rage?

Before Cleo could find a way to frame the question, Patrice supplied the answer.

"I've never met a man as devoted to duty as

Alex was. I think that's what attracted me to him. The total selflessness. The willingness to give two hundred percent, twenty-four hours a day if necessary. I didn't realize until after we'd married he was…"

"He was what, Patrice?"

"I didn't realize Alex was still in mourning for his first wife," she said after a moment. "He'd lost her to breast cancer shortly before we met. I, in turn, lost him to his job until he finally worked through his grief."

Ha! She'd lost Sloan to more than his job. The man was a tomcat. If Cleo had harbored any doubts on that point, he had resolved them this morning during their little interlude on the stairs at La Fonda.

Cleo was in the security and investigations business, though, not the wife enlightening business. Besides, she wasn't ready to show her hand yet, such as it was. Until she found solid evidence linking Alex Sloan to Debra Smith, she was still feeling her way here.

She also had a client to keep safe. Excusing herself, she made another orbit around Marisa. She didn't expect Andrew Martin to show up still sporting the ear studs and Van Dyke beard. Still, she scrutinized every face in the crowd.

Midway through her circuit she spotted Assault Rifle Guy. Modesto didn't acknowledge her with so much as a nod when she sauntered by.

But after she passed, she turned slightly to take a canapé from a waiter's tray, and her hidden camera caught Modesto tracking her progress.

It also caught Alex Sloan weaving his way through the crowd in Cleo's direction. She slowed her pace, intending to allow him to catch up with her. What she didn't intend was for the man to slide his hands down her arms, draw her back against him and plant a hot one on her nape.

"Hello again, Brown Eyes."

"Whoa!" She swung around, controlling just in time the impulse to deck the man. "This is your idea of keeping things private?"

"No, this is my idea of picking up where we left off this morning. The private part comes later."

"Aren't you worried that little smooch on the neck might give your wife the wrong idea?"

"It might," he replied with a slow grin, "if either one of my ex's were here to see it."

The truth hit with a whack. This wasn't Alex Sloan. Eyes narrowing, she looked past the man standing before her. Across the room, the retired colonel approached his wife and slid a possessive arm around her waist. The blonde leaned into him.

"Oooh-kay." Cleo's glance was less than friendly when she brought it back to the colonel's twin. "I don't like being made a fool of, Mr. Sloan."

"Sorry." His gray eyes didn't evince the least repentance. "When you fell into my arms this morning, I couldn't resist. Call me Marc."

She shot another glance across the room. It was uncanny. They were mirror images of each other. Folding her arms, she tapped a foot. "You and your brother play this game often, Marc?"

"Not as much now as when we were younger."

"So was that you or Alex in his bedroom last night?"

The laughter went out of his eyes, replaced by a quickly masked speculation.

"Unfortunately for me, that must have been Alex."

She didn't bother to clarify her question or correct his interpretation of it. She was still torqued at him for messing with her, and at herself for being taken in so easily.

"Right." She made a show of consulting her watch. "If you'll excuse me, it's about time to move my client across the street to the theater."

"See you there, Brown Eyes."

Dammit! She was right back where she'd been this morning. She still didn't have a fix on Alex Sloan. *Had* he been coming on to her last night? Or was he the saint his wife said he was?

Distinctly annoyed with a certain Marcus Sloan, Cleo squeezed into Marisa's circle of admirers. J.L. Evans approached from the opposite direction, tapping a long red nail on her watch.

"Fifteen minutes to showtime, Marisa."

The star tossed back the rest of her drink. She'd downed three so far by Cleo's reckoning—that vodka at the hotel and two Scotches here at the restaurant. She probably needed them. If *The Redemption* lived down to its pre-release reviews, Marisa no doubt wanted to anesthetize herself before the viewers started slinging arrows.

The movie was worse than Cleo had anticipated.

She didn't see much of it. She spent more time watching the audience ahead of and behind her than she did the spectacle unfolding on the giant screen. She couldn't miss Marisa's big scene with a modern-day Archangel Gabriel, though, or her interpretation of how the Virgin Mary came to be with child. The star played it out in graphic, orgiastic detail to the packed and suddenly very quiet house.

Even Cleo was shocked, and she didn't consider herself a prude by any means. She'd dealt with perversion in most of its forms during her years as an agent with the OSI. Since going into business for herself and taking on clients unrestrained by air force rules and regulations, she'd discovered a few additional forms. Nothing this close to out-and-out religious porn, though.

She pulled her gaze from the actress writhing on the screen to the woman seated across the aisle. Marisa was studying the scene with professional detachment. Cleo had to admire her cool, particularly when someone in the audience let loose with a long, loud boo.

Another catcall rang out a second or two later, followed by a gathering swell of derisive comments. Marisa ignored them. So did Alex Sloan and his wife, seated to her right. A few seats away, Joe Garza began to squirm at this treatment of the festival's guest of honor. Marc Sloan, flanking Patrice on her other side, merely looked amused.

Afterward, Cleo was never quite sure which occurred first—the commotion that erupted at the rear of the theater or the sparks that leaped from the mammoth Dolby speaker suspended behind the proscenium arch. She turned instinctively toward the clamor at the back, then spun around again at the unmistakable hiss and spit of an electrical short.

She was out of her seat before the sparks ignited the curtains framing the arch. Lunging across the aisle, she reached past the volunteer escort, snagged Marisa's arm and dragged her to her feet.

"This way!"

Her client didn't need any encouragement. The fire had already made the leap from the curtains to the giant screen. The star threw one horrified glance at the flames now consuming the writhing woman on the screen, and stumbled after her escort into the aisle. Alex hustled Patrice out right behind her.

The sprinklers came on before they'd taken three steps, but that didn't calm the now-panicked audience. Shouting and shoving, the hysterical crowd stampeded for the exits.

10

The frantic mob cut Marisa and Cleo off from the closest exit. Jammed shoulder to shoulder, the moviegoers pushed and shoved through the aisles. Others leaped over rows of seats in a mad race for the rear of the theater.

Snarling, Cleo whirled on the surging mass of humanity. "Do *not* run! Walk!"

Either they couldn't hear her over the shrieking fire alarms and gushing sprinklers, or the memory of the horrific fire that had killed so many nightclub patrons in New Jersey drove them forward. Wave after wave of faces contorted with terror crashed toward her and Marisa. Cleo didn't dare whip out her Glock and fire a couple of warning shots. She'd only add to the panic.

Thank God she'd taken the time for a second walk-though earlier in the day. With the stage retracted, she could get her client down into the orchestra pit and out through the side door opening onto Burro Alley.

"This way!"

Wrenching Marisa's arm, she dragged her away from the crowd. She didn't wait to see if Alex or the others followed. Her responsibility was to her client.

Marisa saw they were headed straight for the scorched, melting screen. Eyes dilated with terror, she dug in her heels. "No!"

"This way, dammit!"

The stink of melting plastic assaulted Cleo's nostrils. She didn't have time to explain she was more worried about toxic fumes from the burning screen than smoke or flames. When Marisa started to claw at the bruising hold on her wrist, Cleo whirled, fisted her free hand and landed a power-packed punch on her client's jaw.

The star's head snapped up. Her eyes rolled back. She started to sag. Cleo caught her before she hit the floor. Grunting, she dragged the actress toward the stairs to the orchestra pit. She had just reached the top step when a figure charged through the darkness on the other side of the pit.

"I'll take her!"

Peter Jacobsen raced toward them, scattering

chairs and music stands. One sleeve of his tux was ripped at the shoulder seam and red scratches decorated his right cheek, but he'd fought his way down from the section reserved for Marisa's entourage. God *bless* all those muscles!

Dumping her client into his arms, Cleo shoved them both toward the door at the rear of the pit. The panel was painted black, like the surrounding walls, but the red emergency exit light glowed like a beacon of hope.

Peter hit the panic bar and slammed out into the night. Cleo followed on his heels and caught the door before it could swing shut. Gulping in the clean, icy air, she made an instant decision.

She'd pulled her client from one danger. Another, in the shape of the as-yet-untagged Andrew Martin, might lurk right around the corner. She had to weigh that "might" against the hundreds of people still trapped inside.

Her gut told her Martin, if he'd stuck around for the premiere, was either caught up in the hysterical mob or strategically positioned outside to watch the exits closest to Marisa's designated seat. Since they'd detoured through the orchestra pit and come out on the opposite side of the theater, Cleo went with her gut.

"Follow this alley," she barked at Peter. "It leads to Don Gaspar Street. The plaza is two blocks up. Our hotel is just off the plaza. Keep

Marisa in your suite until I get there. Don't open the door to anyone but me, you understand? Not anyone!"

"Where are you going?"

"Back inside. Get moving."

She raced back into the pit and spotted Patrice Sloan. Wet hair straggling down her face, the blonde stumbled past the scattered chairs, half dragged by her husband.

"We saw you come this way," Sloan shouted. "Where's the exit?"

"Straight back."

Cleo dodged around them and leaped up the stairs, only to run smack into the arms of another Sloan. Wrenching free, she pointed him in the direction she'd just come.

"Follow your brother!"

Conditions inside the theater were still chaotic. The sprinklers had doused the flames, but toxic fumes lingered in the air. Sacrificing her precious store of oxygen, Cleo cupped her hands around her mouth.

"Over here! There's another exit!"

"This way!"

The deep bellow came from right behind her and almost burst her eardrums. Swallowing a curse, she let Marc Sloan do the shouting while she jumped back down into the dark pit and directed the traffic he sent her way.

The first fire rescue team burst into the theater

a few minutes later. By then Cleo's eyes burned, her drenched clothes hung on her like an icy shroud, and nausea rolled around in her stomach. She'd ripped the pocket off her jacket and slapped the wet fabric over her nose and mouth, but the fumes were making her woozy.

So woozy she had to blink twice to bring into focus the face that suddenly loomed out of the darkness in the pit.

"The cavalry's arrived." Sloan yanked her toward the open rear door. "Let's get out of here."

They'd taken no more than a few steps when something crashed through the stage above their heads. The stage flooring collapsed. Folding chairs and music stands went flying. Sloan spat out a vicious curse and dived for the rear door, hauling Cleo with him.

The next thing she knew she was squatting on a curb, huddled in a warm cocoon with something hard jammed against her cheeks. Everything around her was a blur of black and red and bright, stabbing white.

"You okay?"

The question seemed to come from three blocks away. Slogging through the gray mush in her head, Cleo fixed her eyes on the hand pressing the object against her cheeks. With great effort, she followed the hand to a wrist. The wrist led to an arm. The arm to a shoulder and a face that seemed to swim toward her out of the darkness.

She was pretty sure she knew that face. Frowning, she tried to draw back for a better view. A hard vise at the back of her neck held her where she was.

"Take a few more breaths."

Each gulp tasted dry and cold and cut into her lungs like a glass shard, but cleared the mush in her head.

Oxygen. She was breathing pure oxygen.

Gradually, Cleo recognized that the steamy warmth cocooning her came from a blanket draped over her head and shoulders. She recognized the face that went with the hand holding the portable oxygen bottle, too. More or less.

Dragging in another gulp, she pushed at his hand. The rubber mask fell away, and icy night air replaced the hissing high-test she'd been sucking in.

"Thanks for…" she swallowed, grunting at the effort it required "…pulling me out."

Her throat felt like raw hamburger meat from all the shouting and smoke. Her hair, she discovered when she shoved the wet strands out of her face, had tiny icicles at the tips.

"You're welcome, Brown Eyes." Sloan twisted the shut-off valve on the portable oxygen bottle and signaled to a nearby EMT tech. "She's breathing on her own."

"Let me check her oxygen saturation level."

The medic hunkered down beside her and attached a small clip to Cleo's index finger. The red glow the device emitted a few seconds later seemed to satisfy him.

"Ninety-seven percent. Hang loose and I'll send someone over to help you inside."

Like she could hang any other way at the moment?

Hunching under her blanket, Cleo surveyed the scene. Dozens of emergency vehicles jammed the streets. Red, blue and white strobes stabbed the night. Police and firefighters worked the building. EMT teams circulated through the small, bedraggled crowd outside. Other theatergoers were being herded into the restaurant across the street to give their statements. As she watched, a crew loaded a gurney into an ambulance that took off seconds later, siren wailing.

"How many...hurt?"

"Only a few, as I understand it. The fire was pretty much contained to the stage area. Most of the injured are being treated for smoke inhalation."

Relieved that no one had been trampled in the frenzied rush to safety, Cleo pushed herself to her feet. Or tried to. Her legs refused to support her. Gritting her teeth, she made another attempt. Sloan rose with a good deal more grace and agility than she could summon at the moment, and loaned her a shoulder.

"Thanks," she rasped. "Again."

"You're welcome. Again."

She looked around for the nearest police officer and, spotted one taking names a few feet away. Dragging the blanket over her icicled hair, she gave him her name to add to his list.

"If you'll go inside with the others, ma'am, you'll be warmer there. One of the officers will take your statement."

"Can't."

She had to get back to her client. Now that the wooziness had cleared, she remembered sending Peter off with Marisa and instructions to barricade themselves in their suite.

"Detective Salazar knows how to reach me," she croaked.

When Peter Jacobsen let her into the suite a few minutes later, he was wrapped in one of the hotel's plush robes, and the giant TV in the sitting room was already blaring on-scene reports of the fire.

"Marisa okay?"

The star herself responded. Like Peter, she was swaddled in a warm robe. She was also holding an ice pack to her chin. Whirling on her rescuer, she exhibited all the gratitude of a hyena prevented from gnawing on poisoned meat.

"You slugged me!"

"Yeah, I did."

"Bitch!" Marisa's face flamed under her towel turban. "I don't pay you to manhandle me."

Cleo did a mental ten-count. Her client had just gone through a terrifying experience. She was operating on sheer nerves, lashing out at the handiest object, which in this case happened to be the person who'd raised a nice-size goose egg on her chin.

Cleo managed to hold on to her temper, but Peter's snapped. "For God's sake, Marisa! Cleo saved your damn neck."

"Damn?" Snarling, the star leaped to the attack. "Now it's my *damn* neck? Funny, a few minutes ago you were spouting all this drivel about how it would have killed you if you'd lost me."

Peter's jaw went tight. If Cleo had to bet, she'd guess he didn't appreciate hearing his feelings for the woman categorized as drivel.

"Oh, Christ!" Marisa's mouth twisted in disgust. "Now he's going to sulk."

Discretion, Cleo decided, was the greater part of valor in this situation.

"I just wanted to let you know arson investigators are already on the scene," she said, forcing each word through her raw throat. "I'll check with them and with the police first thing in the morning."

"The police?" Her client's high color drained. "So you think that electrical short wasn't an accident?"

Coming smack in the middle of the woman's big, controversial scene? Not hardly. The timing was too damn coincidental.

"I'm fairly certain the short caused the fire," Cleo managed to say in a hoarse rumble. "Right now I'm more interested in what caused the short."

"Or who," Marisa whispered, the ice pack clenched in her fist.

"Or who."

Cleo wouldn't do her client any favors by dismissing the possibility of human rather than divine intervention. Although God must have been pretty pissed off by that orgiastic scene in *The Redemption*.

"We'll know more in the morning. In the meantime, hold off on any public appearances."

It took Marisa all of three seconds to weigh a possible attempt on her life against the chance to exploit the fire for all it was worth. Shaking her head, she tossed aside the ice pack.

"The phone's already started ringing. Every radio and TV affiliate in the city wants an interview. Peter's been fielding the calls, but I'm not about to pass up this kind of publicity. I need J.L. Where the hell is she?"

"Last I saw her," Peter stated with a touch of acid, "she was fighting her way toward an exit."

The implication was obvious, even to the self-centered star. The color that had fled from her cheeks a few seconds ago rushed back with a vengeance.

"I care about her safety, dammit. But the TV reports said no one was seriously injured."

Seriously being the operative word, Cleo surmised.

"See if you can get her on her cell phone," Marisa snapped. Yanking off her towel, she headed for the bathroom.

Cleo decided it was time to do the same.

"I'm going to take a hot shower," she advised Jacobsen. "Don't let in any of the media until I'm here to vet them."

Cleo meant to spend just long enough under the steaming water to wash the smoke and ice from her hair and bring life back to her frozen toes. When she lifted her face to the hot, stinging needles, though, she started to shake. All over.

Okay, this was normal, she lectured herself. Nothing to write home about. Like Marisa, she was merely experiencing a delayed reaction.

Pressing her shoulder blades to the tiles, she let the water pound into her. It wasn't as though this was her first close call. Just a few months ago, a frantic single mom had hired her to find a runaway daughter. Cleo had tracked the seventeen-year-old through a photographer who specialized in particularly nasty and demeaning porn. He'd tried to escape by flinging a pan of developing solution in her face. Luckily, Cleo could shoot more accurately than he could throw.

Then there was that little incident down in Honduras while Cleo was still in uniform. She and Jack Donovan had dodged several *reeea-lly* close machetes before they battled their way out of that one.

This was the first time she'd almost lost a client to flames, though. Or sucked in fat lungfuls of toxic smoke while hauling said client out of a burning theater. Grunting, Cleo reached for the shampoo. Given a choice between Marisa Conners and the heroin cutters, she'd opt for the dopers.

The plastic tube slipped right out of her still-shaking hand and bounced off the tiles. It rolled around a few times before settling next to the drain. To her disgust, Cleo couldn't seem to summon the will or the strength to lean over and pick it up.

The hot water hammered down. Steam enveloped the enclosure. She was still contemplating the shampoo lying at her feet when she caught a flicker of movement through the foggy glass of the shower stall.

Her chest squeezed hard and tight. Furiously, she blinked the water out of her eyes and made out the shape of a bulky and unmistakably male figure.

Nerves stretched wire tight exploded into action. Kicking the door open, Cleo lunged. She and her unannounced, uninvited visitor went down in a tangle of arms and legs.

11

Cleo pinned the intruder to the bath mat with surprisingly little effort. She discovered the reason for the easy takedown when she flipped her wet hair out of her eyes.

"Donovan!"

Sheer astonishment added a kick to the adrenaline pumping through her veins. Anger galloped right along with it.

"Jesus H. Christ!" Her throat still raw and rasping, she snarled at her OSI contact. "Didn't anyone ever teach you to knock?"

"Life's more interesting this way."

Jack's slow drawl and the fact that he gave every appearance of making himself comfortable on the bath mat reminded Cleo she was wet. And naked. And sitting on the man's chest for the second time in less than two weeks.

"What's with this creeping up on me lately?" Snatching the terry-cloth robe from the rack behind her, she shoved an arm into one sleeve. "Have you developed some kind of death wish or something?"

"Or something." His face registered genuine regret as she draped the robe around her. "No need to cover up. I've seen you, ah, wet before."

"I remember," she huffed, rolling to her feet. "I also remember you dropped out of sight shortly thereafter."

The smile left his eyes. "Yeah, well, that's how it goes in our line of work."

Jack followed her up. He couldn't admit now that he'd never intended to give in to the wild hunger Captain Cleopatra North had stirred in him. Or that the scars from his divorce hadn't yet healed when he'd gotten it on with her in that cave in Honduras.

Hell, who was he kidding? The scars were still oozing. Kate ripped off the scabs every time she called in a drunken stupor. One of these days he'd get past the guilt. In the meantime, he'd keep himself and his hunger for this woman on a tight leash.

Particularly since General Barnes had sent him to discover why one of his former agents had developed such a sudden, intense interest in a certain retired air force colonel. Recalled to his mission, Jack tucked the image of a naked Cleo straddling his chest away for later enjoyment, and followed her out of the bathroom.

"What are you doing here?" she demanded, yanking on the sash of the robe.

"In Santa Fe or in your hotel room?"

"Don't be cute! It doesn't go with your tough-guy image."

Shrugging out of his sheepskin jacket, he tossed it atop the briefcase he'd dumped on a convenient chair before following the sound of drumming water. The bulky jacket had felt just right in the cold December night. After that session in the bathroom, though, he was sweating and as steamed up as her shower stall.

"I'm in Santa Fe because the Old Man wants to know why you were cuddling with Alex Sloan on the stairs at La Fonda Hotel."

He noted the surprise that rippled across her face. Noted, too, the little flicker of caution that followed, but didn't comment on either. The CIA report that Cleo and Sloan seemed to have struck up more than a casual friendship rankled more than Jack wanted to admit.

"I'm in your room because I heard about the fire at the theater. I tried to find you at the scene. One of the EMTs told me you'd blacked out but refused treatment. So when I pounded on your door and got no answer..."

"You dug into your secret-agent bag of tricks, zapped the electronic lock and waltzed in," she finished, shooting a wry glance at the still-open door to her mini-suite. "If the hotel's alarm system works as advertised, security should show in about a minute."

Actually, it was closer to thirty seconds. Cleo gave full marks to the hotel for its efficiency, and her assurances that everything was in order to the serious young woman who responded.

When she closed the door and dragged a hand through her wet hair, it was Jack's turn to feel a ripple of surprise. Unless his eyesight had failed in the past hour or so, her hand was shaking.

Well, hell! He couldn't remember Cleo ever experiencing an attack of nerves during or after a mission. But then she'd probably never dragged a client from a burning building before. Or had to tackle a possible attacker while she was still trying to wash the smoke from her hair.

She had yet to wash it from her throat.

"That's some croak you got working there, North. You sound like you could use a drink."

As expected, the luxurious mini-suite came equipped with a well-stocked bar. Maybe he should give the notion of working in the private sector more thought.

"Make it a Perrier," she grumbled. "I'm still on duty. Or I will be when I get rid of you and drag on some clothes," she added pointedly.

Ms. North didn't know it yet, but the first wasn't going to happen anytime soon. The second…

At the thought of sliding Cleo out of that robe and into nothingness again, Jack closed his fist around the Perrier. Plunking the bottle down on the marble countertop, he added ice to a glass and splashed in the mineral water.

She still had the shakes when he passed her the drink, but he knew better than to give in to the fierce urge to wrap his hand over hers and guide the glass to her lips. After their little tussle in the bathroom, she would probably kick him in the balls if he so much as hinted she wasn't operating on all cylinders right now.

He settled for prowling around her suite while she forced down the Perrier. "What's the story on the fire? The news flashes I caught on the way in from the airport are already screaming arson."

"Figures. The fire chief on scene indicated he was calling in an arson investigation team. I doubt they'll know anything definite for several days."

If then. Jack had worked a case some years ago involving an air force civil servant with a deep, festering grudge against his boss and the system he believed had failed him. Three fires and twenty-six million dollars in damage later, Jack had learned more about accelerants and flash points than he'd ever wanted to know.

"The media are also having a field day with a supposed threat to your client issued by one of the festival attendees. I take it he's the one you asked the FBI to run a voiceprint on."

Cleo frowned at Jack over the rim of her glass. "Told you about that, did they?"

"I'm supposed to be your liaison with the bureaucracy, remember? I've been kept apprised of your activities in Santa Fe."

Some of them, anyway.

"Which brings me back to CIA reports that you've exhibited considerable interest in Alex Sloan. They spotted you getting cozy with the colonel. The Old Man wants to know what you're up to."

So did Jack, although he suspected he might not like the reason behind Cleo's sudden interest in Sloan. If it was professional, she was meddling in something that could get her crosswise of the United States government. If it was personal...

Thankfully, the phone rang before he could decide just how the hell to finish that thought. Shoving his hands in the pockets of his gray cords, he waited while Cleo took the call. The shrill, angry voice on the other end of the line leaped clear across the room.

"I know."

The clipped response set the caller on another tirade.

Cleo raked a hand through her wet hair again.

The mink-brown pelt was longer than Jack remembered, just brushing her shoulder blades. She'd worn it shorter while in the air force. Shorter and curlier.

He liked it this way, though. He particularly liked the way it had tumbled over her slick, naked shoulders a few moments ago.

"Just give me two minutes." Cleo caught his gaze and rolled her eyes. "Two minutes, Marisa."

The phone clattered down. The succinct but highly descriptive phrase she muttered under her breath had Jack grinning.

"We'll have to finish this conversation later. The media are clamoring to interview my client. She wants to hold court in her suite, but hotel security won't let the news crews upstairs without my authorization."

"Later works for me. Need some backup?"

The fact that she actually considered his offer for a second or two told him the fire had upped the risk to her client considerably.

"Thanks, but I've got it covered. Marisa's PR consultant and the studio media rep just showed up. I'll get them to verify the crews' credentials while I sweep them and their equipment for electronic or explosive devices. You're welcome to come along and enjoy the circus, though."

Circus didn't begin to describe it, Jack thought some moments later.

Every local affiliate and independent wanted in on the story. A hyperactive broomstick with spiky black hair and nails so red they looked as though they'd just ripped out someone's heart matched faces to IDs and double-checked credentials against her Palm Pilot. Once the reporters were vetted, Cleo wanded them and every piece of their equipment.

Only then were they allowed to scurry down the corridor and enter the inner sanctum. Jack tagged after a reporter who must have just come from the theater. She had a cell phone jammed to her ear, smelled of smoke and was feeding copy to her editor as she jostled along with the others.

The suite was so jammed he didn't try to wedge his way in. Propping a shoulder against the door, he observed the proceedings from across the room. Marisa Conners sat in the glare of hastily erected portable lights. Boom mikes on extended poles poked at her over the heads of the reporters. A tall, heavily muscled assistant kept them from crowding too close while she fielded their questions.

"Miss Conners! How close were you to the screen when the fire broke out?"

"Too close," she answered, shuddering. She followed that with a valiant attempt to conquer the remembered horror.

She was good, Jack decided. Better than her critics gave her credit for.

"How did the fire start?"

"The arson investigators will have to give you the specifics on that. All I can tell you is that I heard a sort of crackling noise and saw sparks shoot from one of the speakers."

Ignoring the second half of her response, the reporters pounced on the first.

"Do you think it was arson?"

"I don't know." The star's luminous green eyes darkened. "But I *do* know my role in *The Redemption* has stuck a nerve with a number of right-wing hate groups and bigots. One of them even suggested to my face that I would burn in hell for it."

When the reporters demanded more detail, Conners dwelt on the fact that neither the police nor the FBI could identify the individual who'd confronted her at the opening forum.

Jack glanced around and found Cleo standing close behind him. Her expression remained neutral, but he guessed she wanted to wring Conners's neck. Nothing like broadcasting live to a possible perp that you didn't have a clue as to his identity or his whereabouts.

Conners's performance continued for another fifteen or twenty minutes. It ended abruptly when a TV reporter zeroed in on the mottled lump decorating the left side of her chin.

"How did you get that bruise?"

"This?" The actress feathered the swelling

with her fingertips. "I must have crashed into something or someone."

"We heard a woman helped direct the crowd through the orchestra pit. Was that you?"

She hesitated, then gave the reporter a self-deprecating smile. "Everything happened so fast. I really can't take credit for any special heroics."

The muffled snort behind Jack could only have come from Cleo. He shot her a curious glance, but she wouldn't look his way. Her attention stayed fixed on the news crews as her client swayed to her feet.

"That's all for now. I know you must appreciate how traumatic this has been for me. And for my staff," she added with a small smile for the woman hovering just off camera. "J.L. will set up another press conference for tomorrow morning. Hopefully by then we'll all have more information about the fire and who...or what...caused it."

"Quite a performance," Jack murmured as the crews started packing up their equipment.

Cleo's mouth twisted. "Like you wouldn't believe."

"Timely, too. I understand her movie's scheduled to open nationwide tomorrow. Tonight's drama should give it quite a boost at the box office."

"Don't think that hasn't occurred to me. Look, I have to clear the suite and run another sweep. Why don't you wait for me next door?"

He took the key card she passed him and idly flipped it over a few times while she rounded up the crews and herded them toward the door. Marisa Conners's safety was Cleo's responsibility. The Old Man had had other matters on his mind when he'd strong-armed her into taking the job.

But it was looking more and more as though Conners and the controversy surrounding her could disrupt the delicate dance the CIA was doing with the North Korean sound engineer. From all reports, the operatives on the scene had yet to whisk the man away from his associates for a private tête-à-tête. The best they'd been able to do so far was record his presentation and lift portions of the demo film clip to reverse engineer.

The same operatives had noted Cleo's conspicuous presence during the demo and her session with Alex Sloan on the stairs afterward. Now it was up to Jack to find out just what the heck she was up to.

Palming the key card, he headed next door. Once in Cleo's suite, he retrieved his briefcase and dug out the fat manila envelope inside. He started to settle into a chair, but detoured to the counter instead.

The peanuts he'd downed on the flight from D.C. hadn't quite made up for the dinner he'd missed. Stomach rumbling, he poked through the contents of the gift basket.

The salsa exploded in his mouth, but the queso

was rich and creamy. Using tortilla chips to scoop out gobs of the cheesy sauce, he munched half the bag while studying the file he extracted from the manila envelope.

The file was the first thing Cleo spotted after Jack answered her rap on the door. She swept in, jaw tight, and made straight for the bar.

"I'm ready for a real drink now."

Lifting a brow, he watched her down a healthy swig of Scotch. "When did you start tossing back Dewar's neat?"

"When I agreed to provide security for Marisa Conners. Is that an OSI file?"

"It is."

She moved in for a closer look, but Jack slapped a palm over the folder.

"First things first. Let's have it, North. What's your interest in Alex Sloan?"

"Why do you think I have any interest in him beyond the festival and his involvement with my client?"

"Maybe because you were observed getting up close and personal with the man."

"I didn't get personal with Alex Sloan. Wait. I take that back. Are you referring to the first night, when we went chest to chest in his bedroom?"

The glint in her eyes told him she knew damn well he hadn't been briefed on any bedroom business. Jack wouldn't admit to any gaps in his intelligence, however.

"Why don't we start with the incident on the stairs at La Fonda Hotel," he suggested dryly. "We can work our way from there."

"That wasn't Alex Sloan at La Fonda."

"Come again?"

She let the question hang in the air while she hauled the basket of goodies closer and dipped into the salsa. Jack wasn't surprised when she downed the red-hot sauce without a blink. She'd exhibited the same cast-iron taste buds during their foray into the Honduran jungle.

"I'm pretty sure that was his twin." Cleo suspended a chip between bowl and mouth. Jack's sudden slicing frown gave her immense satisfaction. "Didn't you know Alex Sloan's brother was in Santa Fe?"

"Obviously not."

"Tsk-tsk. Your sources should do a better job at keeping you up-to-date. Marc arrived this morning."

Cleo didn't tell him the man's unannounced appearance had taken her by surprise, too. Nor did she read too much into the glance Donovan knifed her way.

"Marc, is it?"

"Hey, he stopped me from taking a tumble down a flight of stairs. That put us on a first-name basis."

He'd also scooped her up when she'd collapsed in the alley behind the theater. Cleo decided not to share that bit of information with Jack.

One, he didn't have a need to know. Two, she hadn't yet sorted through her reactions to that bit of gallantry.

"I'm not the only one who knows Marc is here," she informed Donovan. "He and his brother made side-by-side appearances tonight. Your friends at the CIA probably have him wired by now."

Jack didn't respond. He was chewing over the information she'd just imparted, Cleo guessed, and trying to decide how it affected his appointed task—namely, to discover her real reasons for wanting to get close to Alex Sloan.

She was still debating how much of her personal agenda to reveal when he flipped over the file on the counter.

The tortilla chip crumpled in Cleo's hand. Bite-size bits flaked down on the brown file cover. She recognized the name of the investigating officer printed in block letters on the front of the file.

"I had our analysts run both you and Alex Sloan through the computers," Jack informed her. "We found two links. One, you were both stationed at Luke for an overlapping period of about three months. Two, Second Lieutenant Cleo North worked a murder/suicide involving a sergeant assigned to the same classified project as then–Lieutenant Colonel Sloan. It took awhile to make that link, as the project's name is still masked in the system."

His eyes had gone arctic. His voice was even more glacial. "Tell me about the case, North."

"You've got the file. Didn't you read it?"

"I read it, but I want your take on the investigation. Tell me."

It wasn't a request. It was a flat-out order from a senior-ranking officer who expected instant obedience.

Cleo considered reminding Donovan she no longer took orders from anyone, in uniform or out, but axed the impulse. She was too tired for verbal sparring, and too haunted by the memory of an apartment soaked in blood.

12

"The assistant manager of the Luke all-ranks club called in a report of a disturbance," Cleo related.

Her tone was low and strained from more than smoke. She remembered every detail of the case contained in that fat brown folder, and wished to God she didn't.

"One of the persons involved was threatening physical harm to the other. The security police responded, filed a report of two enlisted personnel going at it verbally. No physical exchange. Since a threat had been communicated, though, the OSI got tagged to follow up."

Jack said nothing, letting her tell it at her own pace, in her own way.

"I interviewed Staff Sergeant Thomas Mitchell and Sergeant Debra Smith separately. They both gave me essentially the same story they'd given the security police. They'd been dating on and off for almost a year, got into an argument at the club, let it escalate into a shouting match. A week later, Mitchell stabbed Smith to death at his off-base apartment, then shot himself."

Cleo looked down at her hands, still dusted with crumbs from the crushed tortilla chip. She'd pulled on rubber gloves that night at Mitchell's apartment. Plastic booties, too, so she wouldn't contaminate the crime scene. To this day, she carried a vivid image of the tracks those booties had made through blood and gore.

"What did you miss?"

The terse question whipped her head up. Her glare left Jack apparently unmoved.

"You obviously blame yourself for failing to substantiate the threat against Sergeant Smith. What do you think you missed?"

"There was a minor discrepancy in their statements. Mitchell claimed they'd argued over what movie to see that night. Smith said they'd argued about money. When I challenged her, she backtracked. Said the fight started because they couldn't afford to blow the cost of an off-base movie with payday still a week away."

"But?"

"But she got nervous," Cleo said slowly. "She

wouldn't look me in the eye. My gut told me she was holding something back, but I couldn't pull it out of her."

"So you zeroed the inquiry?"

Not by choice. Cleo had tried to convince her boss to extend the inquiry and let her have another crack at Debra Smith, but he'd already come under the gun for failing to meet reporting deadlines. He wasn't going to take another hit.

"The incident didn't meet the criteria to justify opening a substantive investigation," she related, her tone flat. "So, yes, I zeroed the inquiry."

Jack studied her through hooded eyes. "What about the murder/suicide investigation? What did your gut tell you about that?"

"At first," she admitted with a grimace, "my gut was too busy emptying itself of everything I'd eaten that day to tell me anything."

For the first time since he'd slapped his palm down on the file, Donovan essayed a smile. "Hey, first big case. Brains splattered on the wall. I'm not surprised you puked."

"It wasn't my finest moment."

"You got better. As I recall, you won more than you lost during your years in uniform."

The reminder that she'd cracked a good number of tough cases helped. Hitching a hip on one of the bar stools, Cleo responded to his question.

"All the evidence pointed to murder and suicide. But it bugged me that we could never pin-point exactly when or where Mitchell got his hands on the 9 mm Kurtz he used to aerate his skull. It was a German model, probably pur-chased outside the States and brought in illegally. In any case, the serial number didn't pop in any databases."

Jack wasn't surprised. Half the air force had transited through the major staging facility at Ramstein Air Base in Germany during the two Gulf Wars. The other half had probably pulled temporary duty in Europe at one time or another. Mitchell could have picked the Kurtz up overseas and failed to declare it on return. He wouldn't have been the first blue-suiter to smuggle contra-band home in his baggage.

At this point, though, Jack wasn't as interested in the 9 mm Kurtz as he was in the possible link between two dead sergeants and a retired air force colonel.

"So talk to me about Alex Sloan. How does he fit into the picture?"

"He doesn't. Yet."

He drummed his fingers on the file. She got the message.

"I struck up an idle conversation with a woman at the Atlanta airport a month or so ago, while we were both standing in line. Right in the middle of it, a couple of slick-sleeves right out of basic walked by. The woman got all choked up and told me her sister had served in the air force. Turns out the sister was Debra Smith."

"Helluva coincidence."

"No kidding!"

The shakes were gone, Jack noted. Cleo vibrated now with a different kind of intensity, one he remembered all too well. It was the kind of energy that challenged everyone around her to keep moving or get the hell out of her way.

The kind, he remembered, that had left a man sprawled on his ass on the spongy floor of a jungle cave, convinced he'd died and his brain just hadn't registered that fact yet.

"The sister told me Debra called her shortly before she was murdered. Said she was having trouble with Mitchell and wanted to break things off. Debra also mentioned a pilot on base. The sister formed the impression she might be romantically involved with the guy."

"The pilot being Alex Sloan?"

"Bingo!"

"What makes you think it was Sloan? Did Debra Smith give his name?"

"Only his handle. The sister remembered it as the Greek or something like that." Cleo pushed out of her chair, too excited now to stay anchored. "I still have friends in the fighter community. I made some calls, narrowed the field down to Alex Sloan. Alexander the Great to a few outside his immediate circle."

"That's what you've been working with? His handle?"

"There's also the fact that Sloan and Mitchell worked in the same classified program."

"Along with fifty or sixty other people."

"I had to check him out, Jack. I owed it to Debra."

Suspicion began to gather in his mind. A slow anger simmered with it. "Back up a second. Are you saying you stage-managed this trip to Santa Fe just so you could get close to Sloan?"

"Stage-managed? That's a pretty good pun, Donovan, even for you."

The smart comeback didn't cut it. Suspicion coalesced into rock-hard certainty. He leaned forward, his anger surging into fury.

"You set it all up, didn't you? The request from Conners to provide security here in Santa Fe. Your show of reluctance to take the job. The request for the OSI to expedite background information on everyone connected with the festival, including its honorary chairman."

"Okay, maybe I—"

"Hell, you probably generated the hate mail Conners received, just to shake her up and convince her she needed extra security."

The accusation brought fire into Cleo's eyes. As furious now as he was, she got right in his face.

"Watch it, pal. I might have made a couple of

phone calls to friends in the security business out
in L.A. and stirred the pot a bit, but I did *not* generate any hate mail or in any way inflate my
threat assessment."

"Yeah, right. Tell it to the marines."

Her lips curled in a snarl. "I'm telling you,
Donovan."

Jack might have apologized if he wasn't so
pissed off. "Dammit, you knew we had a seven
burner working here."

"Not until you dragged me to Washington!
Where, I might add, the Old Man resorted to out-
right blackmail to make me accept this job. So
don't go all hot and heavy with me about stage-
managing things."

With some effort, Jack reined in his temper.
"Okay, we'll call this one a draw. But you'd bet-
ter play it straight with me from this point on,
North."

"Or?"

The pugnacious retort pushed him to the edge
again. "Or we'll yank you out of Santa Fe so fast
you'll have to look behind you to see where
you're going."

Her nostrils flared. He could see she wanted
to fling his words back in his face and remind him
she was a free agent. But she knew damn well
he'd issued a promise, not a threat. She also knew
the government could pull whatever strings necessary with national security at stake.

She *didn't* know her decision to dig into a ten-year-old murder investigation had upped those stakes considerably. The acid that had started churning in Jack's stomach when he'd had the Report of Investigation retrieved from the archives kicked in again.

"I need a drink. Mind if I help myself?"

"Be my guest." Her glance winged to the file. "Mind if *I* help myself?"

"Go for it."

Snatching up the folder, she carried it to a chair. Her face settled into intent lines as she flipped the cover.

Jack figured she would pick up on the significance of the coded entry on the file summary sheet while he downed the Diet Pepsi he extracted from the fridge. She spotted the code before he popped the pull-tab.

"What's this?"

He played it nonchalant, just for the pleasure of seeing her work it out. "What?"

"This."

She stabbed a finger at the computer-generated summary sheet. It was a standard OSI form containing the names of the subjects of the investigation and the investigating agent, a brief description of the crime or incident, and a tab index for the exhibits and attachments.

"Why is there a cross-reference code after Staff Sergeant Mitchell's name?"

"Because he's the subject of another investigation."

Her brows snapped together. He could almost hear the gears spinning as she searched her memory.

"I ran him through the database before I interviewed him ten years ago. I'm certain he came up clean."

"He did. That code refers to an investigation conducted six years after Mitchell murdered Sergeant Smith and shot himself. You'd turned in your shield by then."

"What kind of an investigation?"

"The details are classified. All I can tell you is that CI worked it."

Her eyes widened. "Counterintelligence?"

Cleo had been an air force agent. She didn't need him to connect the dots. "Just tell me this. Did the posthumous investigation relate to Mitchell's involvement with the Harvest Eagle Program?"

"Yes."

"Are we talking an inadvertent leak of classified information here, or something more sinister?"

He could give her that much. It was the reason he'd hopped a plane to Santa Fe. "Far more sinister."

"Holy shit!"

The gears whirred so fast now Jack could almost smell the smoke.

"In Washington, you and your boss inform me Alex Sloan is using his role in the film festival to facilitate an exchange of information between the CIA and a reluctant North Korean sound engineer. Now you tell me classified information concerning a program Sloan once worked might have been sold or otherwise compromised."

"There's nothing linking Sloan to that investigation. Mitchell was and is the only suspect."

"There wasn't anything linking the colonel to Smith's murder and Mitchell's suicide, either. But you've got to be asking yourself now if the colonel's generous offer of assistance with the Korean stems from a desire to serve his country or something more...more sinister."

She sagged against the chair back, her lips pursed in a silent whistle.

The implications were staggering, and she only knew the half of it, Jack thought. Alex Sloan had worked more than the Harvest Eagle Program. During an earlier assignment to NATO, he'd helped develop tactical strike plans against potential enemies the U.S. now counted as close allies. The mere thought that those plans might have been leaked or sold to the wrong people had put the Old Man in a cold sweat.

"We've reopened the CI case. I'm working it personally. We want you to back off, Cleo."

"No way! I worked the original murder/suicide investigation. You can't cut me out now."

"This is OSI business. You don't wear a uniform anymore."

She sprang out of the chair, fully prepared to do battle once again. Jack blunted her attack with the concession he'd had to drag out of the general.

"Here's the deal. You're a security consultant. So you consult. With me. *Only* with me. Fully and completely."

"And if I don't agree to this so-called deal?"

"I take that file and walk. I also shut down your information flow. You'll have to find another way to expedite your requests to the FBI for finger- and voiceprints on this Martin character."

"Dammit, Donovan..."

"Yes or no?"

"Okay! Okay! I'll consult. With you. *Only* with you."

"Fully and completely."

She shot him a poisonous look. "Fully and completely."

Jack wanted to believe it would be that easy. He knew better. Rounding the coffee table, he took her chin in a hard hand and tipped her face to his.

"Don't mess with me on this, North. I'll break you into little pieces."

A low hiss escaped her lips. "You're certainly welcome to try. But you might want to remember whose butt hit the floor first the last two times we tangled."

He hooked a brow. "You think I didn't mean to hit first?"

"No, I don't!"

Jack couldn't help himself. A wicked grin cut across his face. "C'mon, Cleopatra. I was just being accommodating. You know how much you like getting on top."

Her mouth opened. Snapped shut. Opened again. He might not have yielded to the insane impulse to kiss her if she hadn't given such a great impression of a tropical blowfish.

But she did.

And he did.

He made it quick. A hard, fast fusion of lips with an unplanned taste of tongue. As swift as the contact was, it left him greedy for more—and thoroughly disgusted with himself for complicating an already touchy situation. Silently cursing his brief descent into idiocy, Jack snagged his jacket and briefcase.

"I'll leave the file with you. Make sure you lock it in your room safe when you leave." He speared a look around the mini-suite. "You do have a safe?"

"I, uh…" She gave herself a little shake and jerked a thumb toward the bedroom. "Yes. In the closet."

"Good. You've got my cell phone number. Call me in the morning. Hopefully, I'll have something on that voiceprint for you by then."

Cleo nodded, which was the best she could manage with her thoughts ricocheting between Alex Sloan, the potential threat to her client and the kiss Donovan had just laid on her.

"In the meantime," he instructed, his hand on the door latch, "get some sleep. You look like you had to fight your way out of a burning building or something."

She stood frozen, staring at the door after it had snicked shut behind him. The longer she thought about that kiss, the more convinced she became Donovan had done it just to confuse her. Or disarm her. She certainly wouldn't put either past the sneaky bastard.

Geez, what a day! This morning, the man she'd mistaken for Alex Sloan had trailed a thumb over her lips in a decidedly erogenous manner. Tonight, Jack Donovan had done his own thing with her lips and blasted all to hell and back her firm conviction that she was over him.

Okay, so maybe she hadn't put those hours in that damn cave completely behind her. Maybe she got hot just thinking about those sweaty, straining muscles. And maybe she still resented Donovan for not even attempting to contact her after she'd separated from the air force.

He'd never talked about his personal life, but the OSI was a tight community. Cleo had heard about the hell Donovan's ex-wife had put him through. She also knew he'd reconciled with Kate temporarily about the same time Cleo had plunged into the private security business.

From all reports the reconciliation hadn't lasted long, but Cleo had hooked up with her atomic-armed Texas Ranger outfielder by then.

Now Donovan had popped back into her life. And he'd brought with him the file of the case that had haunted her for so many years. Dropping into her chair again, Cleo reached for the Report of Investigation.

She'd pored over the statements and exhibits so many times ten years ago she could probably recite each one verbatim. Still, she started at the beginning of the file and worked her way through it page by page, photograph by photograph.

One in the morning had come and gone by the time she reached the last tab. It contained the only new material added to the file since Cleo had last handled it. The official death certificates, superimposed over the unstamped versions she'd originally put in the file. Copies of the releases and final disposition of remains. The transcript of calls to and from Thomas Mitchell's apartment she'd requested from the phone company, but never received. According to the yellow sticky note still attached to the transcript, it had come in and been misfiled.

Idly, Cleo skimmed the list of calls until she

reached the night of the murder. Ten seconds later, she was scrambling for the phone. Her hand shaking with excitement, she stabbed in Jack's cell number.

He answered on the second ring, his voice thick with sleep. "Donovan."

"Jack, it's Cleo."

"What's wrong?"

"Nothing's wrong. I just need you to exercise your governmental powers for me."

Silence descended, broken by a low growl. "What time is it?"

She checked her watch. "Almost two."

Another growl, louder and more distinct than the first. "This couldn't wait until morning?"

With considerable restraint, Cleo refrained from pointing out 2:00 a.m. *was* morning.

"Just run this phone number for me, would you? Got a pen?"

She waited impatiently while he rooted around, then read him the digits.

"Are you going to tell me what this is about?"

"After you run the number," she promised.

She clicked off her cell phone and dropped it back on the coffee table. Propping her elbows on her knees, she stared down at the report indicating Thomas Mitchell had placed a twenty-minute call to person or persons unknown less than an hour before his approximate time of death.

13

§

Cleo rolled out of bed a mere four hours after closing the OSI Report of Investigation and hitting the sack.

Her throat still felt like someone had taken a cheese grater to it, and her smoke-reddened eyes gave excellent imitations of interstate road maps. She'd caught only a few snatches of sleep, but excitement over that telephone log entry in the Mitchell/Smith file had her energized.

By seven-thirty, she'd downed a breakfast provided by room service and was dressed warmly in tailored black wool slacks, a black turtleneck in whisper-soft cashmere and her caramel-colored blazer. Her Glock went into its holster at the small of her back.

Leaning against the counter that held the coffeemaker, she tossed down a quick cup while she studied the agenda for the day.

It was Saturday, the last full day of the festival. There were lectures and showings scheduled at half a dozen venues around Santa Fe. Another forum session this afternoon. A VIP tea. The big awards ceremony tonight, when the winners in each of the categories would be announced.

Whether her client would attend any of these functions had yet to be determined. Before Cleo could present her recommendations to Marisa, she needed a fix on the cause of last night's fire. Her call to the star's suite roused a sleepy-sounding Peter Jacobsen.

"This is Cleo. I wanted to let you know I'm going down to the theater to talk to the fire investigators."

"Yeah, okay."

"Keep Marisa in her suite until I get back."

"That shouldn't be difficult." Weary resignation colored his voice. "She insisted on taking a couple of pills to help her sleep. She's dead to the world."

As long as the star wasn't dead, period, the pills didn't constitute Cleo's problem. They were obviously Peter's, though. She felt a tug of sympathy for the man, along with a continuing amazement that he opted to remain in such a one-sided relationship. With his Viking good looks

and smooth efficiency, he could have his pick of
employers. Cleo would have hired him in a
heartbeat.

"I'll be back as soon as I can. We'll decide how
to handle the rest of the day's activities then."

She pulled on gloves and a boot-length duster
in warm wool and walked the six blocks to the
theater.

Except for a few cars parked outside a café, the
central plaza was deserted. The shops hadn't
opened yet, and it was too early for the silver-
smiths and artisans to set up their displays under
the overhang of the Spanish Governor's Palace.

Hunching her shoulders against the cold, Cleo
cut a diagonal path through the park in the center of the square. Snow decorated the backs of the
wrought-iron benches and bowed the bare tree
branches. More white stuff threatened in the
clouds hanging low over the adobe buildings.

Two blocks down San Francisco Street, she
spotted the yellow tape closing off the area immediately in front of the historic theater. As Cleo
had anticipated, fire investigators were already
on the scene. So were insurance investigators, she
discovered after fast-talking her way inside. That
wasn't surprising, as Paul Blackman had indicated the Santa Fe Performing Arts Council had
spent millions restoring the theater to its thirties-
era glory. She'd bet the insurance underwriter

would like nothing more than to lay the blame for the fire on faulty wiring, and recoup the losses from the restoration contractor.

She hung back for a few moments, breathing in the stink of smoke and soaked upholstery while she took a wide-angle view of the damage. Fire had blackened the glorious proscenium arch with its decorative tiles and fanciful Moorish arches. The curtains behind the arch hung in scorched tatters.

The giant screen dangled drunkenly, one end of its heavy roll case buried in the hole it had dug when it crashed through the stage flooring last night. The other end hung by a single suspension cable. Cleo eyed the cable thoughtfully as she made her way to the group huddled around a plastic tarp.

The investigators had lowered and disemboweled what remained of the speaker that had sent out the shower of sparks. Melted, mostly unrecognizable components lay tagged on the tarp. Cleo flashed her P.I. license, identified herself as Miss Conners's security agent and weaseled ten minutes from the Santa Fe Fire Department inspector sorting through the parts.

"Too early to say which came first," he said in answer to her question. "The electrical short that generated the sparks, or overheated electro-kindling, which could have caused the short."

"Electro-kindling?"

She hated to display her ignorance, but that was a new one for her.

"See those woofers?" He pointed to lumps of blackened material. "Plastic," he grumbled. "Everything's plastic these days. Coffeemakers, baby monitors, computers, even car bumpers. It's cheaper and lighter than noncombustible metals like steel or aluminum, but ignites like diesel fuel. Electrical appliances used to burn out when overheated. Now they burn *up* and take whole buildings with them. Vehicle fires…"

He shook his head.

"Have you found any evidence suggesting arson?" Cleo asked, knowing it was far too soon for a definitive response, but hoping for an educated guess. The inspector understood the urgency behind her request. He had to know about the controversy surrounding *The Redemption*.

"No evidence at this point, but I'm not ruling it out. Take a look at this."

Hunkering down, he indicated a thin wire. The protective coating had burned away, leaving the twisted copper strands exposed. A tiny globule had formed on one of the strands.

"Like many other metals, copper expands with heat. When it does, it absorbs gaseous elements from other substances around it. Arc beads like this one form and trap the gases as the metal cools."

That much Cleo could follow. He lost her,

though, when he went into a detailed explanation of the differences between carbon monoxide and carbon dioxide gases and those generated by combustible products.

"Bottom line," he summarized, "what's inside this little bead will tell us whether the wire arced and caused the fire, or the components simply overheated and were ignited by a stray spark."

A stray spark sounded purely accidental. The arc didn't.

"Could someone have caused the wire to arc?"

"Sure. I'm not saying someone did, mind you. But all an arsonist would have to do is strip away the protective coating, break a few copper strands and wait for the exposed wire to short. Or he could use a remote device to jump the speaker's normal circuitry and trigger the short. Especially," the inspector added, "if he wanted the pyrotechnics to occur at a particular moment."

"Like in the middle of my client's big scene."

"I hear it was pretty, uh, artistic."

"That it was. Any idea when you'll have something more definitive?"

"Sorry. The days of eyeballing a beaded wire and making a judgment call are gone. We'll send these components to the lab for analysis. Could be a week or more until we have a final determination."

Longer, she guessed, if the insurance investigators didn't agree with the lab findings. Most of the major underwriters retained their own experts. They'd want another analysis. Fires like this one were big business.

Chewing on the inside of her lip, she gestured to the charred remnants of the screen and its massive roll case.

"I assume you're going to take that monster down and analyze its components, too."

"We are. The screen was a secondary contributor to the fire. We'll run tests on the combustibility of the materials used in its manufacture."

"I'd like to know what caused the strut supporting the roll case to fail."

The investigator's shrewd glance went to the stage. "So would I."

Cleo left the theater with more questions than answers. Was the fire one of those freakish, coincidental accidents? Or had someone engineered it? If so, who?

The questions were still swirling inside her head when Peter answered her knock and let her into Marisa's suite. Newspapers covered every horizontal surface. A gleeful J.L. was skimming the headlines while Marisa divided her attention between the big-screen TV in the sitting room and the one blaring in the bedroom.

"We made the morning news," Peter deadpanned. "And every paper in the country."

"Surprise, surprise."

"Want some coffee?"

"Thanks."

"You take it black, right?"

"Right."

Peeling off her gloves and coat, Cleo waded through the stacks of newspapers. Marisa didn't tear her glance away from the TV, where a reporter stood silhouetted against the theater's distinctive facade. The station interspersed her recap of last night's fire with short clips from *The Redemption*.

"Numerous attendees reported that Conners directed them to an exit at the rear of the orchestra pit, at great risk to herself. The courageous star certainly gave new meaning to the title of her stunning tour de force."

Cleo couldn't hold back a cynical smile. Interesting how *The Redemption* had segued from box-office bomb to tour de force overnight.

Peter wore a similar wry expression when he handed her the coffee. Neither of them spoke as the reporter ended with a segment from last night's impromptu news conference, showing a wounded Marisa nobly declining to take credit for any special heroics.

"God, that was great!" A gushing J.L. rounded the back of the couch to beam at her employer. Minus the bloodred lipstick that matched her nails, the woman's face had all the warmth and appeal of unbaked cookie dough. "You played that exactly right, Marisa."

"I thought so." Funneling her hands through her auburn curls, the actress slanted Cleo a cat-like look. "What about you? What did you think?"

She didn't have time to hear what Cleo really thought. Nor would she appreciate hearing it.

"What I think is that we need to discuss what I learned at the theater this morning, then decide how we're going to handle the rest of your sched-ule. Turn off the TVs, J.L."

"Not yet." The PR rep snatched up the remote and stabbed it at the large screen. "We didn't catch the CBS affiliate yet. They might run—"

"Turn them off!"

The terse command raised spots of red into J.L.'s chalky cheeks. She clicked the remote, tossed it onto the sofa beside Marisa and marched into the bedroom to switch off that set.

In the ensuing silence, Cleo recounted the de-tails of her conversation with the fire investiga-tor. She finished with the stark, unsatisfactory truth.

"He can't say at this point whether it was an accident or arson. He won't be able to say for some weeks."

Frowning, Peter leaned his elbows on his knees. "But it could be either."

"Correct." She let that sink in for a few seconds. "If it was arson, we have to ask who triggered it and why. The first, most disturbing possibility is our friend with the fake ID."

Peter moved closer to Marisa as he spoke and gave her shoulder a small squeeze. "Nothing new on him?"

"Nothing yet. I'm hoping for an update on the voiceprint this morning."

Jack had promised to do what he could to expedite that. He'd also promised to check out the phone number Cleo had found in the OSI Report of Investigation.

She slammed the door on the thought. She had to stay focused on one investigation at a time.

"What about all those kooks out there?" Marisa's fingers tightened around her lover's. "The ones who threatened to boycott *The Redemption* when it opens across the country today? Someone has to be organizing and financing them."

"Someone undoubtedly is. Organizing a boycott and participating in one aren't against the law, however. Arson is." Cleo slid her glance from her client to J.L. and back again.

"Do intend to remain in Santa Fe and attend the awards ceremony tonight?"

"I'm presenting the award for best feature film, so yes, I'm going to attend."

Peter gave her shoulder another squeeze. "You're scrubbing everything else on the schedule, right? Except the media-only luncheon J.L. is setting up here at the hotel."

"I hate to hole up and—"

"We talked about this. You'll be the only celebrity at the luncheon. You'll get all the face time you want with the media. The other VIPs will attend the ceremony, but you know the cameras will focus on you. In the meantime, you need to stay safe."

"Hide away, you mean."

"No. Stay safe."

Her temper flaring, Marisa pushed off the sofa. "Look, I know I agreed to curtail my appearances, but that was before the morning papers arrived. Do you see those headlines? Didn't you hear that TV segment? The whole world thinks I'm some kind of superhero. I can't act scared and cower in my hotel room now."

Peter's jaw worked. "What you can do is show some sense for a change. All I'm asking is that you take appropriate measures to protect yourself."

"Providing me protection is my security consultant's job! Why don't we hear her views on the matter before we start jumping down each other's throat?"

As much as Cleo would love to hustle Conners into the limo, whisk her down to the airport in Albuquerque and see her on her way, she owed her client an honest assessment.

"We won't know for some time if the fire was an accident or arson, but I'd say the timing was too damn pat for mere coincidence."

She had to give Marisa credit for not flinching. The star's pumped-up lips tightened, but she said nothing as Cleo continued.

"Assuming someone *did* deliberately engineer the electrical short, the question becomes whether the perpetrator intended to make a dramatic statement or to physically harm you or the other attendees."

"What's the bottom line here?" her client demanded. "Do you think someone wants to hurt me or not?"

Cleo didn't have anything to go on at this point but her gut. She'd ignored her instincts ten years ago and a young sergeant had died as a result. She wouldn't ignore them this time.

"I think someone wants to hurt you."

Marisa's breath left on a long, slow whoosh. Her belligerence went with it. More serious than Cleo had ever seen her, she crossed the room and stripped the situation down to its most basic element.

"My career's riding on this movie. I need to play the fire and the possible threat to my life for all they're worth. Tell me how to do it without putting myself in the crosshairs."

For the first time, Cleo felt a tug of real sympathy for her client. The woman lived in a glass bowl. One of her own choosing, it was true, but even a goldfish deserved a little privacy now and then. She also deserved to know she wasn't risking death every time she stepped out the door. Unfortunately, Cleo's gut told her this wasn't one of those times.

"Okay, here's my plan. First, we bring in more manpower. I've already put in a call to an associate of mine. Goose will be here by noon. I've also asked the festival officials to call in additional security for today's events."

Peter came to stand with them. "Can they arrange more coverage on such short notice?"

"It's done. Second, Marisa doesn't enter any room or facility until I run a sweep."

They would need help for that, too. Donovan was going to regret his rash offer to provide backup.

"Third, one of us stays within six feet of Marisa at all times."

"Consider that done, too," Peter growled.

Wrapping her arms around her waist, Marisa listened closely as her two advisors went over the day's schedule in excruciating detail. She refused to admit the fire had her scared shitless. She _couldn't_ admit it. If she did, Peter would insist on bundling her up and whisking her back to L.A.

She hadn't exaggerated the situation a few minutes ago. She knew damn well _The Redemp-_

tion was her last shot at making it into the ranks of the megastars. She had to stay in Santa Fe, had to take a calculated risk.

But Peter didn't.

The idea of losing his solid presence at her side ripped an unexpected hole in her heart. The thought bothered her almost as much as the prospect of crawling into that king-size bed without him.

Dammit! When had she become so dependent on the man? Torn by the conflicting emotions he always roused in her, she waited until he and Cleo had finished going over the schedule to suggest he return to L.A. without her.

Peter's head snapped up. "No way in hell."

"Look, let's be sensible about this. If there is some kook out there trying to get at me, he'll go for you first if you're in the way."

"That's the way I see it."

"Well, I don't want you hurt."

She saw the tenderness spring into his eyes. He waited for her to say the words she knew he wanted to hear, to voice the feelings she refused to admit, even to herself.

Marisa tried. She honestly tried. The maudlin phrases stuck in her throat.

Frustrated and as angry at herself as she was at him for the pressure he put on her, she tossed her head.

"All right. Stay if you want to. But don't expect

me to be all sweetness and light the next few days. I'm too wound up."

His laughter came fast and rich. Crossing the room, he hooked an arm around her waist and hauled her against his chest.

"I wouldn't recognize you if you were all sweetness and light."

"Bastard."

"Bitch."

The hole in Marisa's heart grew a little more ragged around the edges. She was so close to loving him. She *did* love him, in her own way. She might even have forced the words out if Cleo hadn't chosen that moment to clear her throat.

"Excuse me, folks. Could we get back to business? I want to make sure we're all singing from the same sheet of music before I interview the additional security personnel the festival folks are sending over."

14

Since Cleo had jolted him awake so damn early, Jack put the morning hours to good use. His first call was to headquarters. It took them all of a half hour to run the trace Cleo had requested.

As a result, his second call was to the senior CIA field agent running the Santa Fe op. After a short, one-sided conversation, Charles Porter gave him directions and an access code.

The directions took Jack through a pine-shrouded winter wonderland. His breath clouded in the frigid early morning air when he leaned out the window of the SUV and punched in the security code. A few seconds later, massive bronze gates carved with ancient Southwestern figures swung open.

Jack didn't know Hopi from Ho-Ti, but he had to admit the entrance to Alex Sloan's residence was impressive as hell. It also set the tone for the sprawling adobe structure he glimpsed in the distance. Squinting in the dazzling light, he followed the plowed drive through stands of bare-branched aspen and pines dusted with white.

As instructed, he turned off the main drive and took the sloping ramp to the rear of the residence. The area behind the house was plowed, allowing ample access to the three-car garage. Two sedans and a mud-spattered van were parked some distance beyond the garage.

Jack pulled up beside the van. His boots crunched on the packed snow as he followed a narrow path to a small building sitting by itself among the trees. Like the main residence, the building was flat-roofed and constructed of adobe. It looked like a dollhouse, he decided. Or a small, self-contained hideaway where someone could slip away and indulge secret fantasies.

His face grim behind his aviator sunglasses, he plodded down the path. The shearling-lined sheepskin jacket he'd hauled from Washington felt damn good in the knifing cold. Too bad his well-washed cords didn't provide the same degree of warmth.

The door to the dollhouse swung open when he was still some yards away. Charlie Porter stood silhouetted on the threshold. Jack had worked with the CIA operative before and hadn't been impressed. Tall, heavily muscled from regular workouts, with hair shaved to the scalp to disguise his receding hairline, Porter paid lip service to the concept of interagency cooperation but couldn't quite shake his supercilious air of superiority.

"Donovan."

Slipping off his glove, Jack participated in the male ritual of exerting just enough pressure to demonstrate he wasn't a limp dick but didn't have to prove it by grinding bones.

Standing aside, Porter allowed him entry into what he now saw was a potter's studio. Shelves lined one wall, displaying clay bowls and pots. Most, Jack noted, featured graphics similar to those decorating the bronze gates he'd just passed through. A kiva fireplace occupied one corner, a kiln took up another. The throw wheel, or whatever it was called, had been shoved to one side to make room for racks of equipment.

Sound recording and editing equipment, Jack guessed, although he spotted a few familiar surveillance monitors and sets of high-tech earphones among the scattered racks. Sure enough, Porter's clipped introductions of the other two men present identified one as a CIA intelligence-gathering drone and another as a Ph.D. from nearby Los Alamos Labs. Dr. Lee, a Korean-American, glanced at his watch and reminded

Porter they had to be in town in less than half an hour.

"Yes, I know. What's this about, Donovan?"

"We need to talk privately."

"This way."

Porter led the way to a storage room and closed the door. Jack glanced out the frost-coated window before running an eye over the floor-to-ceiling shelves jammed with supplies.

"This place secure?"

"What do you think?"

Christ, didn't the man ever take the baseball bat out of his ass?

"Well, it's like this, Charlie. My faith in the CIA suffered a slight hit when I heard two of your highly skilled operatives were disarmed by a lone female wielding a sharp stick."

He shouldn't have descended to Porter's level, but the man's sour expression almost compensated for the unpleasant moments Jack knew would come. Almost.

"The casita's secure," Porter snapped. "We swept it, the residence and the entire grounds before we set up shop here."

"How about after you set up shop?"

"We run the routine checks. What the hell is this about, Donovan?"

He hated this. The fact that Cleo had uncovered a link between an air force colonel and a decade old murder/suicide was bad enough. The possibility that same colonel might also be linked to the leak of highly classified information made Jack wish he'd been sent to deliver the news to anyone but Charlie Porter.

"You and your superiors want to know why former Air Force OSI agent Cleo North has demonstrated such an interest in Alex Sloan." Digging a hand into his pocket, he retrieved the scrap of paper he'd scribbled on earlier. "Basically, it's because of this."

"Looks like a phone number."

"It is. Sloan's home number, when he was stationed at Luke Air Force Base ten years ago."

"And that interests me because?"

"Because a twenty-minute call was made to this number from the off-base residence of Air Force Staff Sergeant Thomas Mitchell shortly before Mitchell stabbed his girlfriend to death and splattered his own brains against the wall."

Porter's eyes narrowed. "Domestic murders and suicides don't fall within our purview unless they have—"

"Implications for national security. Yeah, I know. About six years after Mitchell died, a tip from Interpol helped us trace a deliberate compromise of classified information back to him."

"The man was a *spy?*"

"Yes."

"Shit! What kind of classified information did he leak?"

"He was working a compartmented program at the time of his death. The unclassified designator is Harvest Eagle."

The CIA operative went stiff. "Harvest Eagle? Wasn't that the little reverse engineering operation you boys in blue had going on out in the Arizona desert?"

"Something like that."

Even with his security clearances, Jack knew only the bare bones of the program that had picked apart, analyzed and reverse engineered weapons and delivery systems stolen or bought on the black market from a host of foreign sources.

"Alex Sloan headed the Harvest Eagle Program. Staff Sergeant Mitchell worked for him."

"I don't believe this!" Porter's cheeks flamed. "We came to you before we approached Sloan about using his position as film festival chairman to assist us in this frigging op. You cleared the man!"

"That's right, we did. We had interviewed Sloan about the possible compromise, of course. We found nothing linking him to Staff Sergeant Mitchell, other than the fact the man worked for him ten years ago."

"Now you have a phone call."

"We still don't know the significance of the phone call," Jack admitted. "It could have been a desperate cry for help from a subordinate to a superior. Or," he added, playing on Cleo's chance conversation with Sergeant Smith's sister, "the call could have been made by the girlfriend. We're working the possibility Sloan might have been sexually involved with her."

"This is great!" Porter exploded. "Fucking fantastic! Today's the last full day of the festival. I have agents practically living in the Koreans' back pocket and a Ph.D. I need to insert into a sound engineer's intimate circle in less than an hour. Now I've got to worry that the man who helped organize our cover for a highly sensitive project *may* have been screwing the girlfriend of a spy who worked for him ten years ago."

Jack felt a reluctant tug of sympathy for the man. Every undercover agent had watched a carefully orchestrated operation turn to crap at one time or another. This one was definitely starting to acquire a stink.

"That's not all you have to worry about."

"What else do you know, Donovan?"

"I know you didn't see fit to inform us Sloan's brother had arrived on the scene."

Every short, stubby hair on Porter's scalped head seemed to bristle. "What interest does the OSI have in Marc Sloan?"

"Officially, none. Unofficially, we find it interesting he passed himself off as his brother to Ms. North."

On several occasions, which made Jack wonder just how often the Sloan boys switched identities, and why.

"We're also curious about Marc Sloan's sudden interest in recent improvements in swept-frequency acoustic interferometry technology. We understand he requested a copy of the tape of the sound engineer's seminar."

"Yeah, he did. So did thirty other festival attendees."

Some of Porter's antagonism evaporated. Wearily, he scrubbed a hand over his jaw.

"Okay, we were concerned about the brother's sudden appearance, too. When we confronted the colonel about it, he explained he'd invited his twin to attend the festival months ago, long before the North Koreans decided to participate. He says Marc requested the seminar tape because he read about the new sound wave technology and is interested in its commercial applications. He heads an engineering outfit that retrofits cargo ships."

"We know. He's retrofitted several ships in the air force's oceangoing fleet."

That caught Porter by surprise. Evidently the CIA operative didn't know the air force operated a fleet of oceangoing vessels. Jack hadn't known it, either, until late last night. After Cleo had told him about Sloan's brother being in Santa Fe, he'd done some serious background work on the former naval officer and current Fortune 500 exec.

His lips pinched, Porter checked his watch. "I've got to get Dr. Lee downtown. We've spent two days softening up our target. We have to move on him today or we'll lose him."

"Is he ready to talk?"

The other man hesitated several beats. "He's ready. We've stroked his ego until it's the size of Montana. We also fed him all kinds of crap about how he hasn't received the recognition he deserves from the international film community. He thinks we're going to feature him in an article on acoustics in the next issue of *Billboard*."

He reached for the door, apparently torn between the task ahead and the information Jack had just fed him.

"I'll run the information you've given me about this Sergeant Mitchell and his possible link to Alex Sloan up my chain. Don't move on him until I get back to you."

"Sloan is former air force, Porter. The OSI has the stick on this investigation."

"I'm not getting into a jurisdictional pissing contest here, for God's sake! Just give me time to apprise my superiors and get their take on the situation."

"How about this? I'll apprise *my* superior of your request. If he concurs, I'll sit on my hands until I get the nod."

"Fair enough. I've got to roll. The fire last night gave us the opportunity we've been waiting for."

A savage satisfaction colored Porter's voice. "Every eye at every festival event today will be on Marisa Conners. No one's going to notice when we cut our target out of the herd and line him up for a friendly chat with Dr. Lee."

Jack came to a full mental stop, backed up and switched gears. Porter had that right. Every eye *would* be on Marisa today. Convenient. Very convenient.

Had Porter and company planned it all? The public outcry over *The Redemption*. The threats against Marisa Conners. The mysterious heckler. Were they just ways to divert attention from their efforts to extract information from the North Korean? Was that why Jack's contact at the FBI hadn't gotten back to him on the voiceprint match Cleo had requested? Had he been instructed to drag his feet?

When Jack slid behind the wheel of his rental vehicle a few moments later, his chest felt as tight as it had when Cleo had landed on it last night.

His call to General Barnes a short time later was brief, succinct and unpleasant in the extreme.

As Jack had predicted, the Old Man did *not* appreciate learning that Cleo had used him and the OSI in an elaborate scheme to extract information on Alex Sloan. His reaction to the suggestion the CIA might be working an even more elaborate scheme added several new variations to Jack's already extensive repertoire of scatological terms for the Company. Barnes did promise, however, to put his stars behind the request for expeditious handling of the voiceprint.

When Jack caught Cleo on her cell phone and relayed his lack of progress regarding the voiceprint, she grunted in disgust. "I hope you had more luck on the phone number I asked you to trace."

After his conversation with Porter, he wasn't sure when he could give her that information. Or how the hell he'd hold her back when he did.

"We'll talk about that when I get back to the hotel."

"Well, get here fast. I need you."

"Why? What's happened?"

"Nothing yet, but Marisa's determined to make the most of her new savior-of-the-world status. She's going to stick to her schedule of appearances. I've asked the festival to provide additional security. I also have one of my own guys on the way in. Are you still available for backup?"

Despite the knot that had formed in his gut, Jack felt a smile slide into place. It was payback time.

"I'm not sure you can afford me."

"What, you want a retainer fee?"

"Let's just say I expect payment for services rendered."

"Haul your buns over here, Donovan. We'll negotiate payment when and if you render any useful service."

Jack understood the urgency of her request for assistance when he pulled up at her hotel.

News vans jammed the entrance. The lobby was worse. In one corner, a harried-looking official wearing a name tag that identified her as the public affairs coordinator for the festival announced changes to the day's agenda. In another, the rapier-thin brunette Cleo had tagged last night as Marisa Conners's PR rep was detailing the time and precise location of a media-only luncheon to be held here at the hotel.

Elbowing his way through the reporters and camera operators, Jack made it as far as the elevator bank. Hotel security detained him there until he flashed his OSI credentials and gold-plated shield.

Two more security types patrolled the corridor on Marisa's floor. They passed Jack through, but both reached for their weapons when a second elevator door *pinged* open. He caught a glimpse of the behemoth inside and came within a breath of reaching for his own weapon.

Just because the tattooed biker in black leather and chains *looked* liked a recent escapee from a maximum-security facility didn't necessarily mean he was. Looks could be deceiving.

Then again...

When the new arrival took in the two gun barrels aimed at his midsection, a look of wicked enjoyment flickered across his face. "Cool it, dudes. I was invited to this party."

"By whom?"

"Cleo North. Maybe you've heard of her? I expect she's the reason you two are walking this beat."

"And your name is?"

"Dave Petrowski, but y'all can call me Goose."

"Let's see some ID."

"It's in my back pocket. I'm going to reach around. Slowly."

"Correction. You're going to turn around. Slowly. I'll do the reaching."

"Have it your way, dude."

Watching from a few yards down the corridor, Jack winced when the security guard put himself between his partner and the gorilla in black leather. Nothing like turning yourself into a living shield. Lucky for him Baldy didn't take advantage of the opportunity.

Fishing among the chains looped across the man's back pockets, the guard retrieved a trifold wallet thicker than the latest edition of *Webster's Dictionary*.

"Driver's license is in the middle section," Petrowski volunteered. "Right next to my permit to carry concealed."

The man had to be six-six and a good two-fifty. Jack sincerely hoped the tattooed giant was, in fact, the reinforcement Cleo said she'd called in. He didn't relish the idea of having to help the security guards disarm him.

He waited patiently while they contacted Cleo on her cell phone. A few moments later, the door to Marisa's suite flew open.

"'Bout time you got here," Cleo snapped at Jack by way of greeting. "You, too, Goose. Come on in, both of you. We're behind schedule."

The biker retrieved his license from the security guard and hefted a fat duffel bag. Chains clanking, he ambled down the hall and offered Jack a bear-size paw.

"Petrowski."

"Donovan."

"You working for Cleo?"

"Not officially."

Black eyes framed by almost colorless white-blond lashes made a slow trip from Jack's face to his well-worn Ropers and back again.

"Ex-cop?"

A man of few words. Jack appreciated that in a colleague, even if he didn't particularly go for all the extraneous hardware.

"Ex–military cop. Currently special agent with the United States Air Force Office of Special Investigations."

Brows as pale as the lashes winged upward. "You're *that* Donovan?"

The chains danced. The tattooed dagger blade decorating one side of his neck disappeared in the folds of his jacket collar as his shoulders began to shake. Laughter rumbled up from his chest.

"This is gonna be interesting."

15

"Astra Three, this is Astra One."

Cleo returned Jack's wry look while she waited for Goose to acknowledge her transmission. Okay, anyone with a smattering of high school Latin would guess *astra* was code for *star*. But that was the best she'd been able to come up with in the frantic flurry of moving Marisa from El Cortez to La Fonda for her first official appearance of the day.

Cleo had hustled the actress into the hotel through the rear service entrance to avoid the handful of protesters out front. Their numbers had shrunk considerably since yesterday. Hard to work up enough steam to heckle a heroine. Even so, Cleo hadn't drawn a full breath until the doors had swished shut behind her client.

"Go ahead, Astra One."

The wireless headset she was wearing transmitted and received with crystal clarity, yet she had to strain to hear Goose's reply over the clattering dishes and clanking pots in the hotel's busy kitchen.

"We're holding in Area A," she advised. "Are you ready to receive?"

"Roger, One. Extra eyes in place. Proceed to Area B."

Plastering on what she hoped was a reassuring smile, Cleo lined up her troops. "All right, Marisa, make sure you keep close behind Jack. Peter, you stay on her left."

Since Cleo was right-handed, she'd put Jacobsen on the left to maximize her field of fire.

"Everyone ready?"

The two men nodded. Marisa swiped her tongue over glossy, baby-doll lips. Makeup gave her face a healthy glow, but her fist showed white at the knuckles.

"I'm ready."

"Okay, Jack. Move out."

The Old Man would probably choke on his pipe when he heard Cleo had pressed one of his crack agents into temporary service. Tough. She hadn't had time to test the skills of the additional security personnel the festival committee had sent in. She *knew* how Special Agent Donovan performed when the pucker factor rose high enough to put a wiggle in everyone's walk.

She had to admit it felt good to be going into action with him again. They'd only worked that one op together, but those hairy days in the jungle had given her a real appreciation of Jack's skills.

In and out of uniform.

He was the only man who'd ever made her pop her cork with just a few thrusts of his hips. Not that he'd been able to do much else at the time, with his shoulder bandaged and his attention divided between the defenses they'd strung at the entrance to the cave and what was going on inside it.

Cleo didn't kid herself, though. She and Donovan would go their separate ways again after she wrapped up this job—and the other matter that had brought her to Santa Fe. Deliberately, she shoved both Jack Donovan and Alex Sloan out of her mind. She couldn't let herself think about either one of them right now.

So, naturally, the colonel was the first person she spotted when she and her small entourage took the creaky wooden steps to the downstairs conference area. At least, she *thought* it was the colonel. This twin business was a pain in the butt.

Sloan was waiting with Joe Garza outside the packed ballroom. When he started forward, Jack gave him a keen once-over. Donovan had to recognize the colonel from his records. No one could mistake that square chin and military carriage. For reasons of his own, though, Jack chose not to identify himself as air force or OSI. Moving aside, he granted the man access to Marisa.

Sloan took both her hands in his. "Miss Conners, Joe and I want you to know how sincerely we regret the unfortunate incident at the Lensic last night."

"It *was* unfortunate. And damn scary." Sliding into character, she gave him one of her steamy, signature smiles. "Fabulous publicity for the festival, though."

"And for *The Redemption*, of course."

"Of course."

"That kind of PR we can do without," Joe huffed. He, too, stepped forward. "On behalf of the entire organizing committee, I'd like to say how thrilled we are you elected to stay in Santa Fe and appear at the remaining events."

Ha! Cleo just bet they were thrilled. They'd probably kept a couple of lawyers up all night reassessing their liability if their guest artist was injured, disabled or killed.

"Shall we go inside?" Sloan offered her his arm. "I'm introducing you this morning. I'll keep it short," he promised on a dry note, "since we both know you don't need any introduction and I don't want to take away from your time in the spotlight."

That was fine with Marisa. Tucking her arm in the colonel's, she let him escort her into the packed ballroom.

No small breakout room for this one-on-one with the star, Cleo noted. The event was standing room only. It looked as if every festival attendee and official not required to judge the films being shown at different venues across town had wedged inside. News crews from a three-state area jostled for elbow room in the roped-off media section.

As Marisa's party made its way toward the raised stage, the crowd surged to its feet. Thunderous applause broke out, punctuated by cheers and whistles. Quite a change from last night's boos and catcalls, Cleo thought as she searched for Goose and his part-time help.

In deference to the occasion, Goose had shed his leather and chains. Even in a checked wool sport coat and jeans, though, his body art and six-feet-six of solid muscle separated him from the crowd and earned him more than one wary glance from those near him.

When Marisa went onstage, Jack stood close to the stairs on the left side. Cleo covered the right. She pressed back against the wall and skimmed her gaze over the audience while her client mined every last nugget from the standing ovation.

Making sure the cameras had a clean shot, Marisa smiled and waved and worked the crowd with consummate skill. Cleo wished the actress had chosen something other than the flame-red suit that made her such a visible target, but she had to admit it focused all eyes in the ballroom right where Marisa wanted them.

Alex Sloan gave her plenty of time to enjoy the moment before making his introduction. Marisa took the mike next. After glimpsing her client's jittery nerves in the kitchen, Cleo had to admire the performance she now gave. Five minutes into the session, her come-hither smiles and throaty purrs had the camera operators angling for close-ups. Judging by the expressions of the men in the audience, she also had half of them hard.

Except Assault Rifle Guy, Cleo noted as she skimmed the crowd. He and Laser Man had their sights set on the Korean standing a little apart from his compatriots at the back of the ballroom. Without seeming to pay the CIA operatives any particular notice, she watched them ease into position on either side of their target. Moments later, all three had disappeared.

By the time the session concluded, Cleo's nerves were crawling up one side of her neck and down the other. Marisa still had a half hour before her private luncheon with the media and used every minute of it to sign autographs and pose with fans.

Cleo sent Goose and his recruits back to El Cortez for another sweep of the banquet room. Jack tapped a finger on his cell phone to indicate he had to take a call and went out a side door.

With Peter hovering at Marisa's shoulder, Cleo kept a close eye on the throng lined up to speak to her. So close, she had to look twice before she identified which twin had moved into her peripheral vision.

"Morning, Brown Eyes. How's your throat?"

"It's still raw, but I'm not singing bass anymore."

The Brioni tie was gone, but the gray slacks, cashmere sport coat and open-neck Oxford shirt might have come right out of *GQ*.

"I brought you something."

"What?"

She kept her attention ninety percent on Marisa, ten percent on Sloan's smile as he slipped something into Cleo's blazer pocket.

"Open it later, when you're not so busy."

Cleo was as curious as the next woman. She also had a client to protect. She was pretty sure Marc Sloan wouldn't slide an explosive device into her pocket, but it never hurt to check these things out.

The shape of the flat case gave her the first clue to its contents. The embossed name of the jeweler on the lid cinched the matter. Momentarily wrenching her gaze from the two starstruck young women engaging Marisa in conversation, she protested, "If this is what I think it is, I can't accept it."

"Why not?"

"I never accept expensive necklaces before the first date."

Or from the brother of a man who might have been involved with a murdered sergeant.

"We can remedy that situation. Have a late supper with me after the awards ceremony, when you've tucked your client in bed for the night."

"No can do. I'm on duty until I put Marisa on a plane to L.A. tomorrow afternoon."

He didn't give up easily. She suspected it wasn't in his nature.

"We'll make it tomorrow evening, then. I'll re-arrange my schedule and stay in Santa Fe an extra night."

The mellow timber of his voice implied he'd like to spend the extra night with her. All of it. Cleo had to admit the notion didn't totally dis-gust her. The guy was smooth, sophisticated and gorgeous.

As opposed to the individual who reentered the ballroom at that moment. Donovan was gor-geous, too, if craggy features and squinty laugh lines turned you on. And smooth enough when he wanted to be. But sophisticated?

On the outside, maybe. Cleo had seen him in action, though. When she'd hacked through that steaming jungle with the man, she'd watched his veneer of civilization strip away layer by layer.

She'd also been a long time getting him out of her head after he'd dropped out of sight and out of her life. Too long. Sighing, she pressed the jeweler's case into Sloan's hand.

"Thanks, but blue isn't really my color."

He took his marching orders with good grace. "You're right. I would have chosen amber for you, to compliment your eyes. Or yellow diamonds. But you seemed so taken with the lapis. Next time I'll follow my instincts."

Just as Cleo was following hers concerning his brother. Once again she had to fight the urge to divert her attention from Marisa. She itched to pump Sloan for information about his twin, but this wasn't the time or the place.

Tomorrow night, maybe. Since Sloan had offered...

"Give me a call if you do decide to stay over in Santa Fe. I owe you for the oxygen bottle you stuck to my face after the fire."

"Consider it a date, Brown Eyes."

He'd taken only a few steps when Goose's voice rumbled through her earpiece.

"Brown Eyes?"

"It's code," Cleo mouthed into the mike on her wireless headset. She would have preferred not to have broadcast her conversation with Sloan to her entire team, but hadn't dared risk going to nontransmit mode while Marisa remained so vulnerable.

"Roger that, One."

Goose had sounded amused. Jack did not.

"Let's get Astra on the move, One. Some of us have business to take care of that doesn't involve arranging dates for tomorrow night."

Jack caught Cleo alone in her mini-suite after their return to El Cortez. While Marisa primped next door for her by-invitation-only luncheon with the media, he terminated his temporary assignment to the Conners support team.

"I have to drive down to Albuquerque."

"What's going on? Why am I losing my backup?"

"You've got Petrowski and a whole team of hired help to back you up."

Christ, he sounded petulant. Like some horny teenager who'd just overheard his girl getting it on with another guy, he thought in disgust.

Cleo evidently thought so, too. Her jaw set, she looked ready to tackle the matter head-on. Jack blunted the attack with a terse explanation.

"I asked General Barnes to lean on the FBI about that voiceprint. They may have something for us. They want me to come down to the regional office in Albuquerque and take a listen."

"Why the regional office? They have a field office right here in Santa Fe."

"But not the equipment necessary to run the print, evidently." He started for the door. "I'll be back as soon as I can."

"Wait!"

"What?"

"Did you get a trace on the phone number I gave you this morning?"

He hesitated a heartbeat too long. Cleo was on him like fleas on a bassett hound.

"C'mon, Donovan. Give! Who or what did the number track to?"

"The Luke Air Force Base residence of Lieutenant Colonel and Mrs. Alexander Sloan."

Cleo didn't say a word. Not a word. But she looked as gleeful as a chocaholic turned loose in a candy store. Or a former OSI investigator finally handed a vital piece of evidence in a messy, decade-old case.

"We can't move on Sloan yet," he warned.

"Why not?"

He wasn't in the right mood to explain he was waiting for a green light from the CIA. There *wasn't* a right mood for that.

"I'll let you know when it's time. Meanwhile, I'm heading down to Albuquerque. You can reach me on my cell if you need me."

Wet, sloppy snowflakes started plopping against his windshield before he'd cleared Santa Fe. Jack spent the next thirty miles of interstate battling the slush thrown up by the semis that seemed to consider the 75 mph speed limit a personal challenge.

The traffic snarl that resulted after one of those

semis jackknifed ten miles north of Albuquerque
didn't improve his mood. Nor did the hour-long
wait for the highway patrol to clear the wreckage
and restore traffic flow. It was well past two by
the time he reached the city's outskirts, almost
three when he pulled into the parking lot across
the street from the federal building.

Since the Oklahoma City bombing, security at
all federal offices had tightened considerably.
Jack went through one X-ray screening and two
additional checkpoints. The escort sent down to
conduct him to the FBI offices on the sixth floor
waited patiently while the security guards re-
united him with his badge and his weapon.

"I'm Special Agent Roberta Kee."

She had the flat cheeks of a Native American
and the strong, no-nonsense grip of a woman
used to competing in a man's world.

"Sorry to drag you all the way down here, but
I think you'll find what we have for you was
worth the trip. We'll take the elevators."

Six floors up, Kee signed him through another
checkpoint, handed him a badge and escorted
him into an operations center. Banks of computers lined one wall, maps and digital displays
another. With a nod to the agent on duty, she directed Jack to a computer on the far side of the
room.

"The Forensic Audio, Video and Image Analysis Unit at our lab in Quantico analyzed the tape

your agent sent us. What's her name? Caro North?"

"Cleo North. She isn't OSI. She's private."

Kee hooked a brow. "For a P.I., she's sure got friends in high places."

"We hired her as a consultant to work a special project for us."

"If the special project relates to the voiceprint we just ran, maybe *we* should hire the woman. She hit the jackpot with this one."

"I doubt she'd take the assignment," Jack replied, his pulse quickening. "She hates paperwork, and the Bureau is worse for that than the air force. What have you got?"

"How much do you know about voiceprints?" she countered.

"I know you have to match it with a print already on file. And that spectrograph comparisons aren't considered conclusive in a court of law."

"Not yet, but the matches we ran on John Muhammed provided sufficient backup to the DNA and physical evidence to convict the bastard."

Jack had celebrated the Washington sniper's conviction as fiercely as everyone else in D.C. Muhammed didn't interest him at the moment, though.

"It took us awhile to get a hit on this point," Kee related. "Most of the lab's effort these days is focused on the bin Laden and Hussein tapes our sister service keeps sending us from the Middle East."

Her face remained impassive, but curiosity glinted in her black eyes.

"Rumor is, that same sister service is working the transfer of a new sound technology. One that could help pinpoint the exact location where those tapes were cut. Something to do with differing sound waves and acoustic concentrations."

Jesus! So much for the seven burner. Deliberately, Jack slammed the door on her curiosity.

"What have you got?"

Accepting the rebuff with good grace, she handed him a headset. "What we have is a hit on the three-word phrase 'burn in hell.' The voice on the tape North sent us is clear enough. We matched it to a phone conversation we harvested during an electronic search for a suspected Mafia torch job a year or so ago."

Jack's insides went cold. At Cleo's request, he'd run every possible right-wing hate group and religious fanatic who might want to retaliate against Marisa Conners for her role in *The Redemption*. Some of the individuals on the list had criminal records. None of them had direct links to organized crime. The possibility that the mob might be behind the threat to Conners put the game in a whole different ballpark.

"We don't have a hard ID on the torch," Kee informed him, "but we did get a fix on the person he's talking to. Take a listen."

16

Marisa flung herself into the back seat of the limo. She was wiped. Completely wiped.

The media luncheon had given her a rush that had carried her through most of the afternoon. The euphoria had worn off about midway through the tribute's tea, though. Her nerves were now stretched so thin and tight she swore she could hear them humming.

J.L. crawled in after her and took the facing seat. Peter settled beside Marisa. The bald Jesse Ventura look-alike wedged in on her other side. She knew the two men were protecting her with their bulk. Perversely, their very size made her feel caged.

"How much time have I got before the awards ceremony?"

"Two hours," J.L. replied. "Plenty of time to rest before we—"

"Shut the damn car door." Irate, Marisa poked Peter in his ribs. "The snow's blowing in."

He gave her one of his looks. Lord, she hated those looks. Patient and understanding and faintly disapproving, all at the same time. Like she was a child, for God's sake, instead of…

Instead of the selfish bitch who gave him everything he wanted in bed and busted his balls out of it.

As disgusted with him as with herself, Marisa sank back against the leather seat. Why couldn't she get past her hangups where Peter was concerned? Why couldn't she say the words she knew he wanted to hear? What was she so afraid of?

Another failed Hollywood marriage? Another affair like the one she'd had with James Cox on the set of *The Redemption*?

The sex had been great while it lasted, but she and James had banged egos as often as they'd banged each other. She'd known it wouldn't work between them, despite his stubborn determination to leave his wife and move in with Marisa. She'd tried to tell him she wasn't any good at relationships, that she didn't *want* entanglements.

She kept trying to tell Peter the same thing, but he wouldn't go away, no matter how hard she pushed. He just pushed right back in his quiet, solid way.

She hated to admit how much she'd needed him these past few days. Nor would she admit to the fear that had twisted her belly since the fire at the theater. She despised weakness, in herself and in others. Yet she couldn't keep from leaning closer to Peter and drawing from his strength as Cleo hooked an arm over the front seat and turned around.

"The snow is slowing traffic to a crawl. I don't want to get caught in the jam along Paseo de Peralta, so I've instructed our drivers to take an alternate route back to the hotel."

Marisa's limo had a two-car escort now—a lead vehicle packed with extra security, and a similarly loaded chase vehicle. The additional firepower should have eased some of the tension knifing across her shoulders. It only made her feel more trapped.

"I thought you said the FBI had something on that voiceprint," she grumbled. "When are we going to hear from this friend of yours?"

"I told you, Donovan contacted me an hour ago to say the wreck on I-25 had been cleared and he was almost to Albuquerque. He'll get back to us as soon as he has something to report."

Cleo turned around in her seat and tried to concentrate on the road ahead. Impatience for results on the voiceprint waged a constant inner battle with her excitement over the phone trace. She still couldn't believe Jack had waited until he was on his way out the door to drop that bomb on her.

He'd known all morning the number tracked back to Sloan. Yet Donovan had carried the information around with him until Cleo had pried it out of him. And now he expected her to sit on her hands and wait until he gave the signal to move on the man!

Not that she could do anything else at the moment. After she put Marisa on that plane tomorrow afternoon, though, she'd—

"Astra One, this is Lead."

"Go ahead, Lead."

"Looks like some kind of roadblock ahead."

Cleo hit the button to roll down her window, and leaned out. She got a faceful of wet snow, a glimpse of a white-and-black striped sawhorse in the road ahead and a view of the square towers of the Cathedral of St. Louis several blocks away.

"I'm being waved over by a uniform," her point man advised. "Hang tight while I find out what the problem is."

"Roger, Lead."

Sliding the passenger widow back up, Cleo performed an instinctive 360 to check for escape routes. The best she could find was a side alley cutting between two shops decorated with luminaria and red chili wreaths. Nodding at the alley, she asked Randy Scalese if he could handle the tight turn.

"No problem."

"Be ready."

His gloved fists stayed loose on the wheel, but he'd given Cleo sufficient demonstration of his skills to assure her he'd squeeze down the alley if necessary.

"One, this is Lead. The cop says there's an event going on at the cathedral."

"What kind of event?"

"Some kind of an open-air Christmas play."

Well, hell! No one connected with the film festival had mentioned anything to Cleo about an outdoor performance this afternoon. She'd talk to Joe Garza about that later.

"The cop says they've closed off the streets around the church. We have to detour."

"Roger, Lead. We'll follow you."

The vehicle ahead turned right. The limo and the chase vehicle followed. Cleo took note of the uniformed cop manning the barricade as they passed. He was bundled up to his ears against the cold and snow. His upturned collar hid the bottom half of his face. His hat was pulled down low on his forehead. Only his eyes peered out as the limo whisked by, studying the vehicle, checking out the darkened windows.

Cleo twisted in her seat for another look. The

cop's intent stare bothered her. It stayed locked on the limo as it purred down the narrow street.

Frowning, Cleo keyed her mike. "Lead, this is One."

"Go ahead, One."

"What did the police officer say was going on at the cathedral?"

"Christmas carolers and some kind of outdoor play. A living nativity, I think it was."

A nativity. Her stomach did a slow roll. What better time to wreak vengeance on the actress who'd profaned Christ's birth than during a living celebration of the same event?

Gnawing on her lower lip, she dragged her city map from her coat pocket. "Randy, you know Santa Fe better than I do. Where does the street we're on now take us?"

"It'll bring us out on Canyon Road." He shot her a look. "Eventually."

"Show me."

He pulled his attention from the vehicle ahead long enough to stab a finger at the maze of narrow, twisting streets.

"We're here. We want to go... What the hell!"

Red lights flashed ahead. Randy's size-thirteen boot hit the brake. The stretch Lincoln fishtailed wildly on the slick pavement. Cleo had clicked her mike before the limo stopped moving.

"Lead, what's the problem?"

"There's another roadblock ahead. Looks like

a delivery truck. Hell, the thing's parked right in the middle of the street."

Every cell in Cleo's body screamed red alert. Snatching her Glock from its holster, she rolled out of the limo, dropped into a two-fisted protective stance and searched the street behind.

There was no sign of the cop. No sign of *anyone*. The narrow street was deserted except for a few parked cars and the chase vehicle. Her thoughts were racing when the limo's rear door flew open and Goose exploded from the back seat. His semiautomatic whipped from side to side in a lethal arc.

"What do you think? Sniper or direct assault?"

Her frantic mind turned over all the possibilities, came up with the most likely.

"Bomb," she snarled. "Detonated by remote, like the fire at the theater. We've got to get everyone out of the limo! Fast!"

Goose dived for the open rear door. His massive fist closed around Marisa's arm at the same instant the snow-covered pavement under the limo erupted. The force of the blast lifted the Lincoln three feet into the air. It crashed back to the street a second later, a hissing, crackling ball of flames.

17

The explosion slammed Cleo into one of the parked cars. She bounced off it like a yo-yo and landed hard on her hands and knees.

"Cleo! Are you okay?"

Goose's frantic shout ripped her from her daze. She stumbled to her feet, saw that he'd dragged Marisa clear of the blazing limo. J. L. Evans was crawling out of the back seat, her coat afire. Randy Scalese sat slumped over the steering wheel.

"I'm okay. Get Marisa out of here!"

Cleo lunged for the limo. Thank God the reinforced undercarriage had taken the brunt of the explosion! They still weren't out of the woods, though. The blaze ignited by the bomb could reach the gas tank at any second.

Her hired help poured from the lead and chase vehicles. In the few seconds it took for them to reach the burning limo, Cleo had grabbed J.L. and sent her tumbling into the snow to extinguish the flames. She was darting around the front end to help Randy when Marisa clawed free of Goose's hold.

"Peter's still inside! His seat belt's jammed!"

Goose tried to grab the actress again, but she already had a gloved hand on the rear door handle.

"Marisa, no!"

The door whooshed open. Like a living beast, the fire leaped out. Marisa screamed again, threw up an arm to shield her face, stumbled back. Swearing viciously, Goose dragged her away from the flames.

The burst of fresh oxygen from the opened door fed the beast. The inferno consumed the writhing figure in the back seat. Cleo got Randy out, dumped him in the hands of one of the men from the chase vehicle and fumbled for the fire extinguisher in the front console. Arcing a spray of foam through the sliding panel between the front and back seats, she doused the flames enough for the others to cut the seat belt and pull Peter out.

One of the men ripped off his overcoat, dropped it over Marisa's lover and beat at the flames. Cleo threw herself out of the limo and away from the blistering heat.

She had a moment to suck in her breath. Only a moment. Then a pop sounded over the crackling flames and a little spray of slush flew up at Marisa's feet.

Goose reacted instinctively. Flinging the actress down, he buried her beneath his bulk. Cleo and the rest of her team dived for cover. She'd decided to go on the attack before she hit the ground.

Every training manual said to rush the protectee away to safety and let someone else go after the shooter. But Cleo knew she had to take him down. This was no wild-eyed radical or religious fanatic. This was a cold, determined killer. If he didn't get Marisa this time, he would the next.

Scrambling for her Glock, she rolled into a crouch. "Goose! Get Marisa out of here. You two," she snarled at the men closest to him, "go with him."

Goose had the actress in his arms before Cleo pumped out the first shot. Shielding Marisa with his body, he rushed for the closest building. The two security augmentees charged after him.

Cleo and the others maintained covering fire until they'd disappeared inside.

"You!" she shouted at a grim-faced extra. "Call 911 and stay with these people until an ambulance arrives. You two, take the right! I'll take the left!"

* * *

She spotted the dark bulk of the cop's uniform before she'd raced more than a few yards. He saw her coming, assumed a shooter's stance and sighted down the barrel of a silenced automatic. His hand jerked from the recoil as he squeezed off rounds.

Cleo dodged wildly, but didn't stop. Heart slamming against her ribs, she pumped out two shots on the run. The first went wide. The second spun the shooter around.

A barrage of fire erupted from the men racing down the street with her. Blood blossomed in a dozen places on the cop's dark, heavy overcoat. He crumpled. Went down.

Cleo skidded to a stop a few yards from the sprawled body. Her lungs burned. Her eyes teared in the bitter cold. Fat, wet flakes clung to her lashes. Furiously blinking them away, she kept the Glock aimed at the shooter's head while one of her men kicked the automatic from his slackened hold and cautiously knelt to check for a pulse.

"He's dead."

"Roll him over."

They flipped the body over. As Cleo antici-pated, the wire-rimmed glasses were gone and the hair was no longer a rusty-red, but it was Martin. Or whatever the hell his name was.

Lowering her weapon, she waited for her

heart to catch up with the rest of her. She almost had her shakes under control when her cell phone shrilled and had her jumping again. Praying it wasn't Goose calling to say he'd run into another ambush, she snatched the flip-phone from her jacket pocket.

"North!"

"Cleo, it's Jack." His voice came through the cell, low and urgent. "We've got a match. The voice on your tape belongs to a torch for hire. He specializes in remotely detonated devices."

She blew out a ragged breath. "Is that right?"

"The FBI matched him to a fragment of a phone conversation they pulled in during a sweep. They've also matched the person he was talking to. Are you ready for this?"

Hell, no, she wasn't ready! Her brain was still shooting out endorphins and she'd yet to drag a full breath into her tortured lungs.

"It was Cox."

Her mind went blank. "Who?"

"James Cox. Marisa's co-star."

She almost dropped the cell phone. "Are you serious?"

"As a heart attack. Special Agent Kee here notified the L.A. field office. They're sending a team out to pick Cox up. In the meantime, watch your six, woman. The torch might still try to fulfill his contract."

"No, he won't." Her gaze slid to the corpse

sprawled atop the reddening slush. "We just put him out of business. Permanently."

"What happened?"

The question was as sharp as a blade.

"He blew up the limo, or tried to."

"Anyone hurt?"

She threw a glance over her shoulder at the group huddled a safe distance from the still-blazing vehicle.

"Cleo! Were you hurt?"

"No, but Peter Jacobsen's in bad shape." The distant wail of sirens punctuated her reply. "I don't know yet about the others. I have to go. I need to check on Marisa and—"

She broke off, ducking as the limo's gas tank ignited. With a booming roar, what was left of the Lincoln went up in flames.

Goose was in the waiting room outside St. Vincent Hospital's ICU when Jack burst out of the elevator.

"That was fast, dude. You must have laid rubber all the way from Albuquerque."

"I got the feds to chopper me up." Dragging a hand through his hair, he reined his pulse back to a furious gallop. "It took me less time to fly up here than it did to fight my way through the lobby downstairs."

"Yeah, the media's turned out in force. They've been sending an emissary up every fifteen minutes, begging for an interview with Marisa."

"How is she?"

"She singed off her eyebrows and sustained first degree burns to the right side of her face."

"Jacobsen?"

"The E.R. docs inserted a breathing tube, but that's about all they could do for him. They're holding him here in ICU until he stabilizes enough to move him to a burn unit."

"What about Cleo?"

Goose hooked a thumb at the doors to the ICU. "She's in with Marisa. No burns or injuries she'll admit to."

"That sounds like her," Jack muttered.

He didn't want to live through any more moments like the ones that had followed the explosion. Every second it had taken Cleo to get back on the phone to him had been carved into his chest.

"Anyone else in the vehicle hurt?"

"The driver was stunned, but didn't get so much as a scratch. The other woman—Ms. Conners's publicity director—caught her coat on fire, but Cleo rolled her in the snow before it burned through. You probably passed her in the lobby on your way up. So what's the story on Cox? Is that business about him hiring the torch for real?"

"We'll know soon enough. The FBI should have him in custody by now."

"Wait until the dudes downstairs get hold of that juicy morsel. They'll go nuts."

The automatic doors whooshed open, and Jack let out the breath he'd been holding since Albuquerque.

"Who'll go nuts?" Cleo demanded.

"The paparazzi, once they hear the boys in L.A. are bringing Cox in."

"He's already in custody. Whitehorn Studios tracked Marisa down in the ICU a few minutes ago. Wanted to know why the hell the FBI cuffed her co-star and hustled him away just hours after *The Redemption* opened in every theater across the country." Her lips twisted. "Apparently the studio is worried the bust might presage a pornography charge."

"I've gotta see this movie," Jack drawled, earning him a grin from Goose and a dry look from Cleo.

"You'll have plenty of opportunity. After today, it'll probably be the biggest box office draw of all time."

"You think that's why Cox hired the torch? To up his share of the take?"

"That, and to get back at Marisa. Want some coffee?"

He hadn't noticed the coffeemaker tucked in a corner of the waiting room. He hadn't noticed anything beyond the fact that Cleo showed no noticeable wounds or burns.

"Coffee would be good."

While she fetched two cups, he peeled off his heavy jacket. Now that he'd seen for himself she really was still in one piece, his vital organs had resumed their normal functioning. More or less.

"Marisa and I had a chance to talk in the ICU," she told him between sips. "She said Cox was really pissed when she ended their affair and sent him back to his wife with his tail between his legs. He and Caitlin appeared all kissy-face in public, but Marisa's sure she made Cox suffer big time in private."

"So he decided to exact revenge?"

"That's what it's looking like. He also generated a frenzy of publicity for *The Redemption* in the process."

"Thereby ensuring it made millions. Pretty slick."

"Yeah," she muttered into her coffee, "except he hurt a damn good man in the process. The docs don't think Peter's going to make it."

He didn't.

Marisa delivered the grim news when the ICU doors opened again some time later.

To say she looked like hell would have been a gross understatement. A gauze pad covered her right cheek. A thick layer of ointment coated the blistered skin on her temple. With both eyebrows gone, she wore what would have been a look of permanent surprise if not for the tears swimming in her green eyes.

"Peter's dead. His heart stopped and…and they couldn't restart it."

With a vicious oath, Cleo dumped her cup in a wastebasket and crossed the waiting room. There was no friendship between her and her client, and only a modicum of respect. Yet when Cleo wrapped an arm around Marisa's shoulder, the star broke into wrenching sobs and buried her face in her hands.

Jack speared a look at Goose. The bald giant shoved his hands in his pockets, as awkward as most men in the face of a woman's grief. But he'd read the same emotions Jack had in Cleo's expression.

"I've seen that look," Goose muttered. "She's going to blame herself."

Yeah, she would. Jack recognized the signs, understood the bitter self-recrimination that would consume her. She'd lost a man on her watch. She'd take the responsibility and the blame. The corrosive guilt would eat at her from the inside out, just as Sergeant Debra Smith's murder had gnawed at her all these years.

Jaw tight, Jack stood as helplessly as Goose while Cleo put her own emotions on hold to comfort her client.

"I should have told him I loved him," Marisa

moaned, racked by remorse. "I *wanted* to tell him. I just couldn't bring myself to say it."

Cleo hesitated, obviously choosing her words. "Peter knew how you felt about him."

"No, he didn't! I never said it."

"He didn't need the words."

"Oh, God! He took such good care of me. Took care of everything. How am I going to get along without him?"

"Why don't you start by taking care of him?"

Marisa's head came up. "What do you mean?"

"Does Peter have family who should be contacted?"

"I don't… I'm not…"

"They shouldn't hear about this on TV."

Tears streamed down the star's face. Swiping her sleeve across her running nose, she made an effort to pull herself together.

"He has a sister. In upstate New York, I think. He keeps a picture of her in his office."

"Is her phone number in his Rolodex?"

"I think so. Yes, I'm sure it is."

"Is she married?"

"What?"

"If she's married," Cleo said patiently, "we'll need to know her last name."

"Oh. She's single. I think."

"Okay, we'll call your house and ask your maid to look up the number."

Responding to her silent signal, Jack flipped

up his cell phone and dialed the number Cleo gave him. He was still waiting for the maid to supply the information when the elevator doors opened.

"There you are!"

Marisa's PR rep rushed into the waiting room. Her bloodless features sharpened as she swept her employer with a frenetic glance.

"We've got to get you downstairs." Ignoring Marisa's mumbled protest, she almost danced in her excitement. "You're not going to believe this! One of the reporters just got a call from an L.A. bureau chief. The FBI arrested James Cox."

"I know."

"You know?" Her squeak spiraled into a screech. "You know!"

"They think he may have hired someone to get back at Marisa," Cleo explained.

J.L.'s jaw sagged. She gaped at the two women. Recovering swiftly, she grabbed Marisa's arm. "We need to get you in front of the cameras. Like, now!"

"Peter's dead."

"What?"

"His heart stopped."

"Oh, no!"

Evans took longer to recover this time. All of a minute and a half, Jack estimated.

"You've got to talk to the media, Marisa." She laid a sympathetic hand on her employer's shoulder. "This can't come from a hospital spokes-man."

"The hell it can't." With a vicious twist, the star yanked her shoulder free. "I've turned every-thing else in my life into a fucking circus. I'll be damned if I'm going to turn Peter's death into one, too."

"Just make an appearance, then. You don't have to say anything. I'll—"

"No!"

The brunette fell back in the face of Marisa's sudden fury.

"*You* handle the media, J.L. I have more impor-tant business to take care of right now."

Marisa borrowed a cell phone to make the call.

Funny, she thought as she stared at a wall pa-pered in what was probably intended to be a calming pastel print. She'd never talked to Peter about his family. Never asked how he'd spent his time when he'd flown back East for a short visit with his sister.

Now she had to tell a woman she knew only from the picture on his desk that her brother had died. Throat aching, she counted the rings.

"Hello?"

The woman sounded younger than Peter. Years younger.

"Hello?" she said again. A touch of impatience colored her eastern accent. "If this is a telemarketer, you need to know I've entered this number on the no-call list."

"No, I'm not a telemarketer. This is Marisa Conners. You don't know me, but—"

"Of course I know you." Delight chased away the impatience. "You're Peter's Marisa. I get the inside Hollywood scoop about your movies every time he calls. He thinks you're the greatest actor since… Well, the greatest ever. So do I," she added in a polite afterthought.

Marisa couldn't find any response to that. Peter's sister filled the void.

"Look, I probably shouldn't say this, but he's worried about you. The last time he called, he said someone had sent some nasty letters about your new movie. He's probably gotten all protective and overbearing with you. He used to do that with me, too, when we were kids. It drove me nuts, but, well, that's just his way of showing he loves you."

With a silent groan, Marisa pressed her forehead against the pastel wallpaper.

18

The business of death consumed Cleo and her client for the rest of the afternoon. Everyone had to have statements: the Santa Fe police, the FBI, the attorneys flown in by Whitehorn Studios, the media. Especially the media.

That Marisa agreed to a press conference before leaving the hospital didn't surprise Cleo. That she insisted on appearing in front of the cameras with her face still ravaged by fire and grief did. Her voice devoid of any hint of drama, the actress related the details of the attack and Peter's death.

Both Alex Sloan and Joe Garza appeared at the press conference. Speaking on behalf of the festival organizers, Alex expressed their outrage at the deliberate attacks on Miss Conners and her party and their sorrow over Peter Jacobsen's death. Cleo stood at the back of the room with Jack. When Sloan approached, Donovan issued a low warning. "Not a word about the phone trace."

The rigid leash she'd been keeping herself on since the limo explosion almost snapped. "How long do you think I'm going to sit on this?"

"Until I say different."

Jack must have sensed how close she was to breaking free of all restraints. With a quelling glance, he intercepted Alex Sloan.

"Colonel Sloan?"

"Yes?"

"I didn't introduce myself this morning." Reaching into his back pocket, he produced the flat leather case with his shield and ID. "I'm Special Agent Jack Donovan. I'm with the Air Force Office of Special Investigations."

Sloan's gaze narrowed. "I saw you with Miss Conners's entourage this morning. I assumed you were part of the additional security Ms. North brought in and that you were working for her."

"Not for. With. After your call to General Barnes a few weeks ago, he assigned me to act as Ms. North's OSI liaison."

"I see."

Not yet, he didn't. But he would. Soon, Cleo thought grimly as she stepped forward.

"I didn't want to ask Miss Conners her plans with the media crowding around her," Sloan said. "Am I right in assuming she won't attend the awards ceremony tonight?"

"I don't know. I'll find out and have someone contact you or Joe Garza."

"I'd appreciate that. Oh, and my brother asked me to convey his condolences on Mr. Jacobsen's death. He also wanted me to let you know he's extended his stay in Santa Fe."

Jack waited until the colonel had moved away to query Cleo.

"What's going on between you and Marc Sloan? I remember asking you the same question last night. I didn't get an answer then, either."

"Sloan has the hots for me, or says he does."

When she started off, he snagged her arm. "Which is it, Cleo?"

"I haven't had time to find out." She shook her arms loose. "I'll give you an update when I do."

As Cleo escorted Marisa down the hall to her suite at El Cortez, the emotions she'd kept at bay since the explosion were piling up inside her like dark, rolling thunderclouds. She could feel the vicious energy sparking and snapping, demanding release.

Thank God her client had decided to skip the awards ceremony. In contrast to the violent energy building inside Cleo, Marisa looked totally wiped. Her eyes were flat and glazed. Her pouffy lips lacked any trace of color. With her singed eyebrows and bandaged temple, she had the air of a sad circus clown.

A reluctant pity stirred in Cleo. She didn't like the woman, but she had to admit the actress had displayed surprising courage this afternoon when she'd clawed free of Goose and tried to drag Peter out of the blazing limo.

Putting her own raw emotions on hold, Cleo paused just inside the star's suite. "Are you sure you don't want me or J.L. to stay with you for a while?"

"No."

J.L. edged inside and made one last attempt. "I wish you would reconsider and put in an appearance at the ceremony tonight."

"Fuck the awards ceremony."

"Peter would want you to attend."

"Get out."

"Just for a few minutes," the publicist pleaded. "As a tribute to Peter."

"Get out, J.L."

Wrapping her arms around her middle, the actress stared blindly at the wood stacked in the kiva fireplace until Cleo completed her check of the suite. She paused at the door, snared by an obligation to her client that had nothing to do with their contract.

"Can I get you anything?"

"No."

"I'll be next door if you need me."

"Cleo…"

Marisa dragged her glance from the dark fireplace. Her throat working, she ground out a few hoarse words.

"Thanks. For today… Peter's sister…"

Nodding, Cleo let herself out.

Marisa stood where she was as silence surrounded her. She'd had to shut the others out. She didn't want company. She wanted a hit. Or a drink. So much her entire body screamed with the need.

Now that she was alone, though, everything inside her dreaded walking through the suite she'd shared with Peter, seeing his clothes in the bedroom closet, his shaving kit in the bathroom. She knew his death would hit her then, really hit her. She wouldn't wake up next to him in the morning. Wouldn't curl into his warmth, or draw from his strength.

Driven by the guilt and regret she suspected would haunt her forever, Marisa made for the bar. Her hand shook so badly the neck of the vodka bottle chipped the glass tumbler. Still shaking, she fingered the tiny imperfection. The chip was jagged and sharp enough to draw blood. A small teardrop of red slid down inside the tumbler.

Marisa's lungs contracted. Her chest ached so painfully she couldn't breathe. Slowly, she dragged her finger over the jagged edge again. A thin rivulet slithered down the crystal and stained the colorless vodka a watery pink.

With a hoarse groan, she closed her fist around the tumbler and sent it crashing against the wall.

Once inside her own suite, Cleo shed her coat and dropped her Glock on the counter next to the now-depleted pottery bowl. Her eyes locked on the exquisitely crafted turtle, but her mind saw only a snowy street and a blazing fireball.

She knew she didn't feel anything close to Marisa's anguish, but the guilt she'd buried all afternoon was now a towering black thundercloud. She stood at the counter, her sightless gaze fixed on the turtle as she went over the ambush again and again, evaluating her decisions, analyzing her reactions.

She should have questioned the "cop" about the detour herself, dammit, not let the guys in the lead vehicle assume that responsibility. She would have recognized the torch. At the very least, she should have radioed Joe Garza and asked about the event at the cathedral.

Her rational mind knew she wouldn't have had time to radio anyone. The small motorcade had traveled less than a block or two before the lead vehicle hit the brakes. Yet Cleo couldn't let go of the what-ifs and why-didn't-shes.

The acid was still churning inside her when Goose rapped on her door some time later. Jack was with him.

"We're finished here," Cleo told Goose. "Thanks for flying out to Santa Fe on such short notice."

"Sure you don't need me to hang around awhile yet?"

She still had business to attend to here, but it didn't involve Goose.

"I'm sure."

"Fine by me." He tipped Jack a nod. "See you around, dude."

Like Marisa, Cleo wasn't in any mood for company. There was only one thing she wanted from Donovan.

"Do you have the green light to move on Sloan?"

"No."

She pointed to the door. "Come back when you do."

"Pull your head out of your ass, North. It's not your fault Jacobsen died."

She sucked in a swift breath. Trust Donovan to go right for the jugular.

"You were there when I rolled out of the limo, were you? You saw how I wasted precious seconds searching the street behind the vehicle?"

"Goose told me you assessed the situation and made a nearly instantaneous read. He got Marisa out because of your quick call."

"It wasn't quick enough. Not for Peter."

"No, it wasn't." Jack dropped his jacket on top of hers. "So what are you going to do? Beat yourself up over his death the same way you have over Sergeant Smith's all these years?"

Her jaw set. "Back off, Donovan."

"No way, babe."

"Call me 'babe' or 'woman' one more time and you'll be singing Christmas carols two octaves higher."

He didn't appear impressed by the threat. "You're not flying solo on this one, Cleo. We're in it together."

She was spoiling for a fight—verbal, physical, however she could release the beast caged inside her.

"We're not on the same team," she snarled. "We're not even in the same league. You're marching to the general's tune. I stopped living by his rules when I hung up my uniform."

"You didn't live by the rules *before* you hung up your uniform. Barnes swears you're the reason he now chews a bottle of antacids a day."

"Yeah, well, he better keep some handy. I'm done with sitting on my hands."

"Don't even think about it, North. You're not going off on your own."

"Think you can stop me?"

The challenge was raw and blunt and brought a mocking glint to his eyes. He moved across the room with lazy grace.

"Oh, yeah."

The casual approach didn't fool Cleo. Her muscles tensed in anticipation of an attack. She expected him to hook an ankle around hers and try to bring her down. Maybe feint to the left and come at her from the right.

She *didn't* expect him to reach out and snag the waistband of her slacks. Or drag her against him. Or bury his other hand in her hair.

"You want a wrestling match? Fine by me. We'll take it to the mat, Cleopatra Aphrodite."

In the second or two before his mouth came down on hers, Cleo knew she still had a choice. She could let the devil in her rip loose and bring up her knee, or engage in another form of combat altogether.

And that's what it became. The most primitive form of combat. Mouths locked. Tongues against teeth. Muscles straining.

Cleo had enough breath left after the first kiss to call a halt to hostilities if she'd wanted to. After the second, she didn't want *anything* but Donovan naked and in her bed.

The bulge behind his zipper was ample proof he wanted the same thing. She popped the snap on his jeans and gave the zipper a tug. His stomach muscles hollowed under her hand. Flat. Hard. Hot to the touch.

"Cleo…"

The low growl was a warning, but she'd

passed the point of needing one. Slipping her hand inside his Jockey shorts, she palmed his belly. The hair of his groin tickled. The hard, hot flesh her fingers wrapped around sent a jolt straight through her.

She could tell by his reaction they weren't going to make it to the bed. His entire body tensed. His breath ended in a grunt. His flesh leaped in her hand.

She stroked him, not gently, not quite as rough as she wanted to. For all her greedy, selfish need, she couldn't forget this was Jack.

He was rock hard and straining when he brought his hand down, snagged hers and broke the contact. Two seconds later, they hit the Berber carpet.

She landed on her back. Jack straddled her hips, his hands already at the hem of her sweater. When he tugged it up and over her head, she knew a moment of sheer feminine satisfaction at the way his jaw went tight.

"I stopped wearing bras about the same time I stopped wearing a uniform."

"Yeah, I'd noticed."

If he had, he'd never let on. Bastard.

"Makes life more comfortable," she said.

"And convenient."

Contorting, he took a nipple between his teeth. The sharp tug redrew the battle lines.

"Very convenient!"

With a gasp, Cleo arched her back. She was writhing when he yanked at the waistband of her slacks.

"Please tell me you stopped wearing panties, too," he begged.

He discovered the answer for himself before she could provide one. The black, high-on-the-thigh briefs didn't deter him for long, though. He got her near enough to naked for his needs and wedged his hand between her legs. The heel of his hand put maddening pressure on her clit. His clever, clever fingers quickly had her gushing.

When his tongue took over from his fingers, Cleo damn near came right then. She managed to hold on until he dug a condom out of his wallet and sheathed himself. Trust Donovan to go into the field prepared for any eventuality.

She stopped thinking altogether when he positioned himself between her thighs. She'd forgotten the way the muscles in his upper arms corded when he braced himself above her. Forgotten how the wiry hair on his legs rasped against her inner thighs.

She'd remembered the feel of his back under her hands, though. Remembered, too, the powerful flex of his body as he drove into her. Hooking her legs around his, Cleo matched him thrust for thrust. The battle continued until she arched her spine and a low groan ripped from the back of her throat.

* * *

They were both slick with pleasure when Jack dragged his heavy shearling range coat down to cover their naked posteriors. The musky scent of sex mingled with the tang of sweat as he tucked her against him. She lay with her head on his shoulder, waiting for the storm to pass, feeling the thump of his heart against her palm.

"Jacobsen's death wasn't your fault, Cleo."

She didn't answer.

"You took every conceivable precaution to safeguard Marisa." His chin nudged her temple. "You know that."

"I know."

She must not have sounded very convinced. Propping himself up on one elbow, Jack took her chin in his hand.

"Jacobsen would have made it out of the limo if his seat belt hadn't jammed."

Her mind accepted it. The rest of her still had a way to go. "I'm okay, Donovan."

"You sure?"

"I'm sure. Thanks for the sex therapy session. It was very effective."

His grin was pure male. "We aim to please."

"You'll have to tell me what you charge."

"This one's on the house."

Her pleasure was fading. Her gnawing need to finish the other business that had brought her to Santa Fe wasn't. Gathering her scattered clothing, she reassembled herself, then snagged her own coat from the chair.

Jack leaned on his elbow, a frown forming between his brows. "Where are you going?"

"It's early yet. I can still catch Alex Sloan before he leaves for the awards ceremony."

"Dammit, Cleo!"

Rolling to his feet, he yanked on his jeans and stalked across the room. His chest muscles rippled in the overhead light. She could just make out the puckered scar on his shoulder.

"I thought we'd settled this," he growled. "You don't move on Sloan until I give the word."

"We didn't settle anything. You spoke. I listened. We stirred some juices. End of story."

"Not hardly."

When he planted himself between her and the door, Cleo extracted her Glock from its holster. Calmly, she pointed the barrel at the floor, ejected the magazine and checked the rounds. The magazine snapped back in with a lethal snick. She kept the barrel pointed at the carpet, but the message was unmistakable.

"I want an explanation from Sloan about that phone call to his residence the night Debra Smith was murdered. You can come with me or not. Your choice, Donovan."

19

Jack insisted on driving his rented SUV up to the Sloan place. Snow cascaded off the roof when he slid behind the wheel and slammed the door.

Cleo settled into the passenger seat and sent him a sideways glance. His jaw was still locked tight, but he wouldn't have let her walk out of the hotel if he'd really believed she would compromise his investigation or the CIA's operation by forcing the issue with Sloan. Curiosity compelled her to ask, though.

"Aren't you going to notify your buddies in the Company that we're going in?"

He shoved the key in the ignition. "Worried about that small matter of a seven burner, are you?"

"Come off it, Donovan. The festival ends to-morrow at noon. The North Koreans are booked on a flight out of Albuquerque at three-twenty. You know damn well Laser Man and company have by now milked the sound engineer of everything they're going to get from him."

"Laser Man?"

"Porter," she explained with a shrug. "He and his buddy, Assault Rifle Guy, lined me up in their laser sights the first time we met."

"If I were you, I wouldn't remind them of that encounter."

"So are you going to coordinate with them or not?"

"I am. When we're closer to Sloan's place."

He didn't want to get into a jurisdictional pissing contest, Cleo guessed, or give the CIA boys a chance to run interference by letting them know his intentions too far in advance. That was fine with her. She'd just as soon do this one with only Jack looking over her shoulder.

Clipping her seat belt, she hunched her shoulders and waited for the heater to blast away the frigid air inside the vehicle. Her nerves were taut and humming again, but with a tension totally different from the one that had racked her earlier.

The sweaty session on the carpet had eased some of her guilt over Peter's death, which was exactly what Jack had intended. Cleo wasn't operating under any illusions here. Donovan had recognized all too well the volcanic emotions bubbling inside her from the explosion and shoot-out. He'd spent more than his share of months in Afghanistan, dodging bombs and bullets. He'd also shared those knuckle-cracking days with Cleo in the Honduran jungle. They'd jumped each other's bones after during that little exercise, too. It hadn't meant anything then. It didn't mean anything now.

She was still trying to convince herself of that when Donovan took the turnoff that led up to Barranca Road. The sun had already dropped behind the Sangre de Cristos. Dusk purpled the snow-covered peaks surrounding them. The road was a narrow, twisting ribbon of icy slush. Cleo refused to let her glance shift to the sheer drop outside her window.

Jack navigated the steep grade with careful concentration and pulled over about a mile from their destination to punch a number into his cell phone.

"Porter, this is Donovan. I'm on my way up to the Sloan residence."

Cleo couldn't hear Laser Man's reply, but caught the drift of it when Jack responded.

"Tough. It's the right time for me. By the way, I'm bringing Ms. North with me."

She didn't miss the reaction this time. Jack held the phone out to make sure she caught the string of expletives before he cut it off in midstream.

"We'll be there in five minutes. I'll brief you then."

She grimaced at that. "Porter's up at Sloan's place?"

"He and his pals set up their base of operations in a small building at the rear of the main residence."

"I saw it."

That explained the tracks Cleo had spotted in the snow during her initial surveillance. It also explained why Modesto and his buddy had taken such serious exception to said surveillance.

Their headlights picked up the bronze Anasazi figures guarding the entrance to the Sloans' adobe palace a few minutes later.

When Jack whirred down the window and punched in the security code, Cleo didn't comment on the fact that his contacts had supplied him with it. The colonel had obviously agreed to grant government operatives free access to his property. The question now was whether Sloan's motives were as altruistic as everyone had originally assumed.

The possibility the man might be linked to a compromise of classified information made Cleo almost as antsy as the idea he was somehow involved in Debra Smith's murder. She felt as though she'd been dancing around a simmering pot for weeks and was just moments away from prying up the lid.

Once inside the gates, Jack followed the winding, freshly plowed drive through the thick stands of pine and piñon. With the house lights winking in the distance, they turned off on a side road. The steep track circled down to the back of the residence.

Cleo glanced up as she climbed out of the car. The house sat some distance away, two stories of snow-dusted adobe above the underground three-car garage. High in the upper story, the uncurtained corner windows of the Sloans' spa commanded an aerial view of the surrounding countryside.

Squinting, Cleo could just make out a trim figure in black spandex burning up calories on the treadmill. Patrice Sloan had some sort of music player plugged into her ear and her back to the rear windows. Her blond ponytail swung with the same relentless rhythm Marisa's had during Cleo's meeting with the actress in L.A.

"Nice."

The appreciate murmur came from Jack, who'd followed her gaze. His, too, had locked on the distant figure.

"Sloan's wife?"

"Right."

"Lucky man." He realized his error and recovered instantly. "But not as lucky as I got a little while ago."

"Of course not," Cleo drawled.

Grinning, he steered her to the narrow path leading into the woods. They hadn't moved more than a half-dozen feet from their vehicle before Cleo spotted a heavily armed figure in a white ski parka. The figure made no move to disguise himself as they crunched their way along the snowy path to the small casita set back among the piñon.

Interesting. Sentries in camouflage gear didn't usually advertise their presence. Porter must be pretty sure of himself. Either that, or he wanted to make a statement after Jack's terse call.

The sentry obviously announced their arrival. Porter met them at the door to the casita. Light spilled out, silhouetting his muscular frame. Cleo glimpsed racks of equipment in various stages of disassembly behind him.

"Dammit, Donovan, what's with this unilateral decision to move on Alex Sloan? I told you yesterday I'd run the information you passed me about him up my chain and get back to you."

"Yeah, you did."

Jack shouldered past him. Cleo followed before Porter could slam the door in her face, which he appeared all too ready to do.

The inside of the casita looked like a cross between a Pottery Barn and an electronics warehouse. The three men busy disassembling and packing the equipment paused to check out the new arrivals. Two were technicians in white jumpsuits. The third was Laser Man's pal. Cleo tipped Assault Rifle Guy a nod. He returned the greeting with a less-than-friendly dip of his chin.

"Moving day?" Jack asked, surveying the scene.

"We got what we wanted." Porter couldn't keep the satisfaction from his low growl. "Dr. Lee's on his way back to his lab in Los Alamos with a full bag of tricks."

"So you're shutting down."

"Actually, we ceased out operations here right after I talked to you yesterday. We're just cleaning up now."

"And you were going to get back to me when?"

"When I got the green light from headquarters."

"That's what I figured. Consider it green. I delayed approaching Sloan while you worked your op. You're finished. I'm not."

Mouth tight, Porter palmed his shaved-to-the-scalp fringe.

"I'm not asking for permission," Jack informed him. "Just extending you the courtesy you obviously didn't feel obligated to extend me. I'm going up to the house to talk to Sloan. You can tag along if you want. Or not."

Since Cleo had given Jack the same option not a half hour ago, she could have predicted Porter's response. He had no more desire to be left out of the action than Donovan had.

"We're in, Donovan. Tony, you're coming with me."

Modesto abandoned his packing chores and shoved his beefy arms into a parka. The two CIA operatives bundled into their own vehicle to follow Jack and Cleo back up the drive.

The tension in her belly knotted tighter with every crunch of the tires on the freshly plowed gravel. Ten years ago she'd ignored her instincts and ended up with a murder and a suicide. Those same instincts were running riot now.

She'd get some answers tonight. She could feel the certainty in her bones. There were too many tenuous ties between Alex Sloan and the dead sergeants to chalk up to mere coincidence.

"Don't forget," Jack warned as he brought the SUV around to the front of the house. "This is an OSI matter. You're along solely as an observer."

"I got it."

"You're not cleared for most of what I have to discuss with Sloan. I'll have to ask you to leave the room before I question him about Harvest Eagle."

"I've got it, Jack."

Cleo didn't much like the idea of being sent out of the room, but she understood the necessity. She'd settle for watching Sloan's face when he was questioned about the phone call to his residence the night of the murder/suicide. Anticipation thrumming through her veins, she leaned on the door before Jack had brought the vehicle to a complete halt.

Modesto and Porter pulled up alongside them. Stamping her feet in the cold, Cleo studied the floodlit facade of the residence.

"That's strange. The front door's standing open."

He'd already picked up on the slice of light spilling onto the stoop. "Sloan must have seen us drive up."

If he had, he wasn't waiting at the door to welcome them. No one was.

The hairs on the back of Cleo's neck began to itch. She started forward and had taken only a step or two when a sharp crack split the night.

"Down!"

She didn't need Jack's fist between her shoulder blades. She dived into the plowed snow at the side of the driveway, rolled and was reaching for the weapon in her boot before the rifling echo died.

Jack hit right beside her, Porter and Modesto a few feet away. For a heart-stopping second or two, there was only silence.

"Sounded like it came from inside the house," Porter panted.

Their collective search showed only tall, empty windows.

"You and Modesto take the back," Jack bit out. "North and I will go in the front."

He waited only until the two men had disappeared around the corner to spring up.

"Cover me. I'm going in."

Sig in hand, he charged the open front door. Cleo conducted a frantic sweep of the door, the windows, the roofline, searching for a shadow of movement, a red laser eye, a fire flash, anything. As soon as Jack made the stoop, she was up and zigzagging after him.

They burst into the house and stood shoulder to shoulder in the central hall, covering each other's back. Nothing moved. No footsteps thudded on the scrubbed pine flooring. No shots rang out. The only sound disturbing the eerie quiet was the faint drum of the upstairs shower.

Patrice Sloan, Cleo thought, heart slamming against her ribs. She'd finished her workout, had hit the shower. Now where the hell was her husband?

They found him mere seconds later, slumped over his desk in his study. He clutched a .22 pistol in his slackened right hand. Powder burns darkened the small, neat hole in his temple. A glistening red pool spread slowly across the blotter.

Memories of the night that had haunted Cleo for so many years sliced into her even as she spat out a curse and sprang forward. Another room flashed into her head. Another slumped body.

And Debra Smith, sprawled obscenely in a pool of blood.

The realization that she might never get answers to the questions that had brought her to Santa Fe had Cleo swallowing another curse. Fingers pressed against Sloan's throat, she found a faint, erratic pulse.

"He's still alive."

"Call 911 and stay with him," Jack ordered. "I'll search the rest of the house."

She snatched up the phone on Sloan's desk. The emergency notification made, she raced to the downstairs powder room to retrieve a towel. There wasn't really much a nonmedic could do in a situation like this except apply light pressure to the wound and administer mouth-to-mouth if the victim stopped breathing.

She'd picked up the basics of treating head wounds during her days as an air force investigator. More during her years as a P.I. According to the docs, the single most pertinent factor in surviving a gunshot wound to the head was luck. After that, the velocity of the bullet, the trajectory and the area injured all came into play.

At least Alex Sloan had used a smaller caliber weapon than the 9 mm Kurtz Staff Sergeant Mitchell had put to his head, Cleo thought grimly as she pressed the wadded towel against the wound. Considerate of the colonel not to splatter his brains all over the place. The blood was spreading, though. Seeping through the towel and across the blotter. Staining the oak beneath the photograph of Major General Sloan and his two young sons. Swimming toward what looked like a small, ultra-high-tech digital recorder.

At the sight of a red light blinking on that palm-size device, Cleo's already thumping heart took another painful bump.

"Did you record a farewell message?" she muttered to the comatose Sloan. "I hope so, you bastard. Your wife should know why you chose to take the coward's way out."

The thud of running feet jerked her attention from the blinking red light.

"Mrs. Sloan! Wait!"

Jack's gruff shout was ignored. Patrice Sloan burst into the study, her soaked hair streaming over the shoulders of her terry-cloth robe. Water beaded her ashen cheeks and brow.

"Alex!" She stumbled to a halt just inside the paneled room. "Oh, my God! Alex!"

Her eyes were wild with shock, her cry a spiral of pain. Jack crowded in behind her, his weapon still drawn, and steadied her with a quick hand on her arm.

"He's still alive," Cleo assured them both. "I've called 911."

Patrice's horrified gaze whipped up. "He's... he's alive?"

"I've got a pulse. A faint one."

The last shred of color left the woman's face. She looked ready to keel over. Jack tightened his grip.

"Hold on."

"Hold on?" The words rose to a shriek. "We can't just hold *on!*"

Wrenching free of his grasp, she wadded the corner of her robe and rushed toward her husband. "We've got to stop the bleeding."

Cleo held her off with an outthrust palm. "You don't want to cause blood to build up inside his skull. It could put pressure on the damaged tissue."

Or the man could bleed out.

She looked to Jack, praying she wasn't doing exactly the wrong thing here. His quick shrug told her it was a crapshoot either way.

"Alex." With a low, keening sob, Patrice reached out a trembling hand to touch her husband's arm. "I'm here, darling. I'm here."

Jack holstered his Sig. "I'll get Porter and Modesto."

A pumper from the nearby fire station arrived on scene first. The EMTs followed moments later. A SFPD squad car came screeching down the drive right behind the ambulance.

Sloan was still alive when the paramedics lifted him onto a gurney. Patrice climbed in after him. She'd exchanged her robe for slacks and a sweater, but hadn't taken time for socks or shoes. Shoving her bare feet into snow boots, she'd clumped out of the house.

When the ambulance drove off, siren wailing again, everyone reassembled in the study. The flashing red light on the device on Sloan's desk drew them all like a ship's beacon.

Jack and the two CIA operatives had already flashed their IDs at the responding officers. Cleo had her P.I. license and permit to carry handy, but all that government hardware was sufficient to include her in the fraternity.

"You say the victim is a retired colonel?"

Jack nodded. "That's correct."

"And you're here to question him in connection with…?"

"An air force matter."

"I see." The patrolman turned to Porter and Modesto. "What about you two?"

"The colonel was assisting us with a special project."

"Must have been *real* special."

Jack intervened before Porter did his CIA thing and started a territorial brush war. "There's a possibility that device might contain reference to highly classified matters."

"Or just the swan song of an FTF," the patrolman countered.

Cleo had to ask. "FTF?"

"Failed to Fly," Jack explained dryly. "Street slang for botched suicide."

The uniformed looked at him with more approval. "Spend some time on the beat before you started wearing a suit?"

"Eight years. Look, I really need to hear what's on that device. How about we run it, but shut it down immediately if Sloan makes even the slightest reference to the matter that brought me here?"

"Fair enough."

Taking care not to disturb the blood pattern or any of the items on the desk, the patrolman used the tip of his pen to press the play button.

Cleo leaned closer, almost shivering with a combination of tension and anticipation. At this point, she wasn't sure *what* she expected to hear. Certainly not the impatient question that leaped from the wireless device.

"Did you get a trace on the phone number I gave you this morning?"

Blinking in surprise, Cleo recognized her own voice. "That's me," she said stupidly.

"C'mon, Donovan. Give! Who or what did the number track to?"

Jack's reply sounded every bit as terse as it had earlier today.

"The Luke Air Force Base residence of Lieutenant Colonel and Mrs. Alexander Sloan."

"That son of a bitch!" Jaw tight, Donovan

shoved a hand through his hair. "Sloan bugged your room at the hotel. He knew we had him. He was just waiting for us to arrive to put himself out of his misery."

20

"Why would he shoot himself?"

The question nagged at Cleo as she and Jack drove away from the Sloan residence. They'd left their statements and phone numbers with the detectives who'd arrived on scene. They'd also left the Crime Scene Unit hard at work dusting for prints and collecting evidence. Now they were headed to St. Vincent Hospital for the second time that day.

"Why didn't Sloan just wait for us to get there, and answer our questions?"

Jack slewed her a tight look. "Maybe he didn't have any answers. Or maybe he didn't want to face the prospect of being interrogated about his possible involvement in treasonous activities."

"Maybe."

Jack grunted. He was still torqued about hearing his conversation with her broadcast through Sloan's study. Cleo didn't blame him. She wasn't real happy about that herself.

She still couldn't believe she'd missed the bug in her hotel rooms. She'd swept the mini-suite at the same time she'd swept Marisa's. Not with the same thoroughness, of course, but she was ninety-nine percent positive the rooms hadn't been wired. It was the one percent that irritated the hell out of her.

"What are you thinking?" Jack asked, breaking into her latest round of self-recrimination. "That Sloan *didn't* shoot himself?"

She just about jumped out of her seat belt. Every cop worth his salt treated a suspicious shooting as a potential homicide until it was proved otherwise. Yet neither Jack nor his pals in the CIA had surprised an intruder attempting to escape the residence. Nor had the Crime Scene Unit uncovered any evidence of forced entry.

That left only Alex Sloan.

And his wife.

Or the even more bizarre idea that had been forming in the back of Cleo's mind.

"There's another possibility," she said slowly. "What if that wasn't Alex Sloan bleeding all over the desk?"

"The same thought occurred to me, too." Jack

kept his eyes on the steep curves illuminated in the SUV's headlights. "I saw your friend Marc's gear in the upstairs bedroom when I searched the house. I didn't see him, though. Be interesting to see if he shows up at the hospital."

One of the twins was pacing the surgical waiting room when they arrived. Cleo *thought* it was Marc. She was sure when he turned a haggard face in her direction.

"What the hell happened, Brown Eyes? The police won't give me anything except that Alex took a bullet to the head, but Patrice says you were there. You and Donovan."

Before either could reply, the uniformed officer, who'd been tagged to hang at the hospital until the victim was out of surgery, stepped forward. After Cleo and Jack had supplied their IDs, the cop went to refill his coffee and left the three of them alone.

Jack jumped on those precious moments of privacy. When he produced his OSI credentials and informed Sloan he'd traveled to Santa Fe to interview his brother regarding an unspecified OSI matter, the engineer's gray eyes turned glacial.

"Isn't the OSI the air force counterpart to the navy's Criminal Investigative Service?"

"It is."

"And you're saying you're here to investigate my brother."

"I'm saying I'm here to interview him."

Sloan wasn't buying the nuance. His muscles bunched under the hand-tailored çashmere sports jacket. He didn't exactly lean into Jack, but he gave a darn good impression of wanting to.

"The surgeons are digging a bullet out of my brother's brain as we speak, Donovan. If you had something to do with him putting it there, you'll answer to me."

"Is that a threat?"

"Damn straight it is."

"Duly noted. Would you mind telling me where you were at the time of the shooting?"

Sloan looked ready to tell him to shove it. As a former naval officer, he knew the military investigative services held no authority to interrogate civilians—even a high-powered executive who held lucrative government contracts.

"You need to talk to us," Cleo urged Sloan. "Help us figure out the why and the how of what happened."

He pivoted, his gaze slicing into her. "I don't know about the why, but I didn't think there was any question about the how."

"There are always questions. If Alex survives, he can answer them himself. If not, they'll hang over you for the rest of your life. Where were you tonight, Marc?"

"In town, on business."

"What kind of business?"

"If you must know, I was at the jeweler's, returning the lapis necklace. I didn't get to it earlier."

"Where's your sister-in-law?"

"Patrice?" The abrupt change of subject raised Sloan's brow. "One of the aides took her to the nurses' lounge. The aide said they had a hair dryer there. Why?" His gaze switched to Jack. "Does Patrice have something to do with this investigation you say you're not conducting?"

"You tell me."

"Not good enough, Donovan. You have to do better than that if you want my cooperation."

Cleo sensed rather than saw the subtle shift in Jack's stance. He'd decided to move in for the kill. She felt her own muscles knot in anticipation.

"I can't tell you the precise details, but I will tell you this. Ten years ago a staff sergeant who worked for your brother sliced up his girlfriend. He made a call to your brother's residence either right before or right after the murder, then put a .45 slug into his head."

The engineer was too controlled to show in much reaction, but the shock was there. Cleo saw it in the white lines that formed on either side of his mouth and the rigid thrust of his jaw.

"Two men working the same classified program," Jack continued. "Two suicides. What are the odds, Sloan?"

"What the hell are you implying? That my

brother was somehow implicated in a murder?" His eyes narrowed. "Or is this about the classified program? Jesus, it is!"

His control fractured. Openly, searingly angry, he raked a hand through his dark hair.

"You're out of your mind if you think my brother would compromise a classified program in any way, shape or form. Alex spent his entire childhood trying to live up to our father's expectations. He made the air force his life, fought in two wars, earned a Silver Star, for God's sake! He would no more betray his country's secrets than—"

He broke off, his gaze whipping to the woman who stood frozen at the entrance to the waiting room.

"Than he would betray his wife," he finished grimly.

"He knows something!"

"If he does, he's not talking."

Cleo stabbed a forefinger at the elevator button. They were close. So damn close. Every nerve in her body hummed with the certainty that either Marc or Patrice Sloan was concealing something that could explain Sergeant Debra Smith's death.

Neither one would admit it, though. At his sister-in-law's appearance, Marc had shut down tighter than a played-out Texas oil rig. Patrice, too, had refused all comment until a surgeon appeared with the news that he'd extracted the .22 slug from her husband's skull. At that point Patrice, Marc and the uniformed officer had all disappeared into the recovery room.

According to the surgeon, Alex Sloan was comatose and in extremely critical condition. It was anyone's guess whether he'd make it, and if he did, how much brain damage he'd sustained. The surgeon gave him about the same odds of survival the docs had given Peter Jacobsen this morning.

"Two victims in one day," Cleo muttered as the elevator whizzed downward. "That's a new record for me. Since I went private, anyway."

"Yeah, you're racking 'em up."

"Thanks for all the sympathy and support."

"You don't need sympathy. As for support…"

Jack managed a smile. It was the first one he'd given her since they'd rolled around on the floor. "You got everything I had to give awhile ago, North."

She felt a little hitch under her ribs. "You know we have to talk about that."

"I know."

His cell phone chimed. With a saved-by-the-bell grin, he flipped up the lid.

"Donovan." His head cocked. The grin widened. His glance cut to Cleo. "Thanks. I'll pass the word."

"What word?" she demanded as he snapped the phone shut.

"That was Special Agent Kee with the Albuquerque FBI office. You racked up another one."

"Huh?"

"Kee just got a call from her counterparts in L.A. James Cox broke down and admitted he hired the torch to pay Marisa back for dumping him. The L.A. office is going to issue a statement to the press within the next twenty minutes."

She wanted to feel elated at the news. Peter Jacobsen's tragic death precluded every emotion but one. .

"I hope the bastard fries."

"That's looking like a distinct possibility."

God, what a day! And it wasn't over yet.

"I'd better get back to the hotel. Once the media hear about Cox's confession, they're going to storm the place. Marisa's still my responsibility."

She would be until Cleo put her on a plane back to L.A. Hopefully, she'd take care of that task tomorrow. The day's events were starting to wear on her.

Consequently, Cleo was less than thrilled to see the news vans jamming the entrance to the hotel. She and Jack went in through the rear but were spotted by an enterprising reporter who'd camped out by the back entry in hopes of snagging a story from one of the employees. Unfortunately, he recognized Cleo as part of Marisa's entourage.

"Ms. North! Is it true James Cox confessed to trying to kill Miss Conners?"

"That's what I hear."

He dogged her heels. "When will Miss Conners call a news conference or issue a statement?"

"You'll have to ask her media consultant."

"What about the shooting at Colonel Sloan's residence tonight? How does it tie to the other tragic events that have occurred?"

Cleo caught the look Jack threw her. He knew as well as she did the only connection between the attempts on Marisa's life and Alex Sloan's apparent suicide was Cleo herself.

She'd used the potential threat to Marisa as a mechanism to reopen a decade-old murder investigation. She'd been the catalyst leading to a new investigation, one that might implicate the colonel in treasonous activities. She'd also been standing only feet from both Marisa and Alex Sloan when they'd come near to drawing their last breath.

She didn't relish explaining the tenuous links between the week's violent events to Marisa, but she needed to do that before some other enterprising journalist connected the dots. Ignoring the microphone shoved in her face, she used her key card to access the rear entry.

The hotel still had security guards posted on Marisa's floor, more to protect her privacy than her person now. Cleo greeted them with a nod and paused outside the door to her mini-suite to pass Jack her key card.

"Wait for me. I need to talk to my client."

J. L. Evans yanked the door open in response to her knock. "I was just about to call you! Have you heard about James Cox?"

"Yes. Where's Marisa?"

"In the sitting room." The media rep dogged Cleo's heels as she followed the blare of the TV. "An FBI spokesman just made the announcement a few moments ago. He's taking questions now."

Marisa stood like a raging goddess in front of the wall-mounted flat screen. The bandages on her cheek stood out in sharp contrast to her flushed face. She whirled, her green eyes filled with fury.

"Did you hear? Cox confessed to hiring the bastard who killed Peter."

"I heard."

"I hope to God *he* burns in hell!"

Since Cleo had expressed approximately the same sentiments just moments ago, she merely nodded and listened as the FBI agent on TV handled the barrage of questions. The one she'd been anticipating came a few moments later.

When asked if James Cox was in any way connected with the gunshot injury the honorary chairman of the film festival had just sustained, the agent indicated they had no evidence linking Cox to the shooting at the present time. Given the other events that had occurred in conjunction with the film festival, though, they certainly intended to pursue the matter.

Marisa hit the mute button. "Is it true what the local stations are saying? Did Alex Sloan *shoot* himself?"

"It's true he was shot," Cleo replied carefully.

"Why, for God's sake?"

"I can't discuss the details. All I can tell you is he's part of the reason I agreed to provide event security for you here in Santa Fe."

"I don't understand."

Cleo shoved her palms into the front pockets of her jeans. This was where it got dicey.

"I had information Sloan might have a connection to a case I worked ten years ago, while I was still in the air force. I wanted to check him out, using the festival as a cover."

"But you turned down the job the first time Peter called you!"

"That was a deliberate ploy. I guessed you would pressure the festival committee concerning additional security, which you did. I also figured the festival's honorary chairman would turn around and pressure the air force, which *he* did. I caved in to the pressure only after my former boss agreed to provide detailed background dossiers on everyone associated with the festival—including Alex Sloan."

"So…so the whole time you were working for me, you were working for yourself?"

Cleo flinched but didn't shy away from the accusation. "Yes."

She braced herself, anticipating Marisa would work herself into another rage—at the very least, fling the remote at her head. The star looked ready to do both. Her nostrils flared. Her eyes dilated. Her breath came hard and fast.

"Tell me one thing. Did Peter die because you were too busy working this case against Alex Sloan?"

"No."

Cleo's conscience was clear on that. She knew she'd relive those seconds before the limo exploded a thousand times in the months and years to come. God knew she'd relived the horrific scene of Debra Smith's brutal murder at least that many times.

But Jack was right. She couldn't continue to beat herself up over Peter's death. She'd given Marisa her professional best. The star was alive right now because Cleo had insisted on a limo with extra underplating. One of these days they'd both appreciate that.

Not anytime soon, though. And from the sound of it, Marisa carried an even heavier load of guilt than her security consultant.

"Go ahead," the actress rasped, her eyes burning. "Say it."

"What?"

"Peter died because of me."

Shock robbed Cleo of speech. She shot a glance at J.L., whose face went from pale to bloodless.

"Marisa!" the media consultant gasped. "For God's sake, don't spout something like that to the press. They'll take it as a confession and run with it. Next thing you know, you'll be the villain instead of the heroine in this tragedy."

"Heroine?" Marisa turned on her, eyes wide with disbelief. "Heroine! Are you crazy?"

"You tried to save him," J.L. argued. "You broke free of that man, that bodyguard. You raced back to the limo, got the door open."

Cleo bit down on her lower lip. Hard. No way in hell would she add to her client's already staggering guilt. She only hoped the final autopsy report wouldn't suggest that yanking open the limo's rear door had fed the flames.

Sympathy sent her across the room. A grudging respect for the woman who'd emerged from the spoiled star prompted her to lay a consoling hand on Marisa's forearm.

"Listen to me. Peter died because a vindictive, murderous bastard hired a professional torch."

"To get back at me, because I screwed him in every sense of the word."

"You are *not* responsible for what Cox did. Ordinary people might rage at being dumped. They might exact petty forms of revenge. They don't conspire to commit murder."

She could see Marisa wanted to believe her— could see, too, that she wouldn't let herself. The grief and guilt in her face were so naked, so raw, that Cleo ached to turn away. She was as surprised as Marisa probably was when she transferred her hold from her client's arm to her shoulder.

The actress stiffened in the loose embrace, as unsure as Cleo about the shaky bond death seemed to have woven between them. They stood there, awkward, uncomfortable, but somehow drawing strength from each other.

Giving Marisa a quick squeeze, Cleo turned her over to J.L. and escaped.

Jack was waiting when she returned to her mini-suite. He took one look at her face and insisted she needed a drink, a shower and a solid six or eight hours of sack time.

Cleo was too wiped to argue. First, though, she had to attend to a vital piece of business. Digging out her bag of tricks, she conducted an electronic sweep of the entire suite. The phone lines tested clean. Ditto the electrical lines and outlets.

"Nothing," she said, scowling at the flat digital display. "Not so much as a blip."

"Which means Sloan used a wireless intake device to record our conversations."

Not even the CIA could shield totally against the latest crop of high-tech electronic ears. The best of them could pick up a whisper from three hundred yards away. Even the worst of them amplified ordinary conversations sufficiently for a listener parked around the block to record every word.

Most of the parabolic dishes were huge. But a few—a *very* few, Cleo recalled with a sudden hitch to her breath—were small enough to be concealed inside a gift basket.

"Dammit!"

Stalking across the room, she swept the exquisite pottery bowl off the counter, hefted it and smashed it back down. The ancient Anasazi turtle god shattered.

"There it is. The question now is, who put it there?"

With some effort, she resisted the urge to nudge the small, flat disk with the tip of her finger. Her gut told her it wouldn't yield any usable prints. There was always the remote hope, though.

Using the tip of a pen, she flipped the disk over. The battery that powered the device was round and flat. Another flick of the pen pried it out and deactivated the device.

"Okay, Jack. Time to haul out your laptop."

"Let me guess. You want me to run a few queries on Patrice Sloan."

"A few, hell. I want every piece of data ever recorded on the woman. Where she went to grade school. What she ordered last week from her pottery suppliers. Who she corresponds with via e-mail. How much she currently has deposited in her bank account."

"You do know some of that information isn't legally accessible."

"Yep, I know. Let's get to work."

21

Cleo's energy spurt lasted through several iterations of computer queries. Wedged beside Jack on the sofa, she devoured the information they'd gathered so far. It wove an image of a devoted military wife who took up sculpting and pottery as hobbies during her husband's years in service, only to come into her own as a serious artist after his retirement.

"That fits," Cleo murmured as they skimmed an article retrieved from a clipping service's archives. The article detailed a local craft show where the colonel's wife took home top prize in the amateur division. "Patrice told me her husband was a workaholic when they first married. Said it took her awhile to understand he was still working through his grief over his first wife's death."

"Beautiful young bride, lots of time on her hands, picks up hobbies." Jack worked the scroll button. "Wonder what else she picked up."

"Or who. We just assumed Sergeant Mitchell made that call to Colonel Sloan. What if he called Patrice?" Cleo hunched closer to Donovan's solid bulk, her thoughts whirling. "They could have met at a squadron picnic or office Christmas party. Struck up a friendship. Got cozy. Maybe *that's* why Mitchell and Debra Smith had that shouting match a few days before they died. Maybe Debra wasn't getting chummy with the colonel. Maybe she found out her boyfriend was getting chummy with the colonel's wife."

"You're stretching here, North."

"Hey, it happens. How many fraternization or adultery cases has the OSI worked in the past ten years involving high-ranking officers or their spouses? Fifty? A hundred?"

Jack put it closer to two. As Cleo said, it happened, and not just in the military. Rank didn't necessarily confer an automatic ability to keep the zipper zipped. In some cases, just the opposite occurred. Both men and women all too often equated power on the job with sexual prowess off it.

"Did any of the witnesses you interviewed

when you worked the Mitchell case give any hint he might be romantically involved with someone other than Debra?"

"Obviously not, or I would have followed up on it."

"So our only links are still that Mitchell and Sloan worked the same classified program and someone made a call from Mitchell's apartment to the Sloan residence the night of the murder."

"Don't forget the phone call from Debra Smith to her sister. That's what set me off on this quest in the first place."

"Tell me again what she said."

"She said Debra sounded worried, almost scared. She also mentioned a pilot with a funny nickname. I translated that to the Greek, which was Alex Sloan's handle when he was on active flying status."

Jack closed the clipping service article and ran the cursor down the list of items waiting to be opened. He'd mined every database he had legitimate access to and a few that teetered on the edge. He wouldn't jeopardize an investigation by hacking into a protected system without a warrant, but the wizards in Computer Ops had taught him a thing or two over the years.

What he needed to do now was to run the data he'd gathered on Patrice Sloan against the dates of the suspected Harvest Eagle compromise. The information fed to them five years ago from a source inside Interpol had pointed to Staff Sergeant Thomas Mitchell as the most likely source of the leak. They'd scrubbed the deceased sergeant's records and estate with a wire brush and come up empty. If Mitchell *had* tipped off certain foreign governments that the U.S. had harvested their technology, he hadn't done it in exchange for cash.

They'd scrubbed everyone else connected with the program at the time as well, Alex Sloan included. They hadn't screened Patrice Sloan, though. Not in depth, anyway. Before Jack could access the classified database, however, he had to move Cleo out of the room.

She took her marching orders with semi-good grace. "All these years, and you don't trust me, Donovan?"

"What do you think?"

"I think I'm out of here."

Uncurling, she pushed herself off the sofa and stretched. The slice of bare midriff displayed between sweater hem and jeans had Jack sending the cursor skittering across the laptop's screen.

"I'm going to take a shower. And don't come slinking in when the bathroom gets all steamed up," she warned. "You ended up on your butt last time you tried that, remember?"

"Like I could forget?"

With some effort, Jack wiped the memory of

Cleo perched on top of him out of his head and filled it instead with hard-learned lessons from his years in counterintelligence.

Espionage was a high-risk business. There were no statutes of limitation on the crime, and every spy had to worry about detection for his or her entire life. Robert Lipka, a former NSA employee, had been arrested in 1996—thirty years after he'd left the agency and twenty-two years after his last contact with Soviet intelligence.

More to the point, almost every traitor established a signature pattern of suspicious behavior. They had to copy or steal the classified material. Arrange drops. Travel to drop sites. And they always accepted payment in some form—even those who were lured into the game or went into it solely to avenge some perceived wrong. Sooner or later, they all wanted some recompense for the extraordinary risks they were taking.

Propping his laptop on the coffee table, Jack entered a code he changed at frequent intervals and leaned forward. Seconds later, the cover of the thumb-pad slid back. The concealed infrared lens scanned his retina before he could blink. Only after the computer matched the retinal scan to the one embedded in its memory did Jack gain access to the much-sanitized Harvest Eagle files he'd been cleared for.

He skimmed the files, extracted the dates of

the suspected compromises and logged out again. Then he got to work.

Six hours later, he was bleary eyed but infused with so much caffeine he figured he'd get to sleep sometime in January. He also had a lead. Not much of one, but something for the boys back in Washington to bounce against the State Department's computers. Now all he could do was wait.

Well, that wasn't *all* he could do. Shutting down his laptop, he started for the bedroom. The ring of his cell phone caught him on the threshold. Reaching into his pocket, he flipped up the lid before the phone woke the woman sprawled facedown on the king-size bed.

"Donovan," he growled softly, feasting on the sight of Cleo soft and warm and totally unconscious.

"Jack? Iz that..."

He winced as a loud hiccup came over the line.

"Iz that you?"

"Yeah, it's me, Kate. What do you want?"

"I need someone to...to talk to."

Jack's fist tightened on the cell phone. "This isn't a good time."

The sobs came before he could flip the phone shut. Hoarse. Wrenching. Laced with vodka.

"Pleaze! Just talk to me."

With a last look at Cleo, Jack closed the bedroom door.

* * *

Cleo woke to the tantalizing scent of freshly brewed coffee and the vague memory of crawling out of the shower around 1:00 a.m. and into bed for a quick nap while Jack did his thing. The brilliant light slicing through the shutters was her first clue she'd indulged in more than a nap. The digital clock beside the bed confirmed she'd slept a solid eight hours.

Damn! Marisa had reservations on a 1:00 p.m. flight. Unless she'd changed her plans, that left Cleo less than three hours to hustle her client through the media camped out all around the hotel, zip her down to the Albuquerque airport and see her airborne.

She was up, dressed and shoving her feet into heavy socks when Jack rapped on the bedroom door.

"I heard you moving."

She took the steaming mug he offered her with something less than graciousness. "Why didn't you wake me?"

"You were totally zonked. I figured you needed sleep."

She eyed him over the brim of the mug. "You look like you could use some yourself, Donovan. Did you stay awake all night?"

"Most of it."

He scraped a palm across the stubble on his cheek. It was the same tawny gold as his hair, barely noticeable unless you got up close and personal—a move Donovan had apparently decided not to repeat twice in twenty-four hours. Instead, he'd let her sleep. Alone. Undisturbed. Not exactly sure what to make of his forbearance, Cleo added it to their growing list of things to talk about. Later. First, she wanted to find out whether he'd made any progress while she was sacked out.

"Where are we?" she asked, leading the way to the living room. "What's the latest on the Sloans?"

"I checked with the hospital a little while ago. Alex Sloan is still comatose but hanging in there. His doctors are now cautiously optimistic he'll survive, although they won't hazard any guess as to his mental capacity. Marc Sloan spent the night at the hospital, as did Patrice. She went home a little while ago to change clothes."

"What did you find on our gal Patrice?"

"Nothing. She's clean."

"Well, hell!" Scowling, Cleo poked at a shattered pottery shard with the tip of her forefinger. The tiny electronic ear still lay where it had fallen. Jack would send it to the lab to try and trace the make, model and purchaser, but Cleo wasn't holding out much hope.

"Are we back to square one, then?"

"Not quite."

"C'mon, Donovan, spill it! What have you got?"

"I have a U.S. passport issued to one Patricia Hayes."

"Is Patricia Hayes our girl Patrice…?"

"She is. Hayes was her maiden name and the social security numbers match."

"So she was issued the passport before she married Alex Sloan? I don't get the significance."

"Apparently Ms. Hayes didn't submit a name change after her marriage. Instead, she applied for a new passport under the name of Patrice Sloan."

"But the State Department computers would pick up a duplicate issue to the same social security number."

"Such faith in the government bureaucracy is truly touching," Jack drawled. "Particularly coming from someone who usually describes it with four-letter adjectives."

"Okay, I guess I deserved that. Have you asked State to run a search on Patricia aka Patrice to see which passport she's been using?"

"I asked OSI Headquarters to ask State. I also asked for a search of all travel using either passport."

"They haven't responded yet?"

"That's how it works these days. You wouldn't believe the volume of data every intelligence agency and government department has to process now, since 9/11. Unless the query directly involves homeland security or current military operations, it goes into the queue. It'll help that Porter's pushing from his end, too."

"You put Laser Man on to Patrice?"

"Early this morning, when you were making that little snuffling, snorting noise you swear you don't make in your sleep."

"You know, Donovan, telling a woman she snores isn't the best way to talk yourself into her bed."

"That right?" He moved in, backing her against the counter. "What if I tell you those breathless little snorts turn me on?"

"I'd say you were weird."

"Weird bad or weird good?"

Tired and craggy-faced and whiskery, he could still turn on a smile that made Cleo wish she didn't have a client to attend to.

"I'll let you know when I get back from Albuquerque. I've got to put Marisa on a plane to L.A."

"Need some backup?"

"Not with our torch taken care of and the man who hired him in custody." She couldn't resist tracing the tip of her finger along his bristly jaw. "But thanks for the offer."

"Anytime, Cleopatra Aphrodite."

The tender moment was over.

"What is it with this death wish you have, Donovan?"

* * *

His laughter followed her into the hall. The pleasure that deep rumble gave her lasted only until J.L. answered her knock. The media rep's quivering intensity put Cleo on instant alert.

"You're not going to believe this!"

"Try me."

"*The Redemption* broke all opening-day, box-office records!"

Cleo forced her knotted neck muscles to relax. "Nothing like a fiery premiere and a lethal car bomb to stir up interest in a flick."

"The studio wants Marisa back in L.A., like, now. They've got every major network clamoring to interview her."

"What does *Marisa* want?"

"She wants to go home."

Her glee fading, the wire-thin brunette scrunched her shoulders. "Would you believe it? She insists she won't do any interviews."

Cleo wasn't as surprised as she might have been a few days ago. The actress put up a good facade, but there was a lonely, scared woman buried under all those bitchy layers.

"Sounds like she doesn't want to profit from Peter's death."

"That's right," Marisa confirmed, striding out of the bedroom. "I don't."

She was in black, stark and unrelieved. Black slacks, black leather bolero jacket, black silk blouse. Her only concessions to vanity, Cleo noted, were the auburn brows she'd penciled on.

"I'm all packed," she announced.

"I'll call down and have the hotel limo brought around."

"Wait!" J.L. made a last, desperate attempt. "I'm as heartbroken as you are that Peter died, Marisa."

One delicately drawn brow lifted. "Are you?"

"You know I am! But I'm telling you, he wouldn't want you to let your grief get in the way of your career. You can't pass up these media ops."

Marisa cocked her head. She looked older, Cleo thought. More sure of herself. As if she'd been tested by fire—which she had.

"Yes," the actress said calmly. "I can."

"You're thinking with your heart," J.L. protested, "not your head. Exposure like this only comes around once in a lifetime. If you're lucky!"

Too late, the media rep realized what had just come out of her mouth. Bright red spots jumped into her cheeks. She broke the ensuing silence with an abject apology.

"God, I'm sorry, Marisa. I didn't mean that the way it sounded."

Cleo held her breath and waited for the fireworks. They didn't come. Instead of blowing up, the actress stared at J.L with a stricken expression.

"I was just like you, wasn't I?"

Worse, Cleo wanted to say, but she held her tongue.

Marisa gave a long, shuddering sigh and turned. For several moments, she and Cleo faced each other. The bond neither wanted to recognize tugged at them. It was awkward. Uncomfortable. But there.

The old Marisa would have ignored it. The new Marisa—the one Cleo was gaining a grudging respect for—chose to acknowledge it.

"I didn't thank you," she said after a moment. "The extra precautions you insisted on saved my life."

"I only wish they'd saved Peter's, too."

Slowly, Marisa crossed the room and held out her hand. "You did everything you could. Thanks."

"You're welcome."

The actress hesitated a few beats. "I'm sorry I was such a pain in the ass. Here *and* in Cannes."

Cleo answered with a grin. "Me, too."

"I'll call you next time I need additional security."

She managed to keep her grin in place. Barely. "You do that."

And Cleo would make sure she had a conflicting commitment on the opposite side of the globe. She liked this Marisa much more than the old version, but that didn't mean she wanted to make a career of baby-sitting the woman.

"I'll call down to the front desk for the limo and a bellman."

Marisa dodged the reporters lying in wait in the hotel lobby. She wasn't as successful at evading the gaggle at the Albuquerque airport. With a sense of déjà vu, Cleo scanned the crowd of gawkers that had gathered for the star's impromptu news conference outside the security checkpoint.

She couldn't believe she'd arrived in New Mexico only a week ago. Or that the star had stood in this airport only last Wednesday and worked her brand of sultry, seductive magic for the TV cameras. Now Marisa's lover was dead, her co-star had been charged with conspiracy to commit murder and her movie was on its way to becoming one of the biggest box office draws of the decade.

And once Marisa boarded her plane, Cleo just might have a shot at finally laying Sergeant Debra Smith's ghost to rest. The urge to get back to Santa Fe and follow up on the queries involving Patrice Sloan pulled at her with sticky, sucking tentacles.

So much so that she almost missed the figure passing through security. The woman's long, teased hair was black instead of silvery blonde, and oversize glasses shielded her eyes, but one glimpse of her profile startled a shout from Cleo.

"Hey!"

The brunette threw a glance over her shoulder, turned back around and increased her gait.

With a strangled curse, Cleo took off. She fished out her P.I. credentials on the run and flashed them at the startled security agent checking boarding passes.

"Cleo North. I'm in pursuit."

"Hold on a minute!"

With the beefy agent pounding after her, she raced for the metal detector, yanked her Glock from its holster and shoved it butt-first at the nearest screener. The uniformed TSA officer bobbled the weapon like a hot coal.

"Hey! I need to see some paperwork on this."

She didn't have time for paperwork or for explanations. Before she made it through the detector, though, alarms started blaring and a solid phalanx of uniformed security personnel swarmed toward her. Two army types armed with automatic weapons came running. The reporters who'd surrounded Marisa charged across the terminal.

The ensuing chaos daunted even Cleo. Surrounded on all sides, she raised her hands in surrender and went up on tiptoe. The woman had disappeared, lost in the crowd.

With another curse, Cleo dropped back down and braced herself for the firestorm to follow.

22

"Nice going, North."

Donovan's voice floated through the intercom in the airport security holding area. Grimacing, Cleo shot an evil look at the one-way mirror.

"Tell them I'm who I say I am."

He turned away, addressed an unseen presence. "She's who she says she is."

She was ready for Jack's grin when he strolled through the connecting door. She'd had plenty of time to prepare for it, seeing as she'd spent the past hour answering questions, filling out forms and trying to convince the head of airport security she wasn't a terrorist or crazed killer.

The fact that she'd shut down his airport and caused *him* reams of paperwork didn't exactly aid her case. To top it off, she'd had to wait for Donovan to drive down from Santa Fe and confirm her identity.

"Tell me again why you charged the security checkpoint," he said as she signed yet another form and reclaimed her weapon from the official who'd confiscated it.

"Don't be cute. You know why. I saw Patrice Sloan." Or thought she had.

Despite the chaos she'd generated, Cleo had managed to convince airport officials to call both Donovan and the Santa Fe PD. She'd even talked them into conducting a search for the dark-haired woman.

The search hadn't turned up Patrice, but it had produced a reservation in the name of Patrick Hayes on an American Airline flight from Albuquerque to Mexico City.

Patrice. Patricia. Patrick. Cleo was starting to dislike all three intensely.

"I don't suppose anyone spotted her departing the airport."

"You suppose right. Looks like she made it out before you caused a riot and locked it down."

"Figures."

Reholstering her Glock, Cleo yanked her pant leg over her boot top, grabbed her purse and departed the holding area. Jack tipped a nod to the assembled officials and followed.

"Did you get the Santa Fe police to check the Sloan residence?" she asked Donovan.

"I did. They called me while I was on my way down. No evidence of a break-in, but the safe in the bedroom was open and empty. Also, the Jag registered to Patrice wasn't in the garage. It's not in the airport parking garage, either," he added before she could inquire. "I've alerted the Highway Patrol. Also the Border Patrol. My guess is she'll dump the Jag, though. Too easy to spot."

As they made their way past the ticket counters, she Cleo avoided looking at the long tangle of lines. She didn't want to *think* about how many passengers had missed connections and had to be rescheduled. Thank God Marisa had gotten off. The actress had been on the first flight out after operations had resumed.

The automatic doors whooshed open. Cleo breathed in the dry, icy air and followed Jack to the SUV parked in the red zone. Possessing a government-issued shield still carried *some* perks. Good thing, as Cleo had long since sent the limo that had ferried her and Marisa down to Albuquerque back to base.

Sliding into the passenger seat, she clicked on her seat belt. "Does Marc Sloan know his sister-in-law has taken a powder?"

"I didn't notify him, but I'm sure he figured it out when she didn't return to the hospital."

"I don't know about you, Donovan, but I'm

thinking it's time we had a little heart-to-heart with Mr. Sloan."

"Funny, I'm thinking the same thing."

They found him at his brother's bedside in ICU. One glance at his face told Cleo he'd heard the news of his sister-in-law's disappearance. He didn't look happy about it. In fact, she decided, he looked downright dangerous.

"You lost her?" he growled by way of greeting. "You spotted Patrice at the airport dressed as a man and you *lost* her?"

"I lost her. Apparently she has a knack for more than pottery."

"Yes, she's good at a lot of things."

The terse comment wasn't a compliment. Neither Cleo nor Jack took it as one.

"We need to talk to you about your sister-in-law, Marc."

He shot a look at his still-comatose twin, as if worried Alex might hear whatever he had to say about his wife.

"In the lounge."

He led the way, moving with the controlled violence of a caged cat. Once in the waiting room, he shoved his hands in his pockets and took a wide-legged stance in front of the windows.

The smooth, handsome executive who'd saved Cleo from tumbling down the stairs at La Fonda had disappeared. Dark stubble bristled this man's cheeks and chin. His eyes showed the effects of a long, sleepless night. The cuffs of his hand-tailored shirt were rolled up, revealing a smattering of curly black hair on his muscled forearms. He wasn't wearing a tie.

He didn't bother with preambles. "Patrice invited herself into my bed. It happened a long time ago, when she and Alex stopped by Charleston for a visit. At first, I thought she'd mistaken me for him."

"Funny how often that happens," Cleo murmured under her breath.

Not far enough under, apparently. Sloan caught the comment and fired back. "It wasn't funny that night."

"No, I guess not. You were saying…?"

The tendons in his neck corded as he bit out the details of the sordid little tale.

"Patrice was so young then. And more than a little tipsy that night. She was also hurt that Alex had buried himself in his work almost from the day they'd returned from their honeymoon."

"She fed me the same line," Cleo commented. "Said she hadn't realized Alex was still grieving for his first wife when she married him."

"It wasn't a line. Alex buries his emotions. We both do. We got it from our father. The general didn't appreciate mawkish displays of sentiment in his sons."

His closed expression suggested he didn't harbor many warm, cuddly memories of the man who'd adopted him.

"Did you tell your brother about the incident with Patrice?" Jack asked, more interested in the sons than in the father.

"No. He'd lost one wife he loved. I didn't want to be the reason he lost another."

Shoulders taut, he turned to the windows for a moment and gazed at the snowscape outside. When he turned back, the tension was still there.

"I didn't trust Patrice after that night, though. I kept tabs on her off and on for the next few years, especially when Alex was in Saudi Arabia."

Cleo's pulse jumped. If she remembered correctly, Alex Sloan had departed Luke Air Force Base, Arizona, for a six-month stint of temporary duty in Saudi Arabia. He'd then returned to his home base to work the Harvest Eagle Program.

"Did you think Patrice was having an affair while her husband was gone?"

"No, but…"

"But what?"

"I wasn't sure where she was getting her money from."

Jack gave a small, inarticulate grunt. Cleo had spent enough time in counterintelligence to know what he was thinking. Every bastard who betrayed his country usually ended up taking payment in some form.

"Alex had invested heavily in my corporation," Sloan was saying. "I managed our joint assets. I also had a pretty good idea of his other assets. Then one of my corporate vice presidents returned from a convention in Vegas and mentioned seeing my sister-in-law at a high-rollers' table. I was surprised, to say the least."

"So you had her tailed?"

"Yes." He made no apologies. "I found out she made regular jaunts from Phoenix to Vegas and played at high-stakes tables each time."

"What did she say when you confronted her?"

"She said she was bored with Alex away. She also said she had a knack for cards and had won more than she'd lost."

"Had she?"

"As far as I could determine."

"Did you tell your brother about her gambling?"

"No, but I warned Patrice I would if she continued to play at that level. She quit the junkets to Vegas, but needed something to fill her time. That's when she got into pottery. Turns out she had a flair for it."

"A woman of remarkable talents." Without missing a beat, Jack slipped in the knife. "When did you first suspect she was selling classified information on the international black market?"

Marc slewed around. Gray eyes locked with blue.

"Not until last night, when you indicated you were in Santa Fe to investigate Alex. I told you last night, Donovan. I'll tell you again. My brother would never betray the country he's served with such distinction."

"What makes you think his wife would?"

Sloan's jaw worked. "I got to thinking about those junkets to Vegas," he said slowly. "A person who risks high stakes at the tables might get a thrill from taking other kinds of risks, as well."

"We do tend to see a lot of thrill-seekers in the spy business," Jack agreed.

"Spy. Christ!" He dragged a hand through his hair. "I never imagined I'd be having this kind of a conversation about someone in my family."

"Few people do."

"Let me ask you this. In your experience, what do most of these *spies* do when they think you're onto them?"

"Some panic and bolt. Some try to cover their tracks."

"By shifting suspicion onto an innocent victim, then staging his suicide?"

There it was. Flat out and vicious. Cleo could only imagine what it cost Marc to put the ugly possibility into words.

"It's been done," Jack admitted, "but we don't know that's what happened last night."

"Not yet, we don't. But I'll tell you this, Donovan. You'd better find my sister-in-law before I do."

"I'd say Patrice Sloan should do some serious looking over her shoulder," Cleo commented as she and Jack departed the hospital.

"She can look all she wants. It won't help. We'll find her, and sooner rather than later."

"What makes you so sure?"

"She's left too many footprints in the sand."

Cleo wished she felt as confident as he sounded. She was still smarting from the near miss at the airport. Sliding on her Oakleys to filter some of the dazzling afternoon UVs, she crunched along beside him.

"So what's next on your agenda?"

He scraped a palm across his chin. The golden bristles were still there. So were the lines of fatigue etched into the corners of his eyes.

"I should head back to Washington, keep tabs on the hunt for Patrice Sloan."

"Tsk-tsk. There you go, taking another redeye. You can direct the hunt from here. Why don't you stay over and grab some sleep?"

Jack smiled. "Your hotel or mine?"

"I said sleep, Donovan."

"Your hotel or mine?"

It was sweeter this time.
And slower.

The crushing guilt that had swamped Cleo after Peter's death had eased. The quivering certainty that she and Jack were about to break through the haze surrounding Debra Smith's death lifted the burden even more. She felt free and relaxed and eager for pleasure.

Until Jack did his thing with his thumb, that is. When he added an exquisite pressure to the wicked sensations he was rousing with his tongue, Cleo went from eager to greedy. And when he replaced his tongue with his teeth, she jolted into supercharged.

It took just about everything she had, but she managed to hold off her climax until he flexed his thighs and drove into her with a force that left her gasping.

She didn't even realize she'd swung a thigh over his and rolled upright until she felt his stomach muscles quivering under her and heard the laughter rumbling up from his chest.

"Like being on top, don't you, North?"

"Once in a while. Got a problem with that, big guy?"

"No, ma'am. Once in a while works fine for me."

Cleo was still debating how much to read into that when he bent his knees, planted his hands on her hips and thrust upward.

Late afternoon had given way to early winter dusk when Cleo's stomach started making feed-me noises. She pulled herself from a sleepy haze and tried to shift the dead weight draped across her middle.

He wouldn't budge, not even when she stretched across him and fumbled for the phone. She got room service, ordered the house specialty of Steak Diablo for them both, and sank back for another few minutes of snuggling.

"This is nice, North."

His breath was hot against her ear, his arm still heavy on her waist.

"Very nice," she agreed.

With a flex of his biceps, he drew her in to the bend of his hips. "You know, I've been thinking."

"About what?"

"Marc Sloan said his sister-in-law dropped big at the tables in Vegas."

That wasn't exactly what Cleo had expected to hear from the naked male curved around her backside, but it certainly snagged her interest. Wiggling, she maneuvered around until they were face-to-face.

"Sloan also said Patrice claimed to win as much as she lost. So?"

"Could be she wasn't winning *or* losing. Could be she was just laundering money obtained from other sources."

Wide-awake now, Cleo pushed upright, dragging enough of the sheet with her to tuck under her arms. "I thought the 1991 amendment to the

Bank Secrecy Act closed that loophole. All casinos now have to report cash purchases of chips in excess of ten thousand dollars."

"True."

Wedging a pillow under his head, Jack propped himself up. The puckered entry wound high on his shoulder stood out against his tanned skin.

"But Nevada casinos worked an agreement that got them out of reporting aggregates spread across gaming days and venues."

"So a person could buy, say, eight thousand in chips at the craps table, move over to poker and buy another eight thou."

"Correct."

"Then cash the chips in for a cashier's check or money order that could be deposited at any offshore bank with no questions asked."

"Also correct. Until 9/11. The U.S. has flexed considerable muscle in the past couple of years to force closer scrutiny of banks suspected of laundering money for terrorist organizations. Now even such venerable—I use the word advisedly, you understand—such venerable institutions as the First National Bank of Bimini and Century Bank of Nevis are opening their books."

Excitement started to bubble in Cleo's veins. "The financial query you ran on Patricia Sloan came up blank. Think we'll get any luckier with Patrick Hayes?"

"We might."

She flicked a glance at the clock on the night-stand. "How long are you intending to give Computer Ops before you yank their chain?"

His mouth curved. "I was just waiting for you to finish yanking mine, Cleopatra Aphrodite."

She managed to refrain from throwing something at him, mostly because she was too busy admiring the view as he rolled out of bed and pulled on his shorts and jeans. Too impatient to dress, she wrapped the sheet around her and padded after him into the sitting room.

She busied herself with the coffeemaker while he logged on. "Is the data classified?"

His fingers flew over the keys. His intent gaze skimmed the screen. "Not this batch."

Trailing the sheet, she hovered over his naked shoulder as a series of numerical sequences scrolled across the screen. Cleo leaned closer.

"Jack! Are those what I think they are?"

"Depends what you're thinking," he replied with maddening calm.

She pounded a fist on his shoulder. "Jack! Tell me those are bank routing numbers!"

"Okay, okay. They're bank routing numbers." He couldn't keep the fierce satisfaction from his voice. "Seems our Mr. Hayes maintains several offshore accounts. Hmm, interesting."

"What?"

"I'm looking at what appears to be a recent transfer of funds from the Bank of St. Kitts."

"A *very* recent transfer of funds!" Cleo was practically draped over his shoulder. "Who or what did it go to?"

He clicked on the entry and followed a convoluted trail. After several nerve-twisting moments, the name of a travel agency came up on the screen. Another click brought up the information that the agency specialized in securing accommodations at exclusive resorts scattered across the Caribbean.

"You were right, Jack! She *is* leaving footprints in the sand. Literally. We need to call this agency and—"

A sharp rap on the door cut off her gleeful exclamation.

"You expecting anyone?" Jack asked.

"No."

She'd had all the surprises she wanted in the past few days. A fast detour into the bedroom retrieved her Glock. Jack had his Sig in hand when she returned. He angled to the left of the door. Cleo came in from the right.

"Who is it?"

"Marc Sloan." Urgency threaded his voice. "I need to talk to you."

"What's wrong?" Twisting the dead bolt, she flipped back the chain. "Is it your brother?"

"Alex is still holding his own."

"Then what...?"

Sloan strode in. His gaze cut from Cleo's improvised sarong to Jack's naked chest. Declining to comment on the obvious, he made a terse announcement. "I think I know where Patrice might be headed."

"So do we," Cleo informed him. "An exclusive Caribbean resort."

"How the hell did you...?" He stopped, shook his head. "You're good, Brown Eyes. Damn good."

"I can't take credit for this one. Jack—Special Agent Donovan—exercised his OSI muscle. Just out of curiosity, who did you exercise?"

"My entire corporate accounting staff," he admitted dryly. "Alex surprised Patrice with a vacation on a small private island in the Caribbean a few years ago. I remembered him saying how it had called to the artist in her, that she wished she could hide out there forever. Alex was so impressed with the place I looked into leasing a villa for a possible corporate off-site. I was damned if I could remember the name of the island, though, until my people dug it up. I had my staff make some calls and found out the same thing you apparently did. A man by the name of Patrick Hayes leased a villa on Mora Cay just this morning."

He was a half step ahead of them, but then he'd had a whole staff working the phones.

"I've got my private jet being fueled," Sloan informed them. "It's at the Santa Fe airport. We can be wheels-up in half an hour."

Jack included himself in the offer. "Nice of you to invite us along," he drawled. "Mind if I ask why you changed your mind? I thought you wanted to find your sister-in-law before I did."

The executive tipped him a lethal smile. "I decided I'd better have a witness present to hear the truth when I choke it out of her."

23

Some three hours later, Sloan's sleek Learjet swooped down on a crushed-shell airstrip on the private resort island of Mora Cay.

He stepped out into a balmy night filled with the music of rustling palm fronds and distant, crashing surf. Cleo followed, pausing in the open hatch to draw in the thick, almost smothering perfume of frangipani.

He exited after her. He'd left his heavy sheepskin jacket on the jet. Cleo tugged at the collar of her black turtleneck and wished she'd shed a few layers, too. She settled for shrugging out of her wool blazer and draping it over her arm while Jack introduced himself to the constable waiting at the airstrip.

Marc had initially refused to allow his pilot to radio ahead and request assistance from the local authorities. He'd seen the logic, though, when Jack asked if he wanted to see his sister-in-law's lawyer move to suppress on jurisdictional grounds any confession or evidence they might obtain.

That was Donovan. Methodical. Deliberate. By the book.

Most of the time.

The police officer who greeted them was polite, precise, and attired in a uniform that included white Bermuda shorts, a short-sleeved shirt and a pith helmet trimmed with a leopard skin band. Credentials inspected and introductions made, Constable Jacques St. Pierre escorted the new arrivals to his squad car.

"We have verified that a woman matching the description of Mrs. Sloan arrived earlier this evening by chartered flight from Nassau," he informed them in the musical accent of the Caribbean. "She took occupancy of a villa at Oleander Resort. As you requested, I have a man watching the road into the resort. Another watching the villa from the sea."

"Good man," Jack answered.

Wrought-iron gates guarded the entrance to the resort. They weren't as massive or as elaborate as the ones shielding the Sloan residence in Santa Fe, but they still gave Cleo an eerie sense of déjà vu as the constable said a few words to his uniformed officer, who in turn signaled the gate tender to let them in.

The drive led up a steep, fragrant tunnel that gave without warning onto a wide sweep of lawn. Oleander Resort sat atop a slight rise, bathed in moonlight. The bushes that gave it its name grew so tall they almost obscured the pink walls of the main building. Beyond the open-air lobby, small private villas dotted the hillside. Each had its own pool, as well as a Jeep topped by a green-and-white-striped canopy.

"Mrs. Sloan is in number six," the constable informed them.

Cleo's nerves were bunched tight and thrumming as the squad car crunched to a stop in front of the villa. The small unit glowed a pale pink in the moonlight and was fronted by a wooden pergola draped in vines that put out a heavy scent, even in the dark.

She was first out of the squad car. Jack grabbed her arm before she'd gone two steps.

"We're going to do this right. She may be armed. We know she's dangerous."

Weapons drawn, Jack and the constable took the lead. Cleo and Marc were relegated to backup and positioned in the shadows on either side of the pergola. Only when everyone was in place did St. Pierre ring the bell.

Cleo heard its tinkling echo inside the villa

and counted every heartbeat until the old-fashioned iron latch rattled. She scrunched farther back in the shadows, almost smothered by the sickly sweet vines, as the door opened.

"Yes?"

Patrice's look of polite inquiry turned to slack-jawed shock as her gaze dropped to the weapon in the constable's hand. Shock gave way to naked fear when Jack moved into the light spilling through the open door.

"Hello, Mrs. Sloan."

Gasping, the woman stumbled back a step.

When Cleo and Marc moved out of the shadows, her face turned a sickly white. She staggered back another step. Her shaking hand went to her throat.

"Marc?"

Sloan didn't answer.

"Marc, please! Tell me. How is...? How is Alex?"

"Still alive."

The woman swayed, either from fear or relief. "I didn't want to... I never intended to hurt him."

"Bullshit!"

Sloan stalked forward, hands curling. Cleo would have enjoyed watching him hold to his vow to choke the truth out of the woman. Unfortunately, Jack put himself between the two.

"Let's take this inside."

They crowded into a foyer tiled with black

marble. Crystal chandeliers lit the way into a sitting room that ran the entire width of the villa. Sliding glass panels stood open to the night and to the pool shimmering just steps outside.

Still shaken but recovering fast, Patrice followed the constable's instructions and planted her palms against the wall. He patted her down for weapons, found none among the folds of her flowing silk caftan, and informed her they were here at the request of the United States government to question her in regard to an incident that had occurred off Mora Cay.

Her head came up. Her cheeks were still chalk-white, but she met Jack's narrow-eyed look head-on.

"You want to know why I shot my husband."

Marc Sloan started for her again. Cleo hooked her arm through his and yanked him back.

"That'll do for a start," Jack said, not taking his eyes from the woman. "Before we proceed, though, I need to advise you of your rights."

He was making sure they crossed every *T*. Suspects questioned by U.S. authorities on foreign soil in anticipation of a possible trial had the same rights as suspects questioned in the States.

"Do you understand your rights as I've explained them to you, Mrs. Sloan?"

"Yes."

"Good. You were saying?"

"I was saying I shot my husband."

The muscles under Cleo's hand bunched. She could feel the leashed fury in Marc slipping its tether. She dug her fingers in, restraining him, warning him to let Jack handle this.

"Why?" Jack asked.

"I had no choice." Patrice's glance went to Cleo. "When a former OSI agent appeared and questioned my husband about Staff Sergeant Mitchell, I sensed… I guessed…"

"You did more than guess," Jack prompted, forcing her attention back to him. "You bugged Ms. North's hotel room."

"I had to find out how much she knew! Then, when you showed up and she found the record of that phone call Tom Mitchell made to our house at Luke…"

She scrubbed the heel of her hand across her forehead, gathering herself. Her hand dropped, and the ugly truth came out in a rush.

"I knew you'd confront Alex. I had to tell him. We've become so close since his retirement— much closer than we'd ever been during his time in the air force. I thought he'd understand. I was sure he wouldn't let me go to prison, that he'd help me cover my tracks. But when I played him the recording and tried to explain what had happened the night of that phone call, he went stiff and cold and told me there was no way he'd help me cover this up."

"What *did* happen all those years ago, Mrs. Sloan?"

"Mitchell called me. I went to his house and I...I shot him."

"Are you telling me you murdered Staff Sergeant Thomas Mitchell and staged his death to look like a suicide?"

"I had to! He was in a wild panic when he called me that night. His girlfriend..."

"Sergeant Debra Smith." Cleo provided the name through clenched jaws.

"She'd found copies of some of the classified Harvest Eagle files Tom had taken from the office to photocopy. She was going to report him. He panicked, went at her with a kitchen knife, then called me. I had to go over there. I didn't plan on killing him. I swear I didn't! He was so wild, though, I was afraid he'd come at me with that knife. It was self-defense."

"Yeah, right," Cleo huffed. "Just like you shot your husband in self-defense."

Jack silenced her with a furious glance. She'd worked the case ten years ago, but she didn't wear a uniform anymore. This was his show.

"I want to talk to you about the Harvest Eagle Program, Mrs. Sloan, but conversation will have to wait until we get back to Washington and have access to a secure area. Why don't you tell me instead how you got into the business of selling secrets?"

"It started during Alex's assignment to NATO."

Jack's expression didn't change by so much as a quiver of a muscle, but Cleo knew he had to be groaning inside.

"We'd only been married a short while and Alex was so busy, working day and night."

Wrapping her arms around her middle, she the woman turned to stare out over the shimmering pool lit with underwater floods. "I know now it was his way of dealing with the aftermath of his first wife's death, but back then I was bored and lonely and hurt."

"Go on, Mrs. Sloan."

Somehow Jack managed to sound both detached and sympathetic. Cleo, on the other hand, was so *un*sympathetic she was half a breath away from giving the woman a good swift boot in the ass.

"I got into it so innocently," Patrice related in a monotone. "It started with a careless conversation at a party at a foreign embassy. A high-ranking allied officer fawned all over me. Alex was off in a corner talking business and I...I guess I was flattered. I told the man what little I knew about my husband's job. The next time we met, he pumped me for more information. It became a game with us."

She swung back around, defensive now. "I didn't see anything wrong with the game. He was an officer in the air force of one of our staunchest allies…at the time."

The reluctant addendum put white lines at the corners of Jack's mouth but he managed to refrain from comment as Patrice continued.

"After a while, the thrill of the game sucked me in. I started going through Alex's briefcase and passing information to other 'friends.'"

"Is that when you began asking for recompense for the risks you were taking?"

"Yes. That's also when I began milking Alex's subordinates for information."

"Like Thomas Mitchell?"

A grimace of distaste crossed her thin, elegant face. "I should never have involved him. He was too greedy. And too careless."

Jack was noticeably less sympathetic now. "I'll want more detailed information when we get back to Washington. Names. Dates. Drop spots."

"I understand. I'm perfectly willing to provide the specifics."

She drew herself up, in control of herself now. It was obvious she'd thought everything through, even the possibility of being hunted down. Her voice was cool as she announced her conditions.

"In return for my cooperation, I want immunity from prosecution for any and all crimes—"

"No way!"

Cleo's protest was immediate and instinctive. Marc's was more feral. Shaking loose of her hold on his arm, he stalked forward.

"You're going to burn, bitch."

Patrice paled but held her ground. "I've retained an attorney here on Mora Cay. Also one back in the States. Both have assured me that the United States has negotiated no bilateral extradition treaty with this island nation. The government can't force me to leave, and I'll only depart voluntarily if I'm promised—"

"The government can't force you," Marc breathed, his nostrils flaring, "but I can. I operate under a different set of rules than these bureaucrats do."

Cleo didn't particularly like being lumped in with the bureaucracy. She liked it even less when Patrice ignored everyone else in the room to make an impassioned plea to her brother-in-law.

"You have to understand, Marc. I didn't want to hurt Alex! I was devastated that he would even *think* about turning me in. That other shooting, that sergeant… He killed his girlfriend. He deserved to die after what he did to the poor thing."

"Debra," Cleo stated through gritted teeth. "Her name was Debra Smith."

The blonde flapped a hand, as if the victim's identity didn't matter.

The careless gesture set red spots dancing in front of Cleo's eyes. She'd carried the guilt and disgust with herself for failing Debra Smith for ten long years. She was damned if she'd stand by and see her brushed aside so casually by the woman who'd caused her death.

"Her name was Debra Smith," she said again, elbowing Marc out of her way. "And this is in her memory."

The swift fist to the midsection took Patrice by surprise. She stumbled backward, eyes bugging out, and went into the pool butt-first.

24

It was well past noon when Jack located Cleo at the Oleander's outdoor bar. It was one of those wraparound affairs, set beside a waterfall that splashed into a lagoon-shaped pool. A grin tugged at his lips as he took in the gaudy flowered bikini and cover-up she'd purchased at the gift shop.

"At least you're better prepared to go into the pool than Patrice was last night. Her lawyers are going to have a field day with that, by the way."

Supremely uninterested, Cleo slurped piña colada through her straw. "So Patrice-baby can sue me."

He hooked a leg over the bar stool next to hers. The long night he'd spent haggling with Patrice and her lawyer showed on his face. Fatigue shadowed his eyes. The golden bristles that had scraped Cleo in tender places had sprouted another quarter inch or so. She didn't feel the least inclination to trail a fingertip over his chin now, though.

"Did you cut a deal?"

"Yes."

She knew darn well Jack didn't have the authority to grant Patrice immunity on his own. The fact that he didn't try to shift the blame onto his supervisors should have taken some of the edge off her disgust. It didn't.

"She murdered one person, caused the death of at least one other and put a gun to her husband's head. She doesn't deserve anything except a lethal injection."

"What she deserves and what she'll get are two different things. You worked counterintelligence, North. You know damn well we need to plug whatever holes she may have caused over the years or a whole lot more people could die."

"At least tell me she's going to be wearing an orange jumpsuit for the rest of her life!"

"She'll be wearing orange."

That was all he'd commit to. In mature, adult fashion, Cleo responded with another loud slurp.

Jack's grin slipped out again. "The Old Man said to tell you he'd spring for a first-class ticket back to the States if you'd care to accompany me,

Mrs. Sloan and her attorney. We're leaving in an hour."

Cleo had anticipated the offer. She'd put considerable thought into her answer during the hours she'd spent soaking up Mora Cay's brilliant sunshine.

She would always haul around a secret regret for failing to follow her instincts regarding Sergeant Debra Smith. She'd eased a little of her guilt by following up on the tip from Debra's sister and engineering that gig in Santa Fe to get close to Alex Sloan. True, she hadn't expected her behind-the-scenes maneuverings to land her smack in the middle of a seven burner. Nor had Cleo dreamed that her fierce determination to reopen an old investigation would spin out into an espionage case with potentially devastating impact.

In the middle of all that, she'd taken down a torch for hire, helped bust a Hollywood star for conspiracy to commit murder, and lost a good man to a fiery inferno. Cleo figured she'd earned a little vacation.

"I've got the answers to questions I've been hauling around inside my head for ten years," she told Jack. "I think I'll hang around here for a few days and soak up some rays."

He cocked a brow. "With Sloan?"

"Marc is flying out this morning, too. Back to Santa Fe."

No need to tell Jack that Sloan had invited Cleo to go with him. Or that he'd vowed they'd have their first official date as soon as Alex was out of danger and this business with Patrice was settled.

That, Cleo suspected, wouldn't happen for weeks, maybe months. And Donovan would be busy during those months, dragging every detail out of Patrice Sloan, compiling his case, doing what he did best.

"You know," he said, cocking a brow, "we make a pretty good team. In *and* out of bed."

"So what do you think we should do about that, Donovan?"

He flashed her that damn grin, the one that made her toes curl and her internal thermostat kick up a dozen degrees.

"How about I let you know after I finish debriefing the Sloan woman?"

"Ha!" Cleo stabbed her straw into the slushy drink. "I've heard that before."

Laughing, he pushed himself off the stool. Tall and tawny in the dazzling sunlight, he brushed a knuckle down her cheek.

"See you around, North."

"Back at you, Donovan."

She kept her breezy smile in place while he dropped a kiss on her lips. Even managed to return his two-fingered salute with a jaunty one of her own. When he disappeared behind the green-

and-white cabanas, though, Cleo went back to sucking on her straw.

Nothing like shooting herself in both feet. Two drop-dead gorgeous men, one rich, one not so much, both sent off to take care of business. Cleo bet she wouldn't hear from either of them again for a year. If then!

She was wrong. One of them contacted her exactly four months later....

* * * * *

Join Cleo North for another
action-packed adventure in

THE MIDDLE SIN
by Merline Lovelace

Coming from MIRA Books 2009

Please turn the page for an exciting preview.

Cleo lunged at her attacker.

He was huge, six-foot-six of solid muscle wrapped in black leather pants and a sleeveless leather vest that displayed a half acre or so of hair chest.

The scumbag had come at Cleo from behind just as she'd entered the locker room ripe with the acrid tang of sweat and the heat of a mid-April Dallas morning. When he'd whipped an arm around her throat, she'd manage to ram her butt into his midsection and catapult him over her shoulder.

Now she was on the offensive. Launching herself through the air, Cleo angled her attack so her knee hit him square in his gut. The breath exploded from his lungs. His lips curled over his teeth. Under the tattoos decorating his bald skull, he went as white as a week-old corpse.

But before Cleo could take advantage of her momentary mastery, he contracted his stomach. The muscles under her knee snapped together like coiled springs and almost bounded her right off the hulking giant.

Cursing, she dove forward. The heel of her hand was an inch from his nose when he threw up an arm. Deflecting her blow, he heaved his hips upward and tossed her off like a pesky spaniel. She landed hard enough that her eyes watered.

"Dammit, Goose!"

The bald Goliath grinned and made a grab for her. "You're getting soft, North."

This was what she paid him for, Cleo reminded herself grimly as they writhed across the concrete floor. Why she'd turned to him after leaving the air force and starting up her own security-consulting firm. She *wanted* Goose to toss her on her head occasionally—or try to. A girl had to stay on her toes in this business.

Jamming her booted foot against the floor for leverage, Cleo heaved to one side and slammed Goose into a row of metal lockers. Wedged against the unyielding steel, he lost just enough of his maneuverability for her to hook an ankle over his and bring him down. She had his wrist in a death grip and was attempting to shove it up between his massive shoulder blades when the cell phone clipped to her waist pinged.

Cleo froze. It was a special ring tone, one she recognized immediately. Goose recognized it, too. He shot a look of sudden terror over his shoulder.

"That's Mae. For God's sake, don't answer it!"

Struggling for breath, she hunkered back on her heels. Mae was her part-time office manager. The sixtyish retired accountant had recently developed a severe case of the hots for the muscled giant currently pinned between Cleo's thighs.

The cell phone rang again. Short. Sharp. Impatient. She could feel Goose start to tremble beneath her. Mae did that to people.

Surrendering to the inevitable, Cleo unhooked her leg and slid off her trainer's rump. "I'd better take it. You know she only uses this signal in emergencies."

Goose rolled over, his face scrunched in earnest entreaty. "Don't tell her you're with me!"

"She knows we had a training session scheduled. Which *would* have taken place in the gym on a nice, soft rubber pad if my rat-faced trainer hadn't decided to jump me in the women's locker room!"

"You think you're gonna land on a rubber pad out there in the real world, woman?"

Resisting the urge to flip him the bird, she flipped up the phone instead. "It's me, Mae. What's happening?"

"I just took a call from a potential client. He says it's urgent."

"He who?"

"Marcus Sloan."

Cleo's stomach did a quick roll. The image that leapt into her mind was tall, dark and drop-dead gorgeous. Not to mention obscenely rich.

She'd first encountered Marc Sloan four months ago in Santa Fe, while working a case. Sloan had promised to call Cleo and follow up on his not-very-subtle invitations to get her into the sack during those weeks in Santa Fe. After four months of nothing, now it was urgent?

"I told him you'd return his call," Mae announced in her crisp, no-nonsense way.

A moment later, Cleo punched in the long-distance number. The voice that answered was young and flavored with a soft, rolling accent that hinted at mint juleps and magnolias.

"Sloan Enterprises. May I help you?"

"This is Cleo North. I'm returning Mr. Sloan's call."

"Hold, please."

She was handed off to the next echelon of palace guard. This one sounded older, crisper and more difficult to get around.

"I'm Diane Walker, Mr. Sloan's executive assistant. I'm sorry, but I don't show you on the call log, Ms. North."

"Not my problem. He called me."

"If this is in regard to a personal matter, Mr. Sloan has entrusted me to handle his affairs."

Impatient now, Cleo put a bite into her reply.

"I repeat, Ms. Walker, Mr. Sloan called me. My business is with him."

Any notion that the sophisticated executive was calling to pick up where they'd left off a few months ago evaporated ten seconds after he came on the line.

"Hello, Cleo." It was the same sexy baritone she remembered. "Thanks for getting back to me."

"Hello, Marc. How's Alex?"

The last time she'd seen Sloan's twin, the retired air force colonel had been slumped over his desk, blood oozing from the heat hole someone had drilled into his skull with a .22.

"He's walking. Slowly and with a cane, but walking."

"Good to hear. What can I do for you?"

"One of my assistants hasn't shown up for work this week. I'm worried about her and would like you to find her. How soon can you get to Charleston?"

Normally, Cleo went through a detailed intake interview before accepting a job or a new client. North, Incorporated was well-enough established that she could pick and choose her gigs. But Sloan's timing was perfect. He'd caught her just coming off another job and faced with the grim prospect of going wallpaper shopping with Waffling Wanda.

"I can fly out this afternoon."

"That's what I was hoping. My private jet is already in the air. I'll be on the ground at Love Field in an hour."

He was pretty damned sure of himself. Then again, you don't take a company onto the Fortune 500 list by being faint of heart. Which reminded Cleo…

"We haven't discussed fees."

A smile crept into his voice. "Whatever they are, Brown Eyes, you're worth it."

Little shivers danced down Cleo's spine. She could almost feel the crush of Sloan's mouth on hers.

The man was one hell of a kisser. Not as good as Jack Donovan, she admitted, but Cleo and Special Agent Donovan had yet to figure out just what they had going between them. Besides careers that included getting shot at every so often and intermittent sessions of world-class sex, that is.

At the rate things were going, they might *never* figure out just why the heck the air started steaming whenever they got within ten feet of each other. Donovan had e-mailed her exactly three times in the past four months and then only to tell her he was still untangling the web of treason and deceit they'd uncovered in Santa Fe.

Cleo had never been one to sit around and wait. For men *or* for jobs.

"See you this afternoon," she told Sloan.